YEARLING BOOKS

Since 1966, Yearling has been the

leading name in classic and award-winning

literature for young readers.

With a wide variety of titles,

Yearling paperbacks entertain, inspire,

and encourage a love of reading.

VISIT

RANDOMHOUSE.COM/KIDS

**TO FIND THE PERFECT BOOK, PLAY GAMES,
AND MEET FAVORITE AUTHORS!**

ALSO BY WENDELIN VAN DRAANEN

Sammy Keyes and the Hotel Thief
Sammy Keyes and the Skeleton Man
Sammy Keyes and the Sisters of Mercy
Sammy Keyes and the Runaway Elf
Sammy Keyes and the Curse of Moustache Mary
Sammy Keyes and the Search for Snake Eyes
Sammy Keyes and the Art of Deception
Sammy Keyes and the Psycho Kitty Queen
Sammy Keyes and the Dead Givaway

How I Survived Being a Girl
Flipped
Swear to Howdy

Shredderman: Secret Identity
Shredderman: Attack of the Tagger
Shredderman: Meet the Gecko
Shredderman: Enemy Spy

sammy KEYES

and the HOLLYWOOD MUMMY

WENDELIN VAN DRAANEN

A YEARLING BOOK

For my mother,
Sybrichje Marie Agneta van der Meijden Van Draanen,
a woman who's not afraid to be herself.

Special thanks to Leslie Parsons and Bill Hrnjak
for their help with research.

And, as always, eternal gratitude to Nancy and Mark.
In my world, you two are superstars!

PROLOGUE

If I'd asked Grams if I could go, she would have said, "Over my dead body!" But the more I thought about it, the more I realized that I had to go. I mean, it's one thing to hurt *my* feelings, it's another to hurt Grams'. And after Grams came back from visiting Lady Lana—after I'd heard about the things my mother had said and the things she'd done—I knew someone had to do *some*thing, and the only someone I could think of was me.

And once I started thinking about going, well, I couldn't stop thinking about it. And then, when Marissa said, "Oh, let me come with you!" there was no turning back.

We were on our way to Hollywood.

ONE

I couldn't exactly walk from Santa Martina to Hollywood. Couldn't fly, either—not with the amount of money I had jingling in my jeans, anyway. And since I'm not old enough to drive and didn't want to jump a freight train or hitchhike, there was really only one way out of Santa Martina—the bus.

I'd never been on the bus before. Neither had Marissa. Me, I'd never even been out of Santa Martina. Sure, when Lady Lana was still around, she'd drive me up to Santa Luisa once in a while, but I'm talking out of town. Really out of town. I'd never been.

Marissa McKenze, on the other hand, has been everywhere. From Honolulu to Hoover Dam, she's seen it all. And even though she's been on buses before, they've always been youth-group buses or double-decker tour buses. She'd never actually been on the *real* bus. That's right, she'd never ridden the Big Dog.

Getting to the Greyhound station wasn't the hard part. Shoot, it's only a few blocks up from the Heavenly Hotel, so it's practically right across the street from Grams'. Well, almost.

The hard part was catching the bus without cutting

school. That, and not spilling the beans to Grams. And even though I tried to pack light, my backpack still looked like a laundry duffel, and my lunch sack was so stuffed with peanut butter and jelly, I was afraid it would rip before I made it out the door.

Grams didn't seem to notice, though. She was in the middle of brushing her teeth when I gave her a quick kiss good-bye, so all she could do was say, "Hrmm grumm!" and smile at me through foam.

I hurried to school and found Marissa sneaking into homeroom early with a suitcase.

A *pink* suitcase.

Now, there are pinks and then there are pinks. Marissa's suitcase was of the flashy flamingo variety. And it wasn't your average snap-close rectangular model, either. It was a big three-foot tube with a handle on top and fat black zippers everywhere. It looked like something out of CeCe's Thrift Store, except that CeCe would never have stocked it. One side was bashed in, and there was a skid mark right across the middle.

Pink or not, zippers or not, this was a problem. "Marissa! You promised me you'd pack light!"

Marissa did a bit of the McKenze dance, squirming from side to side as she whispered, "It wouldn't all fit. What was I supposed to do?"

"But... Marissa, it's pink! And what did you do? Run over the thing on the way to school?"

I might as well have caught her in the act. She blushed. "Well, it was hard to balance. I tried holding it with my legs, but then I couldn't pedal...."

"So you balanced it on your handlebars?"

She shrugged and nodded and blushed some more.

I've been on Marissa's handlebars. It is one wobbly ride, let me tell you. And every time I do it, I wind up looking about as tattered as her suitcase and I *swear* I'll never do it again.

"Besides, we're going to Hollywood." She checks around to make sure nobody's listening, then sings, "Hol-ly-wood!"

I whisper, "Marissa! We're not going there to get discovered! We're going there to shake some bubbles out of the GasAway Lady's head!"

"Who said anything about getting discovered? People down there are just different. You know, fancy. Didn't you say your mom's staying in some ritzy villa? I don't want to get kicked out for looking like a bum, that's all!"

I look from her to the bulging zippers and back again. "Don't tell me you brought a . . . a dress!"

She starts dancing a little faster. "As a matter of fact, I've got two."

"Two?"

"One for me and one for you."

I threw my hands up. "Marissa!"

"Well . . . ! I just thought we should be prepared."

"Whatever. Just don't ask me to carry that thing. It makes you look like you're running away from home."

She stashed the suitcase behind the coat rack and threw some lost-and-found clothes on top of it, and that's where it stayed until everyone had filed out after the end-of-school dismissal bell rang. But when Mrs. Ambler saw her digging it out, she did a double take, then asked, "Going away for your three-day weekend?"

Marissa says, "Um, yeah."

"Oh?"

Now, when a teacher says Oh? to you like Mrs. Ambler was saying Oh? to Marissa, you can't just pretend you didn't hear. Or nod and smile and leave it at that. You have to *say* something. And the longer a teacher stands there with that Oh? lingering in the air, the harder it is to snow her with something less than the truth.

Sure enough, Marissa stammers, "Yeah...we're going to Holly—" She glances at me for help, but it's too late to bail us out. So she finishes, "—wood."

Up went an eyebrow and out came another "Oh?" And then, "You're both going?"

It seemed to me that Mrs. Ambler was going from curious to nosy in an awful hurry, so I started nudging Marissa toward the door, saying, "Yeah, and if we don't get moving, we're going to miss our ride. Have a nice weekend, Mrs. Ambler. See you on Tuesday!"

But she hurried to follow us, locking up the classroom and falling in step beside us. Suddenly she whips around and blocks our path, whispering, "You girls aren't running away, are you?"

I laugh. "Mrs. Ambler! No! We're just going to visit relatives."

She searches my eyes. "Really?"

I say, "Really," and since I'm not lying, there's not much she can do but believe me.

She lets out a big sigh and says, "For a minute there..."

I nod. "It's the suitcase."

Mrs. Ambler smiles. "Maybe so." Then she asks, "Where's your suitcase, Samantha?"

I pat my backpack. "Got my toothbrush right here."

She turns up the administration building walkway and says, "Well, you girls be careful...and have fun!"

We wave and smile, calling, "We will! Bye!"

The minute she's out of earshot, Marissa whispers, "That was close! Do you think she's going to call home?"

"No." I grab her wrist and check the time. "But if we don't get moving, you're gonna have to lug that thing clear back to your house tonight!"

We unlocked Marissa's bike and wound up wedging the suitcase between the seat and the handlebars. Then, with one of us on each side, we pushed and talked our way toward the bus station. It was actually pretty easy going, and in no time we were jaywalking across Main Street, clicking along the back roads to Wesler Street and through the parking lot of the Greyhound bus station.

We locked Marissa's bike to a rusty rack in the corner of the parking lot, then headed for the glass double doors of the station.

There were five people already in the waiting room. One was asleep, sitting on an old army duffel bag on the floor with his head propped against one of the black plastic chairs anchored to the wall. Another man was huddled with a woman by the soda machine. They both had bleached hair, gelled straight up. He was wearing a gas station attendant shirt tucked into gray businessman

7

slacks, which were tucked into SWAT boots. She had more earrings than Heather Acosta, and nothing of hers was tucked in anywhere. Her bra strap was hanging off a shoulder, her T-shirt was ripped off at the stomach, and her belly button stuck out like an extra eye, fleshy and squinted.

Then there was a farmworker by the water fountain, rinsing his bandanna in the water, wiping down his face and neck. A bent old man in big thick glasses and Velcro-strap sneakers was watching him from across the room, and you could just feel him thinking that people shouldn't bathe themselves in public that way.

Marissa came to a halt in the doorway. "Uh...are you sure you want to do this?"

I wasn't, but I didn't want to let Marissa know that. I whispered back, "We're in downtown Santa Martina, Marissa. What were you expecting? Civilization?"

She let the door close behind her, and as she's dragging her suitcase along, everyone in the building stops what they're doing to check us out. And there's absolutely no doubt about what they're thinking.

Runaways.

Then the guy with the Velcro sneakers rasps up a giant wad of phlegm from the bottom of his throat, snorts any snot he can scare up from his fleshy old nose, squishes the whole mess between his teeth, and swallows.

I cringe and shudder, and Marissa says, "Oh, gross!" We scoot her suitcase toward the counter, and Marissa says to the clerk, "We want to catch the three-forty-five to Hollywood."

He pulls out a couple of tickets. "One way?"

Marissa digs her wallet out of her purse, saying, "Round trip. What return times do you have for Monday?"

He hands her a schedule and has Marissa pass him her suitcase under the counter, then prepares the tickets. And just as he's finishing, he says, "It's pullin' up. Have a nice trip," without even looking up.

I head for the pay phone wedged beside a video game and say, "I've got to call."

Marissa watches the others filing outside. "Just use my cell phone from the bus."

"You brought that thing?"

She shrugged. "Seemed like a good idea to me."

"Are you sure it's going to work?"

"Why wouldn't it . . . Oh, no! It's in my suitcase!"

I raced over to the pay phone, popped in the coins, took a deep breath, and dialed. And after about twenty rings I hung up and tried again, thinking that maybe I'd punched the number in wrong. I mean, I was nervous enough about what I was going to say to Grams that dialing the wrong number sure *was* possible. Again, no answer.

Marissa's starting to dance a little. She whispers, "Sammy, they're getting on!"

I let it ring a few more times, then I slam the phone down and go charging outside. The bus driver's got a cigarette in one hand and is about to close the storage compartment with the other. I call, "Wait! Hey, wait a minute!"

He stops and looks our way. The bus motor is still running, growling and letting out puffs of exhaust. He calls over the rumble, "Have a change of heart?"

"No, we . . ." I point to Marissa's suitcase in the compartment and say, "I need to get something out of my luggage." He frowns, so I add, "Please?"

He helps me pull the thing out and then turns away to finish his smoke as Marissa digs up the phone, zips the suitcase closed, and shoves it back inside.

We tell him thanks and give him our tickets, then hurry up the steps.

And it's funny—being inside the bus wasn't anything like I expected. No people checking each other out like kids do on school buses. No feeling of trench warfare like you get on field trips when the class clowns in back are packing spit-wad straws. Or water balloons. Or stink bombs.

No, the seat backs on this Big Dog were so high that even though I knew they were on board somewhere, the Depot Derelicts seemed to have just disappeared.

It was also the hum. Outside the running engine had sounded like a growl, but inside it was more a hum. A strong, no-nonsense hum. And it drowned out what people were saying to each other, so as we walked down the aisle looking for two empty seats together, it almost felt as though the people on board weren't really there at all. Their very existence seemed erased by the hum.

Marissa let me have the window seat, and I looked down at the station—at cars going along Broadway and a boy cutting through the parking lot on his bicycle. And it felt odd, being up so high, looking out such a large, tinted window, vibrating from the hum. Like I was leaving the planet, not just Santa Martina.

Then the door closed. And as the driver put the bus into

gear and eased out of the parking lot, Marissa handed me the phone and said, "Here. You'll feel a lot better once you take care of this."

She was right. I was feeling queasy. I mean, what was I thinking, going off to Hollywood? I didn't even really know where I was going. Sure I had an address, but the map I'd pulled off the Internet in the library wasn't exactly razor-sharp. And I hadn't really thought through what I was going to say to my mother. I just knew I had to go.

I punched in Grams' number, and while I'm listening to her phone ring, we turn from Broadway onto Main. And then, like in a dream, who do I see in the intersection, crossing the street from Maynard's Market with a sack of groceries in her arms?

Grams.

I want to wave. I want to call her name and explain what I'm doing. Why I couldn't tell her about it before. Why I *have* to go.

But I can't. I can only sit there with her phone ringing in my ear and the hum of the bus purring through me from everywhere else. As we pull away from the intersection and Grams disappears from view, a cry catches in my throat. And even though Marissa's right there beside me, I feel panicky.

Panicky and painfully alone.

TWO

When I did get ahold of her, my conversation with Grams went pretty much as expected. And my grams—who's normally a very sensible person—worked herself into telling me I should take the bus hostage and flip a U-turn home. That actually made me laugh. I reminded her about the first—and last—time I'd tried to drive, and how I'd plowed my way through downtown Santa Martina giving everyone in my wake a heart attack, and then totaled the motor home I was driving and a police car to boot. "Imagine," I told her, "what I could do with a bus."

She didn't find much funny about that, but she did change the subject. She wanted to come, too. She'd take the next bus. Find someone with a plane and sign over her Social Security. Hitchhike. Something.

I just said, "Grams! Grams, stop it! We'll be fine. Stop treating me like a little kid!"

She almost said, But Samantha, you are *behaving* like a child, but she changed her mind at the last second, and what came out instead was, "But, Samantha, you are... going to call me? Every hour?"

"Not every hour, Grams, but I will call. And please,

please don't tell Lady Lana I'm coming. If you do, it will ruin everything!"

She finally agreed, and then all of a sudden she was getting off the phone, telling me to take care and be safe.

The switch in her attitude seemed strange. I clicked the phone off and stared at it, and then it hit me. "Oh, no!"

Marissa asked, "What?"

I turned the phone back on and started punching. "She's going to call Hudson!"

"So?"

"So I've got to get ahold of him first!"

"Why?"

To my relief, there was a ring instead of a busy signal. "Do you want him driving her down so they can both watch over us?"

Marissa cringed at the thought of two senior-citizen chaperones. "He would *do* that?"

"Marissa, he's Hudson! Of course he would!"

Just then Hudson picked up. So I gave him a one-giant-sentence explanation about what we were doing and why, and asked him to please-please-please take care of Grams, but whatever he did, not to drive her to Hollywood.

He asked me a few questions, made me promise to be careful, and then gave me his word. I got off the phone and handed it to Marissa with a great big *pfew!*

Marissa was right. I did feel better. Tons better. And after she got done leaving a "Just checking in, we're fine, see you Monday" message on her parents' machine, we settled in and just talked. About everything from Mrs. Ambler to the Depot Derelicts to Lady Lana and what I

13

was going to say to her. And before you know it, we were making our transfer, boarding another Big Dog for the long stretch into Los Angeles.

After we settled in again, we dug into the peanut butter sandwiches I'd packed, and then, with our tummies happy on the inside and darkness blanketing us from outside, we let the bus hum us to sleep.

The next thing I knew, Marissa was whispering, "Sammy? Sammy, are you awake?"

I cracked open an eye. "Are we there?"

"No, but I think we're close. Look!"

There were more lights than I'd ever seen. Headlights were strung together like white Christmas lights, turning and twisting from highway to highway. Skyscrapers sparkled with office lights. Neon hotel and restaurant signs glowed pink and green and blue. Billboards were flooded with spotlights. The twinkling and shimmering arced away at the horizon, so it felt like we were riding across the surface of an enormous disco ball.

Marissa gasped, "It's beautiful!"

I nodded and whispered, "Wow."

"We are definitely not in Kansas anymore, Toto."

"You can say that again." I eyed her. "You got ruby slippers in that pink suitcase?"

She laughed and said, "Who wants to go home? God, *look* at that!"

We spent the rest of the trip glued to the glass. And when the bus driver took an off-ramp, we were still in a trance. The bus sashayed from side to side, the humming came down in pitch, and it felt like we were coming in for a landing.

But as we purred at an intersection waiting for the stoplight to change, I looked around and realized that up close this place was nothing like it had seemed from the freeway. It wasn't dancing with lights, it was buzzing with them. And they didn't even seem to twinkle anymore. They just made the air a fuzzy gray.

Suddenly the feel of the place was cold and hard. Wall-to-wall hard. The road looked like an asphalt runner on a carpet of dirty cement. And all around were buildings made of cinder block, their windows and doors covered with burglar bars and steel gates.

I peeled myself from the window and leaned back in my seat, but I kept one eye on what we were driving by. Marissa shrank back into her seat, too, and neither of us said anything for a few minutes. Finally I said, "It's not looking so beautiful anymore, is it?"

She shook her head but didn't say a word.

"It's like we've gone from disco to metal."

She frowned. "Death metal."

The bus bounced into the station, and when the driver stood and called, "Hollywood, California," we got up and stretched, then shuffled out the folding doors.

I guess it's not fair to judge a city by its bus station. I mean, if Santa Martina were judged that way, we'd probably have a population of about ten. But there we were—landing in a universe with browning palm trees and cement, populated by skanky people with bloodshot eyes and paper-sacked bottles—definitely judging a town by its bus station.

Marissa whispers, "*Now* what?" and just like her, I was scared. I mean, on my map it had seemed easy. Catch the bus to Hollywood, from there take a city bus to Beverly Hills, walk a little ways, and knock. Ta-da! But a few simple inches on a map translate to a state of confusion in real life. And I didn't see city buses waiting to whisk us away. Only rusty green taxis driven by greasy guys with faded tattoos.

But I didn't want to panic Marissa by letting on that I was scared. So I pointed to where they were unloading luggage and said, "Hey! There's your King Kong carryall—let's go!"

We retrieved her suitcase, then I pulled out my map and said, "Okay, we're right here, on North Vine. Sunset is that way a few blocks. There's bound to be a bus running there."

"Sunset? As in the Sunset Strip?"

I unfolded the map, looking for the answer. "I think so."

All of a sudden Marissa's full of energy again. "Cool!"

Now really, I should've asked. I should've just gone in and asked somebody, anybody, about buses. Or how much taxis cost. Or what other choices there were for getting from here to there. But everybody was so stony. Or strange. And then, when I realized that the guy standing a few feet over from us was peeing in his paper-sacked bottle, I just wanted to get *out* of there.

So we headed up to Sunset. Up to the Strip. And let me

tell you, we figured out in a hurry that this is not a place for lost girls with tattered pink suitcases to be walking around at night. Not that there weren't other pedestrians— there were. And most of them were of the female variety, but they weren't *walking* anywhere, if you know what I mean.

We had trouble not staring as we scurried past them. It was like the stuff you see in the movies: short skirts, high heels, and enough makeup to paint a barn.

What you don't see in the movies, though, is the shivering. And they were *all* shivering. Even the ones wrapped in rabbit. In the movies you can't smell the clashing odors, either. Garbage, musk, and exhaust make for a pretty putrid combination, let me tell you.

The only time I'd seen anything close to this in real life was over at the Heavenly Hotel. Gina and the other people I've gotten to know over there all seem to be edge-dwellers. Like one little tap and they'd be gone, *poof!* over the edge. And it's not just the way they dress or smoke or act. It's more the attitudes they cop. Like their survival depends on getting you before you get them.

After walking about four blocks, Marissa says, "Are you sure this is the Sunset Strip?"

"It must be. How many Sunsets can Hollywood have? Maybe we're just on the bad part of it."

"Well, I don't want to spend any more time looking for the good part of it."

"I'm with you. This place makes the Heavenly Hotel look like Disneyland. You want to go back to the Grey-hound station and ask someone about city buses?"

"No! I want to flag a taxi and get out of here!"

"But, Marissa, that's going to cost—"

"I don't care what it costs! We've got to get out of here!"

Just then a rusty green taxi comes zooming up the street, and what once seemed like a sewage sedan was now looking like a luxury limo. Marissa caught my eye, and that's all it took. She jumped out into traffic and body-blocked that cab, crying, "Taxi! Taxi!"

The cab driver slams on his brakes and swerves to the side, then bolts out the door, screaming, "Are you crazy! You wanna *die*?"

Marissa doesn't budge from in front of the taxi. "Please. You've got to get us out of here. We're kinda lost and—"

"You flagged the wrong cab, girls. I'm on my way in. I'm done for the night."

The whites of this guy's eyes are yellow, and his black hair's greased down into a tiny knot in back. His face is shaved, but there are deep pockmarks across both cheeks, and his teeth are half gone. Not rotten, just missing.

To me, he's scary. Downright scary. But Sunset must've been even scarier to Marissa, because she's jabbering away at the guy like he's a long-lost friend.

"But we can't find a city bus, it's getting late, and we're not sure where we're going to stay...."

The cab driver squints one yellow eye at her. "No? Then why are you killing yourself trying to get there?"

Marissa's like a locomotive gaining steam. "Well, Sammy's mother ran off to become a movie star and she hasn't seen her in over a year. Well, except for a few hours at Christmas, when she gave Sammy a pink angora sweater, if you can believe that. Does this girl look like she'd wear pink *or* angora? Please! And even though her mother landed a commercial, it's for *GasAway.* Tell me, would you want *your* mother to be the GasAway Lady? Would you?"

He just stares like he's having a nightmare.

"And then Sammy's grandmother comes down here to visit her and discovers that the reason Sammy's mother would never let anyone contact her is because she's changed her name to Dominique—Dominique *Windsor*—like she's some English aristocrat or something. And she's going around telling everyone her mother's her grandmother. Can you believe that? Introducing your own mother as your grandmother? And she's not even telling anyone she has a daughter...."

The cab driver pinches his eyes closed and says, "Who's not? The mother or the grandmother?"

"Sammy's mother."

Now, I can't believe that he's even listening to Marissa, let alone trying to get the story straight, but he points to me and asks, "This over here is Sammy?"

Marissa nods. "Yeah. We've been best friends since the third grade, so I told her that yeah, I'd come down here and help her straighten everything out. I mean, it's one thing to ditch your daughter. It's another to pretend you don't *have* one. Do you have kids? What kind of person—"

"Get in," he says, then ducks into the cab.

Marissa stops short, then turns to me and asks, "What did he say?"

"He said, get in."

"Wow...really?"

I nod and ask her, "Are you sure you want to?"

She looks over her shoulder one way at two men eyeing us like a couple of junkyard dogs, and then the other way at the Shiver Sisters. She grabs me and says, "Are you kidding? Get in!"

I mutter, "I'm starting to think I'm a bad influence on you, Marissa McKenze." We wrestle the suitcase into the back, then wedge ourselves around it.

Our knight in rusty armor watches the traffic in his rearview mirror and says, "Where's this mother of yours stayin'?"

I pull the address out of my jeans and hand it to him. "Here."

His eyebrows fly up. "And she can't afford to send down a cab?"

"She doesn't know we're coming. Look, if it's going to cost a lot to get there, maybe you could just, you know, take us to a bus stop or something."

Marissa says through her teeth, "We just *came* from a bus stop!" She leans forward and asks, "Is it very far?"

"Naw. It'll be under twenty."

"Minutes or dollars?"

He studies her in the rearview mirror. "Dollars."

Marissa leans back in the seat, and all of a sudden she's quiet, just sitting there, looking out the window.

The scenery changed almost as quickly. Instead of cement and asphalt as far as you could see, we were now winding through residential areas where stucco-and-tile houses were tucked away behind wrought-iron rails and plants. Lots of plants. Palms, birds-of-paradise, vines— suddenly the place was just springing with green.

Then our rusty knight says, "You girls got no idea what you look like with that thing. If I caught my girls walking Sunset with a pink suitcase, I'd lock 'em up."

I frown at Marissa, but I don't say a word. Marissa, though, asks him, "You've got...you've got daughters?"

He gives her a toothless smile. "Don't believe me?" He pulls down the visor and taps his finger once on each of three pictures. "Shannaya, Angeola, and Sissy—most beautiful girls you ever seen." He eyes Marissa again. "But if they were to start walking the Strip, they'd come home lookin' more like me."

We're both quiet as he zooms us up one street and down another, and about ten minutes later, when he pulls to the curb and says, "This is the one," Marissa and I just stare out the window with our jaws dangling down.

Finally he says, "Go on, girls. I gotta get home."

Marissa gives him a twenty and off he zooms. And there we are, in the middle of the night, standing at the base of about two acres of golf course landscaping, looking up at a house as big as a resort hotel, when it hits me.

She's not coming home.

Ever.

I mean, why? Why would she want to come back to Santa Martina? To some little house or apartment with me, when she's living in a swanky Spanish villa without me?

Marissa whispers, "Wow...."

"Let's just go home, okay?"

"What? To Santa Martina?"

"Yeah."

Marissa looks like she's going to clobber me over the head with her suitcase. But just then I spot someone coming around from behind the house. I watch as she runs across the grass, her slippers popping in and out through the base of her peach-colored satin robe, her hands fisted deep in her pockets, keeping the flaps together.

The woman's hair is short. Very short. And bleached so blond that it's practically glowing in the moonlight. And I didn't realize until she was almost to the sidewalk that this woman—this stranger in the peachy robe and luminescent hair—is my mother. My one and only mother.

And there's no doubt about it—she is fuming mad.

THREE

So much for Grams' promise. So much for the advantage of surprise. We'd made our battle plan and crossed enemy territory only to get ambushed by Peachy Bleachy.

"Get ready," I said to Marissa. "She's going to open her mouth and gun us down."

"That's not... Is that...?"

"Don't tell me you don't recognize the GasAway Lady."

Marissa gasped. "Wow! She has really changed her look!"

My mother didn't start out by gunning us down. Instead she swooped down on us, took a quick look over her shoulder, and said, "Get out from under that streetlight!" Then she grabbed each of us by an arm and hauled us into the shadows of a large lawn shrub. And when she's convinced that no one from the house can see us, that's when she opens fire. "Samantha, I cannot believe you would do this to me! Couldn't we have discussed it over the phone? Every time I call to talk, all I get is attitude. And now this? A *visit*? It was hard enough having your grandmother here—"

"*My* grandmother? According to you, she's *your* grandmother."

"Oh, Samantha, please! Try to understand how things are around here. I explained it to her, and I'm sorry if she took offense, but what could I do? If you're over thirty, you're washed up—*old*. They think I'm twenty-five, okay? And that's plenty old, believe me! So if I'm twenty-five, how can I have a mother who looks like...well, you know!"

"Can't very well have a thirteen-year-old daughter, either, can you?"

She let out a giant sigh. Like I finally understood. "Exactly."

"Might as well change your name, too. And your hair. What's next? You going to add and subtract body tissue until you're just another surgically built bimbo?"

She stared at me for a second, then slapped me, *smack!* right across the face. I wanted to slap her back, but I just stood there with my cheek stinging and my nostrils flaring. And then suddenly there was a rock the size of Gibraltar in my throat. "Look. I was stupid. I thought maybe if I came, you'd—"

"Oh, Samantha, it's not that I don't want to see you..."

There went my eyes, stinging away.

"...I just can't handle this right now. You have no idea about the complexity of the situation."

I forced my voice past the rock. "It can't possibly be as complicated as having to sneak up and down the fire escape every day because you're not supposed to be living with your grandmother! It can't possibly be as complicated as having to convince your school that your phantom mother couldn't attend back-to-school night or the Mother's Day tea or anything else that every other mother seems to be able to attend because she's out of town... *again*."

My mother closed her eyes and took a deep breath. "I am sorry about all of that, Samantha, truly I am, but..."

I dropped for cover, cinching up my high-tops while I tried to blink the tears back. "Never mind. We'll just go back down to the bus—"

"Well, it's a little late for that tonight, don't you think?" She pinched her perfectly plucked eyebrows together and said, "You've got to *promise* me, though—if anyone does see you, you're my nieces, you're...what? From Kansas? And you're taking the first bus back in the morning."

I was too tired to argue, and one look at Marissa told me that she was, too.

"Well? Samantha? Is that so much to ask?"

It was, but there's no way the woman who'd given me a pink angora sweater for Christmas would understand that. So I just sighed and shook my head and watched her eyebrows ease back into place.

"Well, let's get you inside, then." She eyed the suitcase and said, "Sorry to disappoint you, Marissa."

Marissa mumbled, "That's all right, Ms. Keyes," which made my mother say, "Please. You've got to call me Dominique. Aunt Dominique, I suppose."

Marissa shrugged. "Yes, ma'am."

Dominique frowned, then hurried off across the lawn, watching the house the whole time to make sure no one had spotted us. And while we're lugging along our stuff, struggling to keep up, she's keeping her voice low, saying, "I've already switched rooms with LeBrandi for the night. Mine's a single, and she's got a double. Max is still interviewing to fill the vacancy Opal left, so we'll be safe for one night."

"What did you do when Grams visited?"

My mother frowned over her shoulder at me. "Max and Inga were in Austria visiting relatives." She shook her head. "This . . . *this* is a whole 'nother story."

I was trying my best to walk beside her, but somehow every time I caught up, I couldn't keep up and wound up marching along like a dog at heel. On top of that, I wasn't even close to keeping up with all the names she was throwing around, and something about that bugged me. "Who are Max and Inga, and why are you afraid of them?"

"I'm not afraid of them. They're amazing people, but there are terms. Strict terms. And if you don't abide by them, you wind up like Opal."

"What happened to Opal?"

"She got kicked out, pure and simple. I never thought she had much talent to begin with, but then she started acting like this was a resort. She missed a few classes, a few physical regimens, spent all her time sunning at the pool and talking on the phone. And then she broke curfew one too many times."

"Curfew? You have a *curfew*?"

"That's right. And I'm violating it as we speak."

We tiptoed along a stone walkway, through an arched gate, and around the side of the complex. We passed a bunch of big trees and palms, a small garage, and then a large formal garden that looked like it had been groomed by the Fussy Florist. In the middle of the night, in the middle of winter, there were *flowers* blooming, and not a leaf on the ground.

When we rounded the corner to the back side of the mansion, my mother kept on walking, but Marissa and I stopped and stared. A pool with crystal-clear water was shimmering blue in the moonlight, and all around it were white lounge chairs and tables with royal-blue umbrellas. The terra-cotta deck was bordered with walkway lights and periwinkle vines, and forty degrees out or not, it didn't matter—all of a sudden I *had* to go swimming.

A voice from the shadows snapped me out of it. "Who's there?" it said, but the sound was soft, almost musical, and it had an accent that seemed to round off the edge in the question.

My mother comes scampering back. "Reena, it's only me. Dominique."

A screen door opens, and a large woman dressed in a muumuu the colors of a parrot steps out. She points to us and says, "And whose chil'ren are they?"

Lady Lana stammers, but in a heartbeat Dominique takes over. "They're my nieces. From Kansas. They're leaving first thing in the morning."

The door that this Reena person had come out of was the entrance to a small cottage that wasn't part of the main building. And behind its screen door I could see someone else watching. Watching and listening.

Reena looks us over and says, "Are they hungry?"

Lady Lana gives us a worried look. Like she's been

asked to change a strange kid's dirty diaper. "No...I... Reena, we don't have time to eat! If Max or Inga sees me, I'll wind up like Opal!"

The screen door opens with a little squeak, and out steps a girl with long beaded braids, wearing an oversized UCLA T-shirt and toe rings. And as she comes away from the cottage and into the moonlight, she says, "Come on, Dominique. You don't have to play that game with us. You know you've got nothin' to worry about. Not with Max, anyway." She looks us over, too, and says, "You're right, Mama. They're definitely hungry."

Good ol' Lady Lana. It takes a perfect stranger to inform her that her kid is starving, and all she can do is look at us with horror—like we're Pampers, Extra Poopy. She turns to Toe Rings and says, "Why did you say that?"

Toe Rings shrugs and asks us, "You girls hungry?"

In the middle of our nods, my mother interrupts. "No, I mean about me playing games. I'm not playing games! You think I want to be caught breaking curfew?"

Reena shoots her daughter a sharp look, but Toe Rings frowns and says, "What's it matter, Mama?"

Reena mumbles something back, then disappears into the cottage. Toe Rings shakes her head, then says, "You're in some spot, huh, Dominique?"

My mother glances at Marissa and me with a flash of panic in her eyes. But she lowers her voice and asks, "Hali, what are you talking about?"

Hali eyes us, too, and says, "Oh, *you* know....The question is, what's your answer gonna be?"

Now, I am absolutely clueless about what they're discussing. But as the color drains from my mother's face, I can see that she's not. She says, "I . . . I don't know what you're . . ."

Hali *tsk*s and whispers, "Like I said, you don't have to play games with *us*, Dominique. Just be straight about it. What are you going to tell him?"

I thought my mother was going to faint. Her eyes open real wide, and she whispers, "How did you . . ."

Hali shakes her head and says, "He tells Mama everything. You should know that by now."

"Can we please discuss this later?"

"No problem there. Just don't be playing that tearful-fearful game with Mama. She's been nothing but good to you. The least you can be is straight up with her." She turns to go, then says, "Oh, Mama says you and LeBrandi made the final cut for some big part on *Lords*. Congratulations."

She starts to walk away, but my mother chases after her. "What? Are you sure?"

"Oh, whoops. Well, like I said, Max likes to talk to Mama."

My mother's cheeks have gone from ash white to fiery red. She whispers, "But you're sure?"

"Oh, yeah. Final audition is Monday. He's probably planning to announce it at breakfast tomorrow."

"Does LeBrandi know?"

"LeBrandi? I ain't tellin' that twit jack."

My mother studies her a second. "What did *she* do to you?"

"Nothing to me. But when Mama spotted her sneaking around the grounds after curfew, LeBrandi called her the

Jamaican Jailer and told her if she said anything to Max or Inga, she'd get her deported."

"She said *what*? When did that happen?"

"Oh, an hour ago. Which is why Mama noticed you. She's a little jumpy, you know?"

"I can't believe LeBrandi said that!"

"Yeah, well, that's 'cause you got more class than her. You watch your back, Dominique. That girl's a cat."

Just then Reena comes out of the cottage carrying two lunch sacks. She hands one to Marissa and one to me, but she doesn't let go of mine. She holds on and just stares at me. Then, soft and low, she asks, "What's your name?"

My hand is next to hers on the paper sack, and I want to let go and back away, but it's like I'm frozen to this sack dangling in the air. I choke out, "Me?"

She nods.

"Sammy. My...my name's Sammy."

My mother can't help herself. "Actually, it's Samantha."

Reena doesn't seem to hear her. She leans in even closer, then looks in my eyes like she's reading a crystal ball. "What's your *las'* name?"

Her eyes are deep brown. Almost black. And even though she's looking at me real intensely, there's a softness to them that seems to be begging me to trust her. A softness that scares me.

It barely comes out a whisper when I say, "Keyes."

She hesitates. "Not Windsor?"

I shake my head, then I back away a step, clear my throat a little, and say, "My name's Sammy Keyes, and this is my..." I glance at my mother, who's all in a panic, and finish, "My cousin Marissa."

Reena doesn't look at Marissa. Instead she turns to my mother and whispers, "Go along, Dominique. It's late."

Marissa and I murmur our thanks for the food, then follow my mother along the path, through a jungle of ferns, palms, and periwinkles, to the mansion's back door.

At doorbell height there's a grid of number keys. Like someone took apart a pay phone, shrank the number pad, and mounted it in the wall. My mother punches in four digits, and to me it looks like a little ritual. Like she's making a speedy little sign of the cross at the Altar of Stucco.

When a green light glows at the base of the keypad, my mother faces us and says, "That was close back there." She turns the door handle, takes a deep breath, and whispers, "Not a sound. Not a peep. Just follow me."

This was not easy to do. The moment we stepped through the door, it felt as though we'd been transported from the Mediterranean to Egypt. From the back door clear through a central open area to the fancy glass double doors at the front of the house, the place looked like an Egyptian museum. There were urns on black marble pedestals, ancient-looking torches strapped to the walls, and Plexiglas cases with cracked and crumbling artifacts in them. Jewelry, plates, scraps of cloth, slabs of stone with hieroglyphics—I felt like I was on a tour through a mansion on the Nile.

And as we tiptoed along behind my mother, we couldn't help gawking. Or talking.

31

Marissa gasped, "Is that a real sarcophagus?"

"Shhh! Everything here is real. Samantha, don't touch!"

"I'm not! I can't!"

"Well, get away from there!" She rubbed her temples. "Oh god, you're giving me a headache!"

I tried to pull myself away, but I couldn't. The sarcophagus was like the coffin of King Tut, upright, staring at me from behind half an inch of Plexiglas—the large eyes, lined in black, seemed to pierce right through the case, like time and space and man-made displays couldn't contain them.

"Is this Max guy Egyptian?"

"No! His father was some kind of ambassador, so the family spent several years in Egypt when Max was growing up. Now come!" She grabbed me by the arm and yanked, then dragged me past a black marble fountain in the central open area, around the corner to the base of a stairwell. Then she turned and whispered, "Please, *please,* don't make any noise."

We nodded and followed her up the tiled steps to a hallway that was about as wide as a road. There were fresh flowers in vases on hall tables, brown leather-back chairs, and Oriental rugs running end to end over the polished hardwood floor. My mother tiptoed along in her peachy robe, pointing to doors, making stiff little hand signals and mouthing, "Bathroom…phone room…my room," and then, right next door, "We're in here." It was like getting a tour from a mannequin mime.

She hurries us in, then closes the door without a sound and lets out a windstorm sigh. "Okay. Here we are. Marissa, you can put that down by this bed. I'm afraid the two of you will have to share. Or one of you can sleep on the floor. There are extra blankets...."

After everything we'd walked past and seen, I was expecting the room to be big. Big and fancy. But it wasn't. There were two twin-sized beds with matching ivy-patterned bedspreads, two dressers with vanity mirrors, matching writing desks, and a closet. And even though everything was clean and tidy, it looked more like a budget motel room than a suite in a fancy villa.

Lady Lana sees what I'm thinking and says, "Our bedrooms don't have to be elaborate, Samantha. We don't spend much time in them—we're here to work. And it's a lot harder work than you've ever imagined." She motions around the place. "My room's even smaller. One bed, no window—which is why it's not exactly convenient to have guests."

Guests. I bit my lip and asked, "Where's the bathroom?"

"I pointed it out to you as we were walking past it!"

"That's the bathroom for everybody?"

"Yes. Four showers, four toilets. There are twelve of us, so most mornings you wait in line."

Marissa parked her suitcase by the bed as she studied the room. "It looks like this used to be bigger. Like they subdivided it or something."

A perfect little eyebrow arched up on Lady Lana's brow. "Exactly. They made these little cubicles out of the original rooms twenty years ago, when Max first started the agency. He used to be a director and a producer. He's even written a few features."

"Uh...what about the phone room?"

"What about it?"

"Is that for everyone, too? I mean, can I call Grams? I promised."

My mother says, "You stay here—I'll do it," then wrinkles her nose and adds, "And eat those horrid sandwiches, would you? They're smelling up the room!"

We loved the horrid sandwiches. They were some kind of salty fish on buttered bread, and I could've eaten three of them. We sat on the floor and inhaled them, then chased the sandwiches down with bananas and sodas.

When my mother gets back, she says, "She sends her love and a reminder to call when you know which bus you'll be catching home." Then she sits down in front of the mirror and starts dealing with her face. First she smears cream all over it, then she starts plucking microscopic hairs from her eyebrows. And let me tell you, she is on nub patrol like I have never seen, squinting into the mirror, turning from side to side, tracking down enemy hairs to seize and destroy.

And I know she's not going to tell me what that whole exchange with Toe Rings was about, and I know that asking is going to get me seriously snapped at, but after I finish my food I decide to try anyway. "So who was that girl with the braids?"

"Reena's daughter. Reena cooks, Hali cleans."

"Isn't she kinda young to be a maid?"

"Oh, I don't know. The story I heard is that she was going to UCLA but had to drop out because they couldn't afford it. She *is* smart, but she can also be somewhat brash, which is not very becoming."

I hesitate, then very quietly I ask, "What did she know that got you so upset, Mom?"

She stops plucking, turns to me, and whispers, "Samantha, it's imperative that you call me Dominique. At all times. Even when you think no one else can hear." Then she goes back to looking in the mirror.

I just sit there waiting for an answer to my question, and when one doesn't come, I try again. "Okay...so, Aunt Dominique, what did she know that got you so upset?"

Pluck, pluck. Pluck.

"Well, if you don't want to tell me, I could make some pretty wild guesses instead...."

Pluck, pluck...pluck!

"Let's see...maybe..."

She eyes me through the mirror. "If you really must know...," she says, then turns to face me, "Maximilian Mueller has asked me to marry him."

FOUR

She might as well have stuck my finger in a light socket. "To *marry* you?"

"That's right. So now maybe you understand the complexity of the situation a little bit?"

A tidal wave of panic was crashing all over me. I mean, my real father was a stranger. A big unknown. Someone my mother refused to discuss until I was "old enough to understand." And now here she was, talking about marrying someone else I didn't know and could never know because, according to her, I didn't exist.

I choked out, "But isn't he . . . isn't he *old*?"

My mother went back to searching for wayward eyebrow hairs. "Sixty-two is not *that* old."

"Sixty-two!"

Pluck.

"Well, if I can't be me because you can't be over thirty, then how can you say—"

"Samantha!" she hissed. "It's not the same thing!"

"Why not?"

"He's a man, and he's not trying to be an actress!"

I wanted to say, What does *that* matter? but what came out instead was, "Well, do you *love* him?"

She frowned at herself in the mirror. "We can see how far *love's* gotten me!"

That shut me down cold.

And as she's working her eyebrows, Marissa holds on to my arm and whispers, "She didn't mean it like that."

My mother stops mid-pluck and looks at me in the mirror. "No, Samantha, I didn't mean it like that. This really has nothing at all to do with you."

"How can you *say* that? You're gonna marry some guy who's old enough to be my grandfather, who doesn't know who you really are or that you have a—"

"Stop!" she whispered fiercely.

I stopped, all right. Just clammed up and looked down. And while my eyes are burning like they've been doused with acid, Marissa says to her, "You're afraid of losing everything, aren't you?"

I looked through my tears at Marissa. It didn't even sound like her. She sounded calm. Older. And there was so much understanding in her voice that my mother turned completely around in her chair, gave Marissa a few painful blinks, then burst into tears. "Why can't I just be an actress? Why do I have to go through this nightmare?" She looks at me and says, "If I don't marry him, it's all over. I'll be back waiting tables at Big Daddy's like I never left town, and Samantha, that's going to kill me. Do you understand? Kill me." She pushes the tears up and away with her little fingers. "And I can't afford to just leave here and live on my own. I'll never find another setup like this! I'm not out a nickel until I actually get work—do you think there's another place around that does that?

No! Which is why we're all willing to stick to their ridiculously strict schedules and regimens. They want to make us stars as much as we want to be stars, because that's how they make their money."

Marissa says, "So if you say no, you think he's going to make you leave?"

"I have no doubt about it. Max is a very proud man, and I'm sure he'd hold me to my contract, which means I'd probably never work again."

Marissa asks, "Can he *do* that?" and I add, "Yeah, isn't that blackmail?"

She shrugs. "He hasn't come right out and said any of this. It's just my intuition that it's what I can expect."

Marissa says, "Maybe you're just worrying too much."

"Yeah. Maybe he does this all the time. How many wives has he had, anyway?"

She looks right at me. "One. He never remarried after his wife, Claire, died. Have either of you ever heard of her? Claire Lewellen."

We both shake our heads.

"Neither had I, but she'd be a hard act to follow. Max's office is a veritable shrine to her. She was a very glamorous starlet, and from the way Max talks, she would've had a room full of Oscars if she'd lived."

"What happened to her?"

My mother shrugged and said, "She died in a car wreck near Malibu."

"A long time ago?"

"According to the newspaper article hanging in the reception room, it's been twenty-five years."

I thought about all this a minute, then asked, "So why you?"

She frowned at me. "Don't sound so incredulous, Samantha."

I *was* incredulous. I mean, after all these years of *not* getting married again, why now? And why, of all people, my *mother*?

She looks down and sighs. "He says we're destined to be together. He says he's been waiting for me since the world went dark. He says he can't turn back now, and he can't go forward without me."

For a moment the room is heavy with silence. Then Marissa says, "It sounds like he's in love with you."

My mother looks at Marissa, her eyebrows practically screwed into a knot on her forehead. "Except that when he proposed...he called me Claire. He swears he didn't, and I *was* in a state of shock, but still...."

We all sat there a minute, quiet. And it was strange. In a way I was upset. Very upset. But in another way, the whole situation seemed distant. Like it was happening to someone else. My mother had transformed herself into someone new, just to be mistaken for a person who'd been dead for twenty-five years.

Oh yeah, that was worth the effort.

Finally I shook my head and asked, "So what are you going to do?"

"Samantha, this is not the picture I had for my life, but there's probably not a woman at the agency crazy enough to turn him down. LeBrandi said she'd do it. She said she'd do it in a heartbeat."

I blinked. "You *told* her about it?"

"I had to tell *some*one! And LeBrandi and I have been through a lot of auditions together, so yes, I confided in her." She eyed me and said, "And what I told her was that I couldn't do it."

"Really?"

"Yes, but what she said makes a lot of sense. I'll lose everything if I turn him down, and think about what I'll get by becoming his wife! The man is extremely wealthy, but aside from that, imagine how my career would take off! I have every reason to believe he'd put the same effort and dedication into promoting me that he did into promoting Claire."

It was like she'd zapped me with a stun gun. I couldn't move, I couldn't speak. I couldn't even blink. Marissa, though, was functioning just fine. She says, "But how can you marry him when he thinks you're Dominique Windsor? Don't you need birth certificates and blood tests and stuff to get married?"

My mother rubs her temples and whispers, "I know. I do have a fake driver's license, but—"

That brought me around in a hurry. "You do? How'd you get *that*?"

"Oh, Samantha, not now. It's way easier than it should be. The point is, I've been trying to figure a way out of this nightmare ever since he proposed. I know everything's on the verge of blowing up in my face, but I've been trying to keep the lid on it long enough to make the final audition for Jewel. And now, according to Hali, I've got that! If I can land that part...if I can just land that part, I'll be able to go out on my own and not have to deal with this nightmare anymore. I'll be able to get an apartment, and you"—she comes over and holds my hand, squeezing it hard—"you can come and live with me."

I didn't squeeze back. I just sat there, looking into the eyes of this person who used to be my mother. And what I felt was nothing. Nothing. The thought of moving into an apartment with her didn't make me happy. It didn't make me angry. It left me completely numb.

She lets go of my hand and says, "This isn't just a pipe dream, Samantha. I have wanted to be an actress my entire life. You of all people know how much I've given up to get here, and at this point I'm not going to let anything stop me." She cocks her head a bit and asks, "Do either of you ever watch *The Lords of Willow Heights*?"

Marissa says, "Oh, yeah. I've seen it."

"You know Jewel? Sir Melville's dearly departed wife? All these years he's pined away for her. No other woman could take her place . . . and now she's back! Or will be, as soon as they cast her. Bad case of amnesia. Doesn't remember Sir Melville or their children. . . ."

I couldn't believe what I was hearing. Talk about typecasting! I mean, my mother sure wouldn't have to do much acting for that part. And I was burning to ask her why it was okay to play a mom on TV but not in real life, but before I could get myself slapped again, Marissa says, "*That's* the part you've been talking about? You're going to be *Jewel*?"

"I don't know that yet, but I *am* very close. And since you know who she is, you can imagine what a complete cattle call it was when they first held auditions. But here it is, down to final callbacks, and I'm still in the running. It proves that I'm not just here wishing I was good at this—I really *am* a good actress!"

Marissa asks, "How many people made the final cut?"

"When I got picked for the GasAway commercial, it came down to me and one other actress. I don't know this for certain, but I have a hunch that it's a similar situation now."

She turns to me and says, "I can't believe how much better I feel for having told you all of this. Things are not cushy for me here, they're not fun, and it's important to me that you understand that I'm not just some ding-a-ling down here having a little crisis."

Some ding-a-ling having a little crisis! I couldn't help it—I busted up. And the funny thing is, she did, too. And we're sitting there, looking at each other, laughing, and it feels strange. Like we're speaking a long-lost language.

Finally she smiles at me in a way that completely dissolves my heart. It's so sweet. So kind. So loving. Then she whispers, "I've missed you, Sunshine," but before I can get anything past the bowling ball in my throat, she pats my knee and says, "We really should get to bed. Breakfast is at seven, and that's when Max gives assignments and makes announcements. And I've got to get rid of this headache before then."

So Marissa pops her nightgown and a toothbrush out of her suitcase while I dig a T-shirt and toothbrush out of my backpack. And we're almost at the door when we hear, "Wait a minute! Where are you going? You can't go out there!"

Marissa and I look at each other and then at my mother. Finally Marissa says, "I can't go to bed with sardine breath!"

"And I really have to pee, Mom."

"Samantha!" she hissed. "Call me Dominique!" But she let us visit the bathroom, and in no time Marissa and I were back and under the covers of Opal's old bed, trying not to sprawl into each other's territory.

I did fall asleep for a little while, but then I rolled into Marissa, which didn't bother her but woke me right up. I lay there for the longest time, staring at the ceiling, listening to Marissa breathing beside me. Finally I propped myself up, and there's my mother, sleeping on her side, snuggled up in bed with moonlight from the window washing across her.

I couldn't help staring. She looked so beautiful. Like a fairy, snug in a bed of ivy leaves. And even though she'd abandoned me, even though she could barely admit that I was her daughter, even though there were times I knew she wanted to just wish me away, I couldn't stop looking at her.

I wanted to kneel beside her and just be near her, because now I knew she was still there; I'd seen a flash of her when she'd smiled at me. Yes, somewhere inside this stranger was my real mother—the one who'd raised me until I was almost twelve; the one I'd followed like a kitten, trusted like a scout. But bit by bit she'd been disappearing, and I didn't know how to stop it. I missed her hair. Her eyebrows. The freckles across her nose. The laughter in her voice.

43

And it felt like if I fell asleep again, I'd wake up to find a complete stranger where my mother had once been.

I don't remember falling asleep, but I do remember waking up. Something banged against the wall near the head of our bed, and it banged hard. Marissa slept right through it, and when I propped myself up, my mother was gone and the alarm clock across the room was glowing 3:30.

For a moment I panicked. Where had she gone? Then *thump!* something from the other room banged against the wall again. "Marissa?" I whispered. "Did you hear that?"

She didn't budge.

One more *thump,* this time quieter. "Marissa!" I shook her.

"Wh . . . what?" She sat upright. "What's wrong?"

"There's something banging around next door. Listen!"

She moaned, "Sam-my!" but she did hold still and listen. And what did we hear?

Nothing.

A minute later the door opens and my mother comes tiptoeing in. She takes one look at us and whispers, "What are you two doing up?"

"There was some kind of banging next door. Did you hear it?"

She shook her head. "These walls are like paper. You get used to it."

I watched her ease back into bed and asked, "Where'd you go?"

"To take some aspirin." She looks at the clock, then

turns her back on us and practically sobs, "God, if I feel this miserable at breakfast, I'm going to die."

I knew better than to talk. If there's one thing Lady Lana can't stand, it's chatty girls when she's trying to sleep. Marissa remembered, too. She buttoned her lips with two fingers, then mouthed, "Good night."

They were both asleep in no time, but I just lay there, watching the moonlight dance through the blinds, thinking about my mother marrying Max; about her auditioning for the part of Jewel; about whether there'd ever be a day when I'd have to decide if living with her was worth leaving Grams and Marissa.

What I should have been thinking about was the banging.

FIVE

The alarm rang at six-thirty. And that's when I learned that my mother doesn't even wake up the way she used to. No snooze button. No moaning and groaning. No Oh, *please!* from under the covers. Instead, she clicked off the buzz, swung out of bed, smiled, and cried, "It's gone! It's completely gone!"

I wanted to moan and groan and say, Oh, *please!* from under the covers, but instead I asked, "Your headache?"

She stands up. "Yes! C'mon, girls. Rise and shine! I told LeBrandi we'd switch back right at six-thirty. She's got to get her things, and I've got to get mine." She comes over and sits on my edge of the bed. "Samantha, I'm really sorry about this. About all of this. And I'll come home the first chance I get so that we can talk—now that I know you want to talk. But I think you can see that this is not the time to discuss things. *If* I get the part of Jewel, *then* we'll have some options. But in order for me to do that, I've got to live and breathe nothing but Jewel so that I can become sort of a reincarnation of her."

Marissa sits up and rubs her eyes. "Why can't you just be a new Jewel?"

My mother takes a deep breath and lets it out slowly.

"Jewel is already an established character. And sure, it'd be a lot more fun for me to do my own interpretation of her, but this is a big, *big* role. The casting director has made it very clear that the producer wants to fill the part as closely as possible in likeness, manner, and voice to the old Jewel, so that *Lords* fans will embrace her return. Once you're accepted by the viewers, then you can start making subtle changes."

"Is that why your hair's all . . ." Marissa ruffled the top of her head, trying to find the words.

"Exactly. It has really helped me get into character. Max says it also shows commitment, which is something this casting director is looking for. And now that I think about it, it may have helped LeBrandi and me to make the final cut."

"LeBrandi did her hair like that, too?"

My mother nodded. "We did it at the same time. It was scary"— she grinned at us —"but fun."

Marissa says, "But I don't get it. If Jewel's got amnesia, maybe she doesn't remember how she used to be. I mean, she doesn't even know who she is, right?"

"Marissa, all I can tell you is that if this is what the producer wants, this is what you try to deliver."

"What happened to the old Jewel, anyway? Did she die in real life?"

"No," my mother says, standing up. "The truth is, she got too old and too fat. Now come on, girls. Let's get going."

We got dressed quickly and stuffed our jammies away, and we were following her to the door when she says, "Why don't you wait right here." She checks her watch.

47

"If LeBrandi's not ready, I don't want you standing out in the hallway with that suitcase."

So she goes out while we wait. And when she isn't back a minute later, I stick my nose out and look up and down the hallway.

Marissa says, "Well?"

"She's gone."

She looks out, too, checking both directions. "Where'd she go?"

"I have no idea."

She points to the left. "That's her room, right?"

"Yeah."

"Maybe she went inside."

Just then we see her, scurrying toward us from the bathroom. She comes inside the room, shuts the door, and says, "The room's locked, she's not in the bathroom, she's not in the gym . . . do you think she's still asleep?"

She's really just talking to herself, so she doesn't wait around for an answer. She goes back to her door, knocks, and whispers, "LeBrandi! LeBrandi, wake up!"

I ask, "Don't you have a key?" but then I look down at our doorknob and notice that it doesn't have a keyed lock. All of the doors just have privacy locks like you find in people's bathrooms.

So I say, "She must be in there. You wouldn't lock it unless you were inside, right?"

She knocks a little louder. "LeBrandi! LeBrandi, it's getting late!"

Marissa offers, "Maybe she locked it by accident. I've done that before."

My mother comes back and says, "What am I going to do?"

I shrug and say, "Just break in."

"Break in? How? I'm not going to rip the door off its hinges."

"No, Mom—"

"Samantha!" She barked it like a dog with laryngitis.

"Sorry! Aunt Dominique."

"Well, what? How would you get in?"

"All you need is something like a cake tester."

"I don't happen to *have* a cake tester!"

"Anything skinny and hard. A paper clip. A piece of wire. A bobby pin?"

She's all over it. In two seconds flat she's got the drawers of LeBrandi's desk flying in and out, but the best she can produce is a pencil.

"No. It's got to fit into that little hole in the middle of the knob."

She starts tearing through the empty drawers of Opal's desk. "Well, help me look! Maybe there's something in LeBrandi's dresser."

So we go rummaging through LeBrandi's underwear and stockings, bathing suits and polo shirts, and find absolutely nothing that will work. Then a pair of socks stabs me. Just digs in and jabs me. I squeal, "Owwww!" then yank my hand out of the drawer as blood erupts from my ring finger.

My mother whispers, "What happened?"

I stick my finger in my mouth and mumble, "I got jabbed by a sock!"

She frowns. "Jabbed by a sock? And you're *bleeding*?"

I check my finger, then pop it back inside my portable blood vacuum. "Grm-hm."

Marissa's looking through the drawer. "Which pair?"

"They're sort of an olive green . . . yeah, those! Careful!"

Now, to my mother, bleeding is like farting. It's just not something you do in polite company. And if you do have an accident, well, you excuse yourself and leave the room before anyone realizes what you've done.

But I didn't have anywhere to go, so I just stood there, sucking on my finger while Lady Lana wrinkles her nose like the room is full of gas. Then Marissa untucks a pair of socks and gasps, "Look at this brooch!"

It's a large gold oval pin with a red stone in the middle. And even though the stone is too big to be a ruby, from the way it's cut and set, it sure seems like *something* expensive.

My mother gasps, too, and very gingerly takes it from the palm of Marissa's hand. She looks at the front, then the back. And when she sees the spear of gold used to pin the thing on, she says, "That would draw blood, all right."

I nod and say, "It'll also open a door."

It's like she'd forgotten. "Oh!" She hands me the brooch. "Here!"

So I take the thing, and that's when I see that the design etched in gold around the stone isn't just swirls and swiggles. It's two snakes. Intertwined. And I don't know why, but all of a sudden I get the creeps. Like I hadn't just been jabbed by a brooch—I'd been bitten by a snake.

I look at my mother and say, "These are *snakes*."

She jumps back and looks around frantically. "Snakes? Where?"

"On the brooch, Mom. Right here."

She takes a quick look at it and says, "So what?" Then she adds, "And it's *Dominique*, Samantha."

"Oh, right."

I don't know why the snakes bothered me. Snakes are actually pretty cool. Unless they're coiled up and rattling, ready to inject you with poison, that is. But as I grabbed my backpack and followed my mother next door, I kept looking at the snakes, twined together around the stone, and something about it felt strange. Foreign. Like this brooch didn't belong anywhere near California.

Then I remembered the decorations downstairs and asked my mother, "Where do you think LeBrandi got this?"

She looked around nervously, then checked her watch. "I don't know. I don't *care*. Would you just open the door?"

So I did. I pushed the pin in, popped the lock out, opened the door, and stepped aside.

My mother blinks at me. "You made that look so easy...! Where'd you learn how to do that?"

"It *is* easy. And everyone knows how to do that." I look at Marissa standing there with her suitcase. "Don't they?"

She shrugs. "That's what I do whenever Mikey locks himself in my bathroom...but I think I learned it from you."

My mother peeks into her room, then motions us in, whispering, "She's still asleep! I can't believe it."

51

Other than the light from the hallway, it's pretty dark inside the room. But I can see the silhouette of someone in the bed against the wall. My mother sits on the edge of the mattress and shakes her a little, saying, "LeBrandi? LeBrandi, it's time to get up!"

Something about this is giving me the creeps. And it's more than the fact that my mother's room is like a little cave, small and dark and cool—it's the air. It feels like it's charged wrong. Like the ions are clashing, and *angry* or something.

So I put the brooch in my sweatshirt pocket and flip on the light.

My mother jumps, but LeBrandi keeps right on sleeping, the covers tucked up to her neck as she faces the wall. My mother shakes her again. "LeBrandi! Wake up!"

That's when I notice the orange vial of prescription pills sitting all by itself on the dresser, which butts up to the head of the bed. I whisper, "Look!" and point.

She grabs the pills and reads the label, saying, "I told her to stop taking these! She's missed morning conference twice already because of these!"

I moved a little closer. "Sleeping pills?"

"Yes." She hands them over to me, saying, "Opal got her started on them." She shakes LeBrandi again, only this time she shakes her hard. "LeBrandi! Wake up!"

Now, the first thing I notice when my mother hands me the vial is that it's empty. No rattle of pills inside. Then my mother rolls LeBrandi onto her back. And while she's smacking LeBrandi's cheeks with her fingertips, saying, "Wake up! LeBrandi, wake up!" the air seems to be zapping all around me. I mean, one look at LeBrandi and I know.

No matter how hard my mother slaps her, she's never going to wake up again.

SIX

It's creepy enough finding a dead body. But when that dead body looks just like your mother, you get more than the chills. You get sick to your stomach.

And while my mother's busy slapping LeBrandi's cheeks and I'm trying to keep the fish in my stomach from swimming too far upstream, Marissa grabs my arm and gasps, "They could be twins!"

I just nod.

"And she looks..."

I choke out, "I know," then swallow hard and clear my throat. "Mom...Mom, stop it. She's dead."

"What?" She looks from me to LeBrandi, then back at me. "She can't be!"

"She's *blue*, Mom."

My mother takes LeBrandi by the shoulders and shakes her. Hard. Then she looks at me and gasps, "Oh my god!" and she's off like a shot, out the door and down the hall.

Marissa says, "Shouldn't we try CPR or something?" but I just stand there with the orange vial in my hand, staring at this fuzzy blond woman with blue skin.

"Maybe take her pulse...?"

"Marissa, it's hopeless! Look at her!"

"Well, shouldn't we at least *try*?"

I felt like saying, *You* try! but instead I put the vial on the dresser, dropped my backpack off my shoulder, and sat down on the edge of the bed. Marissa parks her suitcase beside the bed and sits on it, then looks at me like, Well?

So I pick up LeBrandi's wrist and press against the inside with my fingertips, looking for a pulse.

Touching her is giving me the creeps. Her skin isn't like ice or anything, but it's cool and pale, and her fingers are arched straight up at me.

I put her hand back by her side and whisper, "Nothing."

Just then a woman in purple-and-green plaid pajamas and purple cottontail slippers comes barging in. She gasps, and the rag-wrapped pigtails on top of her head seem to flex toward the ceiling as she says, "Oh my god—it's true?"

We just look at her.

"She's *dead*?"

"I . . . I think so."

"I overheard Dominique on the phone . . . and . . . and . . . oh-me-oh my, oh-me-oh-*my*!" she whimpers, hopping around like the Plaid Rabbit, late to tea. Then her nose twitches up and down really fast and she cries, "This is terrible, just terrible!" and barges right back out the door.

Thirty seconds later she's back with two other women, and in no time more show up. And pretty soon we're having a pajama party of brightly colored women playing Pass-the-Vial and wailing Why-oh-why-LeBrandi.

Then suddenly the Plaid Rabbit gasps and slams the vial

back onto the dresser, and when everyone else looks where she's looking, they all go wide-eyed and silent, shrinking back against the walls. And let me tell you, Marissa and I shrink back, too, because coming straight at us is a mummy.

A real live mummy.

That's what she looks like to us, anyway. She's got white gauze wrapped around her hands, around her head and most of her face, and she's wearing a white robe, crossed tight at the neck. She shuffles toward us in heavy woolen socks, and the minute her eyes land on me, I scramble to the side too.

See, she's got eyes like a tiger, yellow and fierce. And I'm not talking yellow like our cab driver's had been—no, her *irises* are yellow. And as I'm hugging the wall, Tiger Eyes takes one look at LeBrandi, then turns on Marissa and me. "Who are you."

It's a command, not a question, but still, it needs an answer—one I tried hard not to choke on. "We're Domi...Dominique's nieces."

"This is not a hotel."

"We...we came to...to surprise her, and...and um... well, we're leaving this morning. We didn't know."

"Hrrmm." She turns back to LeBrandi, then sees the vial on the dresser. She picks it up and shakes it at the other women. "This should be a lesson to you, girls! You see where this can lead?"

Just then my mother appears, her shoulders cradled in the arm of a man with a white moustache wearing a shiny gold robe and black slippers.

Right away I know that this man is Maximilian Mueller. There's just an air about him. His hair's damp and styled back, and the part down the side is as sharp as the edge of his moustache. His face is tan, and shiny from shaving, and his hazel green eyes look magnified to about three times normal size by the lenses of his boxy tortoiseshell glasses.

Soap and aftershave fill the air like incense as he pats my mother's shoulder and says, "Take a deep breath, Dominique. Inga and I will handle this."

As Max walks in, the Pajama Platoon seems to let out a gigantic sigh of relief. And when they see their friend Dominique crying, they all start bawling. The Plaid Rabbit grabs my mother by the arm and says, "Why, *why?*" and another lady with plum red hair sobs, "She was so beautiful!"

The Mummy frowns. "Shoo! All of you, shoo! Go on to your rooms and get yourselves ready for breakfast," she says, then adds, "Except you and your nieces, Dominique. You should explain to Max and me why LeBrandi is in your bed. Has it to do with unexpected company?"

Dying must rank higher than bleeding or passing gas in my mother's book of social no-nos, because she didn't even nod. She just stared at LeBrandi with a horrified expression on her face, getting paler and paler by the second.

The Mummy points to the writing-desk chair. "Maxi, let her sit down."

He swings the chair around, and my mother sort of dissolves onto it. Then the Mummy says softly, "Perhaps if you didn't look at her...?"

57

My mother blinks, then tears her eyes away from LeBrandi and stares at her feet instead.

And then, does the Mummy let my mother recover a little and suggest maybe taking this discussion elsewhere? No. She sits right down on the edge of the bed and says, "Now then, tell us what happened."

So my mother does. And even though she tells everything pretty much like it happened, the whole situation is giving me the creeps. A mummy on the bed with her back to the dead, my mother brushing away tears as she speaks, Mr. Max looking oh-so-sympathetic and never taking his eyes off my mother—it's like we're in the middle of some weird soap opera instead of a room with a real live dead body.

Now, maybe Max and Inga are hanging on my mother's every word, but I'm not. I'm more checking out Max, worrying about my mother actually *marrying* this guy. I mean, maybe he's really rich, but what kind of man wears a gold lamé robe and turtle-shell glasses?

Not anyone you'd want to call Dad.

'Course then again, there was Lady Lana, with fuzzy blond hair and pencil-sharp eyebrows—someone I *had* been known to call Mom.

When my mother gets to the part about the vial of pills, Max leans over and takes the bottle off the dresser, and as he does, a long gold chain with a key dangling from it swings forward from the flaps of his robe. He tucks it back away, then murmurs, "Why didn't I see it? It should never have been like this!"

Inga says, "Maxi, don't do this to yourself! Who was to know she was so troubled?"

Just then Hali comes into the room, and if it weren't for those beaded braids, I might not have recognized her. Instead of a UCLA T-shirt, she's wearing a simple black dress with a white apron over it, and her toe rings are tucked safely inside black nurse shoes. Her face also seems stiff, almost blank, and she doesn't look at us at all. Or LeBrandi. Instead she looks straight at Max and says, "There's an ambulance here. Mama's bringing them up."

Max nods, then says, "Help Dominique and the girls down to the reception room, would you? And bring them some coffee and juice. Inga and I will be down shortly."

Hali gives everyone in the room sort of a roving sneer—well, except LeBrandi; she doesn't even *look* at her. Then she flags us along with a wag of the head and leaves the room.

I grab my backpack and Marissa wrestles with her suitcase, and just as we make it out the door, here comes Reena in a getup just like Hali's, hurrying alongside two guys in orange jumpsuits. They rush past us, and while Marissa and I are kind of rooted to the floor, Hali says, "Dominique, have them park that suitcase next door, okay? They look ridiculous hauling that thing around."

"What's that?" She looks at us like she'd forgotten we were there. "Oh, yes, yes, of course."

So we throw Marissa's suitcase and my backpack on the bed where we'd slept, then come back out to see Hali and Reena off to the side, whispering fiercely to each other while my mother's hovering near her own doorway, eavesdropping.

59

She sees us and comes away, saying, "They radioed in a 'code blue'—do you know what that is?"

I shrug. "Blue body?" I turn to Marissa. "You think?"

Reena takes off down the hall, then Hali says to us, "Let's go, lambchops."

She leads us down the stairs, past the marble fountain, into Little Egypt, then marches through the foyer without a word. And it's starting to feel like she's going to march us straight outside when suddenly she pivots to a halt by a tall black door that's got four-foot stone urns on either side of it. She pushes the door open, steps aside, and puts an arm out, saying, "Wait in here. I'll be back with coffee."

My mother slumps into a black leather chair by a window, and when I try to say something to her, she snaps, "Shh! Let me think, would you?" So Marissa and I sort of stand around awhile, then start checking out what looks like the Mueller Agency Hall of Fame. Framed photographs and magazine covers tile the walls from end to end, clear up to the ceiling, and even I have to admit that some of these people chumming up to Max in the photographs are famous. Real famous. Marissa says to my mother, "Max is the agent for all these people?"

She blinks at her a few times, then says, "What was that? Oh. Oh, yes." Then she adds, "Or was." She gets up and starts pacing around the room, muttering, "Why does he want us here? What is *taking* so long?" She turns to me. "Don't slip up, Samantha. Say as little as you can get away with. You too, Marissa." She slumps back into the chair. "Oh god, what a nightmare!"

Now, it seemed to me that my mother was more con-

cerned about us giving her away than she was about her
friend having died. And I was trying not to be too upset
with her about it, especially since—as much as I tried to
tell myself it wasn't my fault—I was pretty upset with myself. I mean, I had heard thumping. Loud thumping. And
sleeping people do not thump. They snore, or drool, or
make little whistling noises, but they don't thump. Not
like that, anyway.

So what was all that thumping for? Had LeBrandi been
calling for help? It hadn't even *resembled* an SOS, but
maybe she was too out of it to do anything more. Maybe
if I'd gone next door...

I sat beside my mother and whispered, "Do you think
that bumping I heard last night was her calling for help?"

"Oh, Samantha. Are you sure you didn't just imagine
it?"

"I did *not* imagine it! What if she was trying to call for
help? What if—"

"Oh, please. Don't do this. How were we supposed to
know?" She hesitates, then says, "It would probably be a
good idea not to bring it up at all. It'll . . . it'll only com-
plicate matters." Then she gets up and starts pacing again.

I had so many questions logjamming in my brain that I
probably would've started pacing the opposite side of the
room if Marissa hadn't distracted me. "Hey!" she says
from a narrow table across the room. "You look gorgeous
in these pictures!"

My mother barely tells her, "Thanks," and keeps right
on pacing.

This I had to see, so I join Marissa, who's busy turning

the pages of a large black binder. She flips back to my mother's pages and says, "Check these out. Isn't that head shot great?"

I'd never seen my mother in black-and-white glossy before—only in full-spectrum color, which, believe me, includes some scary hues that not even Crayola's come up with yet.

But with all those colors filtered out, what was left was someone beautiful. There was a spot of light in each eye, and with her hair blowing back and her chin up and out she looked absolutely glamorous.

Like a movie star.

Which is probably what I should've told her, but instead I blurted out, "But you don't look anything like this anymore." She stops pacing and flashes her eyes at me. "I . . . I mean your hair and everything."

She takes a deep breath and says, "Hopefully after Monday that won't be an issue."

On the left page of my mother's section is the head shot, and on the right is what looks like an oversized postcard that takes up the top half of the page, showing my mother in three different poses and outfits. In one she's wearing jeans, a flannel shirt, and a cowboy hat, and she's leaning against corral fencing, looking ladylike but completely at home with a lasso in her hand. Like she could ride a rodeo bull sidesaddle if you asked her to.

In the middle picture she's walking along the shoulder of the road in an evening gown, holding up a gasoline can with a you-win-some-you-lose-some look on her face, and in the third picture she's at a breakfast bar scooping cereal up to her mouth while she pores over the *Wall Street Journal*.

Even *I* have to admit that this Dominique Windsor person seems like she can handle any role. From roping cows to selling chow, she's your girl—which I suppose is how a person with a distinct aversion to anything even remotely associated with intestinal distress landed a commercial for GasAway.

Anyway, underneath the oversized postcard is a list of acting experience and credits. I happen to know that my mother hasn't exactly been Thelma Thespian for at least a decade, but according to her résumé, she has.

On the top of the list there is, of course, GasAway. Something I wish she *would* lie about. But beneath that is a whole string of credits: the role of Belle in *Beauty and the Beast;* Maria in *The Sound of Music;* Sandy in *Grease.* The list fills the page, and in almost every credit she's the leading lady.

One look at my mother, and I know she knows what I'm thinking. She's stopped pacing, her hands are on her hips, and her jaw is set. And before I can say anything, she snaps, "Well, you can't get in here with no experience!"

"So you just—"

"Shh!" She comes over to us and whispers, "Yes. But I could play any of those parts if I had to."

Marissa says, "And they're all theatrical, so you don't have to have video clips?"

My mother looks at her with surprise. "I'm glad it wasn't that transparent to Max! I had some dummy press clips made up, but he barely glanced at those."

I must've looked shocked, and I guess I was. I mean, first she gets a fake driver's license, then she dummies up newspaper clippings; who *was* this woman? Certainly not the person I knew back in Santa Martina. She laughs and says, "Sorry to disillusion you, Samantha."

Marissa looks back at the credits and asks, "But why did you pick Great Falls, Montana? Is there even a Grande Theatre there?"

My mother winks at her. "Nope. Got torn down a few years ago. You know how people are, not supporting the arts and all." She leans a little closer and whispers, "Actually, it was a good thing I'd been to Great Falls, because when Max learned during my interview that I was 'born and raised' there, that's practically all we talked about. Turns out *Claire* was from there."

"His wife?"

"That's right. Fortunately for me her family moved when she was two, so he really didn't know anything about it." She pulls a little face. "That doesn't mean I wasn't sweating it out for a little while there, though!"

It's funny. In all my years growing up with her, my mother had never admitted to a lie. There were things she just wouldn't talk about, but I always thought that was because if I did force her to talk about it, she would wind up lying, and lying was something that was—I don't know—*beneath* her.

But looking at her now, I realized that lying wasn't beneath her at all. She did it all the time! And as she smiled at me from across the room, she seemed proud of herself. Like, wow, hadn't she gotten away with murder?

I didn't know what to say to her, and I couldn't stand to look at her a second longer, so I joined Marissa, who was taking refuge in the pages of the big black binder.

Marissa turns over a couple of pages, then says, "Recognize her?"

I didn't need to check the name at the bottom of the page. Even with her hair dark, her eyes open, and no blue in sight, I knew it was LeBrandi.

We both shuddered as she turned the page.

I guess my mother was feeling bad about what she'd told me, because she comes up behind us and whispers, "Everyone around here does the same thing, Samantha." She points to a list of credits on the Plaid Rabbit's page. "Do you really think Tammy was ever on Broadway? Please. She couldn't act her way out of a speeding ticket. And—"

I turned on her. "Oh, yeah? Then what's she doing here?!"

Our eyes locked, until finally my mother looks down and says, "I'm sorry. You're right. There's no need for me to start getting catty. But Tammy *is* sort of... I don't know... skittish. Like she's afraid of her own shadow. Every time she gets a little nervous, she has to go to the bathroom. She auditioned for the part of Jewel, too, and wound up excusing herself in the middle of that. Opal and LeBrandi told me it was all a big act, but I don't think so. Who'd want to embarrass themselves that way?"

Marissa says, "Speaking of Opal...," and points to the name OPAL NOVAK beneath the next headshot.

My mother says, "She's still in there?" and is about to

add something more when Hali walks into the room. Hali slides a large coffee-table book about Cleopatra aside with a big silver tray loaded with decanters and cups. She looks right through my mother, saying, "There's cocoa here, too." She turns to go, then changes her mind and looks directly at my mother. "Max says he'll be right down. You know what you're going to tell him?"

Now, she's not talking about dead bodies in bed. And it's really starting to bug me how everyone seems to have their mind on something *besides* LeBrandi, so I almost feel like cheering when my mother says, "Hali, we're here to discuss LeBrandi. And I would appreciate it if you wouldn't bring that other matter up again. It's really none of your business."

Blood rushes to Hali's cheeks, and I can tell from the way her nostrils are flaring out and her eyes are pinching in that it's not embarrassed blood—it's *angry* blood.

She checks down the hallway, then closes the door and snaps, "You are *so* wrong about that, blondie!"

"*Blondie?* Now wait just a minute...."

Hali steps forward, practically breathing fire through her nose. "Why would a man his age, who has everything and is surrounded by beautiful women, suddenly want to get married? Have you stopped to ask yourself this? Or are you so wrapped up in your own magnificence that you think he could actually be in *love* with you?"

My mother stands there, wide-eyed and petrified, and chokes out, "Hali, stop it! What's wrong with you? Why are you acting like this?"

Hali shakes her head from side to side, the beads in her

hair clicking together. "It's a no-brainer, Dominique." She gives my mother a really disgusted look, then flings the door open and marches out.

My mother stands there staring at the empty doorway with her mouth gaping open. Finally she looks at me and shakes her head. "What was *that* all about?"

Now, I had no idea why Hali was so mad, but I did have a pretty good idea what she was driving at. And to tell you the truth, I probably should've been revolted, but I was mostly feeling relieved. I mean, if my hunch was right, then there was no way I'd ever have to call Max Mueller Dad.

She studies me and asks, "You do know, don't you?"

I look at Marissa and can tell by her expression that she's figured it out, too, and that she doesn't think it's such a hot idea to fill my mother in on it, either. But I take a deep breath and say, "Maybe you should sit down...."

"Don't be ridiculous, Samantha. Tell me!"

I hesitate, then try, "Max doesn't have *every*thing, you know."

I hold my breath, but no lightbulb appears over my mother's head. "Samantha! Just tell me, would you?"

I shake my head and whisper, "Does the word *heir* mean anything to you?"

SEVEN

She should've sat down. Instead, she blinked at me for maybe eight seconds, then fainted. Just crumpled to the floor like she was a marionette and someone had cut her strings.

And maybe I should've been sympathetic, but to tell you the truth, I thought it was stupid. It was so...so... Hollywood. And if you ask me, it was bad manners, too. Way worse than passing gas or bleeding. I mean, if you cut the cheese, you get some air moving or light a few matches. It's no big deal. If you cut your*self*, well, you just apply pressure and a bandage and try not to drip on anything. But if you faint? There you are like a big ol' blob of Jell-O, sprawled out on the floor with a stupid look on your face and the flaps of your robe hanging wide open. And then people have got to attend to you. You know, make sure you're breathing, fix your clothes, get you up on a couch, and try to revive you. It's a lot of work and worry, and for what? Give me a bleeder with a belly full of beans any day of the week.

Anyway, we did get my mother up on the couch, and just as I was fixing her robe, who walks in?

Max.

He's traded in his robe and slippers for a sports coat, some slacks, and loafers, and he must have put on a second coat of aftershave, because right away I feel like I'm going to sneeze. He takes one look at my mother and says, "What happened here?"

I fight back the tickle in my nose as I say, "She fainted."

He sighs and says, "This whole ordeal has been so draining." Then he sits beside her on the couch and rubs her hand, saying, "Dominique ... Dominique!"

It's obvious that he's not seeing the hundred pounds of stubborn Jell-O Marissa and I have just wrestled up onto the couch. What he's seeing is Dominique Windsor, love of his life, and the look on his face is making me sick. He's like a big old bug-eyed fly hovering over my mother, and I'm just itching to swat him away. So I say, "Don't you have some smelling salts or cold water or something around here?"

He gets up and smiles at me like I'm a genius. "Better yet," he says, pulling up the key from around his neck, "I've got whiskey."

"Whiskey!" I follow him to an inner office door, saying, "She doesn't need whiskey! She's already passed out!"

He smiles at me again, only it's not a condescending smile or even a mocking one. It's kind. Gentle.

And I hate him for it.

He says, "They use it to revive people all the time." He slides the key into a heavy-duty Schlage deadbolt, opens his office, then hurries around behind his desk. "I keep it on hand for hospitality reasons—you'd be surprised how many people will accept a drink in the middle of the day."

He sits down in a high-back leather roll-around chair and opens the bottom right drawer of his desk, saying, "It's an unfortunate aspect to this whole industry, I'm afraid. High stakes breed shattered nerves." He pulls up a dark amber bottle and a shot glass. "Prayer and meditation are much more effective than booze, but I've given up trying to convert the people in this town. The bigger picture is just not within their focal range."

He's about to close the drawer when suddenly he stops short and starts digging through it. A few seconds later he looks up at me and gasps—like someone's stuck his rear end with a pin. "They're gone!"

Marissa calls from the other room, "She's coming to!"

I look over my shoulder, then back at Max. "What are gone?"

"The Honeymoon Jewels." He chokes out, "But how can that be?" then dives back into the drawer to paw around some more.

It feels like I really shouldn't be there while he's so upset, but I can't seem to leave either. His office is like some kind of strange chamber. It's a lot smaller than the reception room, and it feels heavy. Dark. Partly that's because there are no windows, but also the furniture is chunky and heavy-looking. And black. Just like the waiting-room door that Hali had let us in through.

But it's the *stuff* that keeps me from backing out of there. Like, in one corner there's this headless mannequin with skinny white arms, wearing a deep purple cape over a full-length silver dress. Next to the mannequin there's a large chest—like something you'd pull off a pirate ship, only it's painted a brilliant tomato red. Behind the desk there's an ebony harp with a singing angel's head, and alongside it is an antique armoire with a twisting design of inlaid roses.

Then, on the left wall, there's a small black vanity table with a tarnished brass birdcage sitting on it, and beside that is this tapestry, four feet wide, running from the floor almost clear up to the ceiling. It's got six large hieroglyphics woven into it, each surrounded by smaller Egyptian-looking shapes and designs.

Now, maybe this stuff would've looked good if it was split up and put in other rooms with other similarly weird stuff—like that tapestry would've fit just fine out in Little Egypt—but all of it crammed together made me feel like I was in an attic instead of an office.

Then I remembered what my mother had said about Max's office being a shrine to his wife. And as I looked around, I realized that this was probably all *her* stuff. Max had put his massive desk smack-dab in the middle of his little temple to Claire.

In the few seconds it had taken me to check out the room, Max had torn that drawer completely apart. He sits up and says again, "But how can that be?" Then he leans back in his chair, and his whole face—his forehead, his cheeks, his moustache, his *ears*—crawls back, like someone's tightening his scalp from behind. "Opal!" he whispers, and suddenly his face becomes flushed, and a new wave of aftershave fills the air.

Serious storm clouds are forming behind that man's boxy glasses, and I'm not carrying an umbrella, if you know what I mean. So I inch my way toward the door while he pours himself a shot of whiskey and downs it.

Marissa comes up to me carrying a cup from the tray that Hali had brought in, and says, "She's fine. I'm going to get her a glass of water. I'll be right back."

I sit down next to my mom and say, "There's no way you can marry that guy."

She says, "Shh!" then whispers, "What's he doing in there?"

"He's doing shots."

"What?"

"Well, he went to get some whiskey to revive you, but then he noticed that some jewels are missing, so he decided to drink it himself."

"Some *jewels* are missing? What jewels?"

"I don't know. He called them the Honeymoon Jewels."

"*Honeymoon* jewels?"

"Yeah. I think he thinks Opal stole them."

"Opal? How could she...?"

"I don't know!" I whisper, checking over my shoulder. "What I do know is that if all that stuff was Claire's, then Lover Boy in there is crazy."

My mother looks down.

"Well *is* it?"

Very quietly she says, "That's what I've been told."

"Doesn't that kind of freak you out?"

She shrugs. "He loved her. Completely. It's actually very romantic."

"It's *weird* is what it is!"

72   Just then Max pokes his head out, and he doesn't even

acknowledge that my mother has come to. He just says, "If Inga doesn't come down in a few minutes, you're free to go," and closes the door.

"Free to go?" my mother says. "I don't like the way that sounded!"

Just then Marissa comes in with a cup of water, saying, "I passed by the dining room. Everyone's in there eating, and it smelled so good. God, I'm starved."

My mother takes a sip of water and says, "I couldn't eat a bite," then she adds, "Why don't you drink your cocoa, Marissa, that should help."

So Marissa and I drink cocoa while my mother has her water, and we're all just sitting in silence, wondering how long a "few minutes" should be. And I'm sort of looking over Max's Walls of Fame when I notice a photo near the center of the wall. The photo's framed just like the rest of the pictures, and it's black-and-white like a lot of them, but it's not a portrait or a magazine cover or a candid with Max chumming up to the star. It's just a nice picture of a woman in a dainty beaded cap propping her face up with one lacy-gloved hand.

What made me put my cocoa down and pulled me up and over to the picture was not wanting to get a closer look at *her*. It was her neck I wanted to see. She was wearing a lacy blouse with a high collar, a long string of dark beads, and a ring. And half hidden behind her hand was a brooch.

My hand shot into the pocket of my sweatshirt, and there it was, warm and hard, the brooch I'd used to open the door.

I didn't need to pull it out of my pocket to know it was the same piece of jewelry that was peeking out from behind that lacy glove. And I didn't need my mother to tell me that this was Claire or that the brooch in my pocket was part of the Honeymoon Jewels. My brain made those connections like a bear trap snapping shut.

My first impulse was to go up and knock on Max's door and hand it over. I mean, I wasn't guilty of anything. He'd *have* to believe how I'd found it. But then I remembered how many times adults *haven't* believed me, and I don't know—something told me that knocking would only get me tangled up tighter in this sticky mess called my mother's life.

So I motioned my mother over and pointed to the photo. "This is Claire, right?"

She nods and takes a sip of water.

I point out the brooch in the photo, then give her a sneak peek at what's in my hand. "What do you want me to do with this?"

At first she gapes at me. Then she grabs the brooch and compares it with the picture. And when she's positive that they're the same, she gives it back to me like it's burned her. "Put it back where you found it. Right now. Go! There's no way you want to be caught with this in your possession."

"But—"

"They'll find it when they pack up her stuff. Go!"

A "few minutes," it seemed, were up. Marissa and I scooted out of there and snuck back upstairs to LeBrandi's room. And we were so busy looking over our shoulders as we slipped through the door that we practically had a heart attack when we faced forward and saw Hali standing next to the bed we'd slept in.

She scowls at us, then starts tearing apart the bed.

I catch my breath and say, "What are you *doing*?"

She pulls up hard on the fitted sheet, lifting the whole mattress a few inches before it flops free. "What I've been doing since I can remember—following orders." She peels off the sheet, covers and all. Then she throws the ball of bedding on the ground, walks right across the mattress, and starts tearing apart the bed my mother had slept in. "Inga seems to think Dominique will be traumatized for life if she has to sleep in LeBrandi's sheets again, so I've been told to launder these and the ones next door." She strips the bed and drags the bundles out the door, muttering, "They all get to hang around and gossip about LeBrandi, but can this wait? No. It's got to be done *now*."

When she's gone, Marissa shakes her head and says, "I wouldn't want her working for me."

I check down the hall, then close the door and push in the lock button. "What do you mean?"

"That is one major chip she's got on her shoulder."

"Yeah, but you know what? She wasn't like that last night. I mean, she had attitude and everything, but she wasn't *mad*."

Marissa shrugs. "Yeah, but still—she shouldn't take it out on us."

I took out the brooch and started buffing away fingerprints with the bottom of my sweatshirt, thinking that even though Hali had seemed mad—especially at my mother—I got the feeling that it really wasn't any of us she was mad at. It was something much deeper. Like overnight she'd become angry at the whole world.

Marissa says, "That's good enough, Sammy. Put it away!"

The pair of socks the brooch had come out of was sitting unrolled on top of the other balls of socks in the drawer. I picked one up, then gathered it down to the toe, thinking that I could pick the brooch up with the sock and not have to touch it again.

Then my thumbs felt something that does not belong in the toe of a sock.

Paper.

So I stopped, looked at Marissa, then pushed the toe end inside out. And onto the dresser fluttered a small scrap of folded paper.

Now, I don't know about fingerprints and paper. And maybe I was being paranoid, but something about the whole situation told me to pull the sleeves of my sweatshirt over my hands and *then* unfold the scrap. So that's what I did.

77CURIO was all that was written on it.

Marissa whispers, "What's that mean?"

"I don't know. It looks like a license plate number."

I could hear Hali thumping the mattress around next door, and when she banged against the wall, it reminded me of what I'd heard the night before. I had *not* imagined it! No way. And wondering what that thumping had been about gave me the shivers. Clear up and down my spine.

I scooted the scrap next to the brooch on the dresser

top, then gathered the sock again and pinched them both inside the toe. Marissa whispered, "You sure you want to do this?"

"No, but I'm doing it anyway." I tucked the socks inside each other, popped them into the dresser, and closed the drawer. "You-know-who told me to, and besides, I just want to get rid of the thing. It's giving me the creeps."

"So what are we supposed to do now? Go back down there?"

"I guess. I sure don't want to stay in here."

"Can we maybe go find something to eat?"

"Sure. Let's ask Hali."

Marissa grabs my arm. "Let's not."

Now, it's probably not very polite to go up to someone who's busy being mad at the world and ask her for food. It doesn't rank as high as fainting, but it's definitely somewhere in the top twenty. Especially when the person who's mad at the world is sweating away, rolling up bedding and throwing around furniture.

So we just stood in the doorway, watching as she flipped the chair upside down on the desk and then popped the wastepaper basket between the legs of the chair.

When she finally sees us, she says hello with a scowl, then picks a pair of my mother's shoes up off the floor and puts them next to the chair.

I take a step in and ask, "What are you doing?"

"Got orders to vacuum, too." She eyes me with a smirk. "You here to help?"

I hesitate, then step all the way in. "Sure."

She stops what she's doing, stares at me for a few seconds, then throws her head back and laughs. Not an oh-you're-so-funny laugh, a hysterical laugh. Like she's on the verge of completely losing it.

Very quietly I say, "I'm serious, Hali. We'll help." I look over my shoulder. "Won't we, Marissa?"

Marissa says, "Uh...sure," and steps around a bundle of bedding to join us.

Hali stares at me, then at Marissa, then back at me. "It's Sammy, right?"

"That's right."

She sighs and says, "God, I'm sorry I've been such a witch. I'm just freaked out about something, and I'm finding it hard to deal."

"Well, it's pretty easy to see you're mad about something."

She shakes her head. "I'd like to hang 'em both."

I took a stab. "Inga and Max?"

She snorts and says, "Yeah, her too."

Marissa whispers, "What's up with those bandages she wears, anyway?"

Hali takes a rag out of her apron and starts wiping down the dresser. "You go in to get beautiful, you come out looking like a monster."

"What?"

"Her plastic surgery was a disaster. They did some sort of skin peel, but she had a weird reaction to it, so now they're planing off the scars and grafting skin and trying to fix her up with some sort of intense skin rejuvenation program. I haven't actually seen it, but Tammy did, and I know it really freaked her out."

Now, while Hali's explaining about Inga's cosmetic fiasco, she's buffing the dresser with a dust rag. And while she's talking, little snapshots of the morning start flipping through my brain —LeBrandi, dead in bed; the vial of pills on the dresser behind her; people passing the vial around; Tammy slamming it back on the dresser. And these snapshots keep bringing me back to the dresser.

The dresser.

Slowly a chill comes over me and holds on tight. And all of a sudden it feels like I'm trapped in a walk-in freezer— I'm cold, I'm panicky, and I know I can't get out without crying for help.

"Hali," I say, but it's no cry at all. It's barely a whisper. "Hali!"

"What?" She stops mid-swipe. "Don't you go fainting on me, girl. What's wrong?"

I sit down on the edge of the mattress and ask, "Was there a glass in here?"

"What?"

"When you were cleaning up—did you find a glass?"

"No."

I turn to Marissa. "Did you see one this morning?"

Marissa shakes her head.

"Is there a cup, a bottle, *anything* in the trash can?"

Hali checks. "Two Kleenex and a pantyhose wrapper. What are you getting at?"

"What happened to the vial?"

"What vial? Oh, her sleeping pills? I don't know. Maybe the paramedics took it."

I sat there a minute, trying not to shiver, but the more

I thought about it, the more I knew that there was too much wrong here for me not to be right.

Hali puts her hands on her hips and says, "What is up with you, girl?"

I look at her and whisper, "She didn't have water."

"What?"

"Water. How could she have swallowed all those pills without any water?"

EIGHT

The moment it was out of my mouth, I wished I could take it back. I mean, who was I to say LeBrandi didn't swallow a fistful of pills without water? Maybe she had super-slick saliva that slid those suckers straight to her stomach. Maybe she just opened her throat and shook 'em down whole. Or maybe she'd gotten up, put all the pills in her hand, walked clear down to the bathroom, and downed them a few at a time while she gulped water under the faucet.

Right.

And what about the banging? I mean, you don't usually bang like that against a wall if you're drugged up with sleeping pills. You don't do that if you're dying of natural causes, either. Well, unless maybe you're choking, but I hadn't noticed any boxes of bonbons or half-eaten sandwiches waiting to be bagged and tagged as evidence.

No, you bang against a wall like that in a struggle. In a fight.

In a murder.

And if she *was* murdered, well, who in the world had wanted her dead?

The obvious choice sizzled like a branding iron against

my brain. I jerked back and tried to run from the idea. It had to be someone else! It had to be. I raced through some other possibilities, starting with Max. LeBrandi had Max's brooch in her sock drawer and . . . and that was an obvious dead end. Max didn't even know that the Honeymoon Jewels were missing until a little while ago.

Okay. Hali and Reena. Yeah! They'd been really upset with LeBrandi. But in my heart I knew—this was stretching things way too far. I mean, you don't kill someone over calling you *or* your mother a Jamaican Jailer.

Then it flashed through my mind that really, it could be anyone. Anyone at all! Someone could have come in through the window—no, there was no window. Okay, the door. I got up and checked the doorknob and then the jamb. No splintered wood, no stressed or pried-up metal. Whoever had come in had just walked in.

As I factored in the security system, the possibilities were coming down fast. Twelve women, plus Inga and Max, and Hali and Reena. And even though I didn't know anything about most of them, I did know a lot about *one* of them. Someone who was desperate enough and determined enough to do something as drastic as murdering LeBrandi.

My mother.

It was a horrible, panicky thought, but it rang so completely true. Getting the part of Jewel meant everything to my mother. It would mean she was a "real" actress, and it would mean getting away from Max—from the whole prospect of marrying Max *and* from the danger of being found out. For my mother to admit now that she was

Lana Keyes, truck-stop waitress from Santa Martina, would kill her. Absolutely kill her.

She'd also been gone—mysteriously gone—at the exact same time I'd heard the thumping from LeBrandi's room. And when I'd mentioned the thumping, my mother had wanted me to believe that I'd imagined it.

And what a quick and easy diversion the vial was! All she had to do was throw the pills out.

Or flush them down the toilet.

And even though she'd been very upset—even though she'd looked shocked and pale and frightened by LeBrandi, dead in her bed—I was starting to get the picture that my mother *was* an actress.

A very *good* actress.

I stood there panting for air, not knowing what to do. It was a perfect setup. My mother's fingerprints, her strands of hair, fibers from her clothes—any evidence that might be used against her *couldn't* be used against her. They were all things that you'd expect to find there. It was *her* room.

And her alibi would be airtight, except for one pesky little thing.

Me.

Hali pulled me out of my train wreck of emotions. "What are you doing over there?"

I came away from the door. "N-nothing."

"Well, what were you saying?"

I shook my head. "Never mind. It was stupid."

But Marissa's caught on. "Wow," she says, but then adds, "Well . . . she could've gone down to the bathroom.

Sleeping pills don't kill you right away, do they? There'd be time."

I try to sound confident as I say, "Yeah. I'm sure you're right," but in my heart there's a cloud the size of Kansas moving in, and it feels heavy and dark.

And evil.

And for the first time in my life, that little part of my brain that helps me figure out what to do is quiet. Completely quiet. It's not knocking or nagging, not shaking or flagging. It's like a mute in there, arms crossed, eyes closed.

I wished with all my heart that I knew there was no way my mother would have killed LeBrandi. But I *didn't* know that. She'd made a new identity, complete with fake ID, phony newspaper clippings, and concocted acting credits. She'd spun herself into this person I barely knew and sure wouldn't trust.

Hali puts her fists on her hips and says, "Are you suggesting...," then shakes her braids and mocks me with, "...foul play?"

I kind of toe the carpet with my high-tops and mumble, "Well, are they gonna...you know, check into it or something?"

"Why should they? Pills on the dresser, girl in the bed...." She rolls her eyes. "And I don't see any blood around here, do you?"

I shake my head, but what I'm thinking is, Just the way Lady Lana likes it.

"So you wanted to help? Here," Hali says, then heaves me the giant wad of bedding off my mother's mattress. She points to the other two bundles and says to Marissa,

"You get one and I'll get the other. The chute's past the stairwell at the end of the hall. In a cubby on the left."

I followed them like a zombie down to the end of the hall. And just before we turn left, Marissa points to some double doors straight ahead and says, "What's in there?"

"His Majesty's suite. He lets me in once a week so I can clean." Hali sneers. "The prince."

"Lets you in?" Marissa nods at the security panel. "He's got a different code?"

"What, are you kidding? He's Max."

The laundry chute's just a big wooden cabinet door that swings down instead of to the side. Hali pulled it open, crammed her bundle in, and away it whooshed. Marissa did the same, and when hers had disappeared she giggled and said, "Cool! Where's that go?"

"Down to the laundry room, right by the kitchen."

"But it doesn't just plop. You can hear it slide!"

Hali gives her a weak smile. "Work here a week. The thrill will be gone." She holds the chute open for me. "Well? That your new security blanket or what?"

I pried my arms open and dumped my bundle, and as it whooshed happily down to the laundry room, that big cloud in my heart got two shades darker.

Marissa asks Hali, "Is there, you know, any possibility of maybe getting something to eat around here?"

Hali nods her head in my direction. "You think that's what her problem is?"

Marissa shrugs. "Could be."

"A little cup of cocoa wouldn't cut it for me, either. Come on."

She leads us downstairs, through Little Egypt, past the dining hall, and into the kitchen, where Reena's working away at a large stainless-steel sink, rinsing plates with an overhead sprayer. When she sees Hali, she shuts off the water and tries to talk to her, but Hali just steams right past and says to us, "Let's get the wash going first, okay?"

She pushes through a white metal door, and we follow her into the laundry room, where our wads of bedding are poking out beneath the laundry chute's swinging door. Hali says, "Separate those, would you? Sheets and cases, blankets, and spreads."

So Marissa and I pull the bundles completely out of the chute and separate them as Hali stomps around, ratcheting the dials and pulling on the water in all three washers. Then she takes a huge container of liquid soap and glub-glubs some into each machine, not even bothering to measure. "Sheets and cases in this one, spreads in this one, and blankets here."

Marissa scoops up the blankets. "You think these'll all fit?"

Hali nods. "I know they'll fit. Just cram 'em in there."

I tried not to think about it. I just picked up the pile of sheets and pillowcases, walked them over to the machine, and stuffed them around the agitator. And I kept reminding myself that really, there *was* no evidence, so it was fine to wash the bedding. F-I-N-E, fine. But still, as the sheets swished back and forth beneath the growing tide of suds, I felt like an accomplice.

An accomplice to murder.

And I felt like I couldn't tell anyone about it. Not even Marissa. It was too horrible. Too unbelievable.

And too embarrassing.

I mean, how many people do you know whose mother would go and kill someone—not for love or hate or revenge or even raving mental lunacy, but so that she could play an amnesiac on a soap?

Welcome to my nightmare.

Hali clanged the lids closed and headed back to the kitchen, saying, "So, what can I get you girls? Eggs? Toast? Waffles?"

I almost said, Nothing. But then I realized that I was starving. Starving for something I wasn't going to get in Reena's kitchen—or probably in all of Hollywood.

Oatmeal.

Grams' oatmeal.

All of a sudden I missed her like I never had before. She was like her oatmeal—warm, hearty, and dependable.

My mother, on the other hand, was like some fancy, finicky soufflé—beautiful on the outside, full of nasty asparagus tips and onions on the inside. And where oatmeal can hold a spoon straight up in a hurricane, little things like drafts and clanks and bumps will collapse a soufflé into a pathetic heap of unresponsive goo.

And I was busy wondering how a person as fragile as a soufflé would go about killing someone when Marissa nudges me and says, "Sammy? What do you want?"

I just blinked at her.

"For breakfast?"

"Oh, doesn't matter."

So Marissa says to Hali, "Anything's fine. Whatever's easy."

"What's easy is cereal. Two bowls of that?"

I say, "Sure," and Marissa—who's dying for waffles, toast, *and* eggs—says, "Uh...sure" too.

So Hali scoots around the kitchen, banging and clanging her way around her mom. And Reena's trying to talk to her with her eyes, but Hali's not making contact. Instead, she calls over from a cupboard, "You got a preference? It's mostly oat bran and whole-grain stuff like muesli. Oh, wait! There's Rice Krispies. You want those?"

Like Rice Krispies could hold a spoon straight up in a hurricane. Please.

But Marissa says, "Sure," so Hali pulls down the box and shoos us over to a small plank table that's pushed up against the wall. We sit at each end of it while Hali clanks bowls and spoons in front of us, thumps down a gallon of milk, slides a sugar bowl across the table, and flips us some napkins. And as she's doing all this, she's moving faster and faster, and I can just see her stewing about something, getting madder and madder.

"Hali," I whisper. "What is going *on?* What are you thinking about?"

She stops and looks at me and then literally *seethes,* "Like it would've killed the creep to spring for tuition."

"What?"

"Never mind," she snaps, and then stares. Just stares. Not at us. Not at what's on the table. Just kind of through everything, off into some private dimension. And when she comes back to earth, she looks at each of us, says,

"That Nazi!" then flies around the kitchen, slamming drawers and cupboards until she's got her own cereal-chomping equipment. She scoots up a chair, sits down between us, and says, "Pass the Krispies."

Take snap-crackle-pop, add scoop-shovel-slurp, and you've got what Hali did through three big bowls of Rice Krispies before she belched and started on a fourth. And just as she's sprinkling on the sugar, I look up and freeze because there in the kitchen doorway, with her hands on her hips, is Inga.

Inga the Angry Mummy.

And even though it's a big kitchen, she's filling the whole thing with big bad mummy vibes like you wouldn't believe. And there's no doubt about it—they're aimed straight at Hali.

Hali scowls at her. "What's your problem, Inga?"

Inga's yellow eyes pop right open, and over from the sink, Reena gasps, "Hali!"

Inga steps into the kitchen. "My problem? It would appear my problem this morning is you."

Hali laughs. Just throws her head back and laughs. "You got no idea how right you are." Then suddenly she stops laughing and stands. "The help's not supposed to be eating on the job, is that it? I gotta clock in and clock out to have a snack? This whole arrangement is a joke." She points to Reena. "She's a joke. You're a joke. Your brother's a joke. This whole place is one big stupid joke."

Reena whispers, "Hali, *please*...."

"They're Nazis, Mama!"

It was like setting the Mummy's fuse. She fizzed and

spattered at the mouth while her eyes got bigger and bigger beneath her bandages. And for a minute there I thought she was going to explode and plaster the room with cotton shrapnel. "Nazis? You ignorant, insolent child! How *dare* you!"

Reena races over to Hali, grabs both her hands, and pulls her away from the Gauze Grenade, pleading, "Hali, go. Go to the house. I'll be there in a minute."

Hali shakes her off but then bursts into tears and charges out of the kitchen. And the door's barely swung closed when *whoosh!* it swings back open again.

Now, I was expecting it to be Hali, charging in for another attack, but it wasn't Hali. It was the Plaid Rabbit. Only she wasn't looking like a rabbit anymore—well, except for that nose of hers, twitching away. But she wasn't hopping around. She was shaking. "Inga! Do you know where Max is?"

Inga hadn't quite defused. "No! Why should I know where he is?"

"I've got to find him! Do you have any ideas?"

"Did you check his office?"

Twitch. "Yes."

"Did you *knock*?"

"Yes."

"His suite?"

"Yes!"

"Then I don't know—go look around!"

But Tammy doesn't leave. Instead, she looks over her shoulder, then steps completely into the kitchen, holding the door with the palms of both hands as it swings closed behind her. She leans forward and whispers, "There are two policemen and a homicide detective here, Inga. They want to talk to Max."

"A homicide detective? What for?"

I held my breath and waited for the words I knew were coming next.

"LeBrandi didn't overdose on sleeping pills...LeBrandi was murdered!"

NINE

Now, you would think that when someone comes into a room and makes the announcement that a person's been murdered, *this* would be a time for people to faint or gasp or cry out in disbelief. But nothing like that happened. Tammy's hands stayed plastered to the door, Reena clutched a dish towel, squeezing one end like she was milking a cow, and Inga just stood there, frozen like a museum piece. The only sound was the quiet *swish-swish* of the washing machines next door.

Marissa nudges me across the table and whispers, "You were right!"

I couldn't even look at her. I just stared into my cereal bowl and felt myself shrivel up inside.

Finally Inga says, "Surely there's been a mistake!"

Tammy shakes her head. "She was *suffocated*."

"Come, now! How can they tell that? And they've only had her a couple of hours!"

"Look, Inga. They took a blood test, all right? And it came back negative for drugs, all right? Other than that, I don't know! Go ask them yourself, would you? I can't find Max, so you go talk to them!"

Inga says, "Take me to them," and off they go.

When they're gone, Reena takes a deep breath, hangs up the dish towel, and leaves, too.

Marissa says, "Why would someone have killed her? *Who* would've killed her?"

I just keep looking down at my soggy cereal, wishing with all my heart that I didn't know.

Marissa drops her voice and raises her eyebrows. "Oh, this is creepy. This is just too creepy! It happened, like, right *next* to us. I mean, if there wasn't a wall there, we'd have seen the whole thing! God, who do you think did it? Do you think it's someone who lives here?" She raps me on the head with her knuckles. "Sammy? Knock, knock! Are you in there?"

I mumble, "Yeah. I'm right here."

She stares at me. "What is *wrong* with you?"

I sit up a bit and say, "Nothing. I'm fine. How am I supposed to know who killed LeBrandi?"

"But..." She looks at me and shakes her head. "Don't you even care?"

"Well, sure. Okay. So who do you think killed LeBrandi?"

"I don't know, but I'll bet it has something to do with that brooch."

"The brooch?"

"What if that stone *is* a ruby? My mom's got a necklace that my dad gave her—it's a single ruby set in a hanger, and it's nowhere near the size of the stone in that brooch, but still, it was real expensive." She leans in a little and drops her voice. "And what was *LeBrandi* doing with the brooch if Opal stole it in the first place?"

I blinked at her. I'd been so wrapped up in my mother that I hadn't even thought about it, but she was right. Maybe LeBrandi had stolen the brooch from Opal. And maybe Opal knew it and was so mad about it that she'd come back for revenge.

But how'd she know to go to my mother's room? That didn't make sense at all. But maybe they had talked. Maybe she did know! Maybe my mother hadn't killed LeBrandi after all!

It was like Marissa had pulled a rip cord to my brain. I could feel it sputter to life, smoking and choking my old thoughts out, revving up until it was running clean and strong and *fast*. "Okay. Opal stole the jewels out of Max's drawer—LeBrandi saw them or found out about them somehow, and managed to lift the brooch off Opal before she moved out. Or maybe she blackmailed her for it. You know, I won't rat on you if you cut me in?"

Marissa nods. "Okay, but then what?"

"Well, the jewels are hot. You can't *wear* them, so they're only valuable if you can find someone who's willing to buy them off you."

We look at each other and at the same time we whisper, "Seventy-seven curio!"

Marissa says, "Maybe it's a street address?"

I count on my fingers, 7-7-C-U-R-I-O. "A phone number?"

Marissa points to a telephone mounted on the wall near a fire extinguisher. "You want to give it a try?"

I take a quick look around, then scramble for the phone. The number rang. And rang. And rang some more. And

I was about to give up and hang up when a man with the voice of a grizzly bear says, "Cosmo's Curios."

I cleared my throat and said, "Uh...can you tell me what your hours are?"

"Nine ta six," growled the grizzly. "Closed tomorrow and Monday."

"Uh...and where are you located?"

"Sixty-six thirteen Hollywood Boulevard." He slurped something from a cup. "You buyin' or sellin'?"

"Uh...selling."

Slurp. "Well, come on in. I'll make ya a good deal."

When he hung up, I turned to Marissa and said, "Sixty-six thirteen Hollywood Boulevard." I hooked the receiver back on the wall. "C'mon!"

"Come on? Come on where? How are we going to get to sixty-six thirteen Hollywood Boulevard, and what are we going to do when we get there?"

I peeked out the kitchen door, my brain still running full throttle.

"Sammy, don't just leave! Where are you going?"

"Shh! I have to try something. Come *on*!" I waved her along, and we tiptoed down the hall, past the dining room, then took a right through Little Egypt to the back door.

Now, when my mother had let us in the night before, all I'd really seen was the pattern of the entry code, and even though I didn't know if I'd be needing it or not, I didn't want to leave without being sure I could get back in. So I made Marissa wait inside while I went out and closed the door behind me.

First I checked the handle. It was locked. I punched in 2-8-6-4.

Still locked.

I tried crossing over the other way with 2-8-4-6, and bingo! I let myself in.

I grinned at Marissa and whispered, "The code's 2-8-4-6, c'mon!" I dragged her out the door, down the steps, past ferns and palms and periwinkle vines, clear over to Hali's cottage. "I'm praying the code hasn't been changed since Opal got canned."

"Praying? First you don't care, now you're praying? God, you're acting so weird today!" Then she mutters, "You're reminding me of Hali!"

I knocked on the frame of the cottage's screen door and called, "Reena? Hali? Hello...?" as I peeked into the front room.

A door inside slammed, and Hali's voice cried, "I don't care, Mama! I don't *care*! He's a coward! A fraud! A *liar*! And you! You should've told me *years* ago! Like it's not my right to know?"

Marissa grabs my arm and whispers, "Sammy, we shouldn't be here."

And we're about to hightail it out of there when a voice behind us says, "They're not answering the door?"

How we let Tammy hippity-hop up behind us is beyond me. But there she was, towering above us, twitching her nose like she's hot on the trail of some fresh-sprung clover. We step aside and she moves forward, calling through the screen, "Reena! Hali! They're calling an emergency meeting in the dining hall. Max wants you there right away!"

Inside the bungalow, the voices stop. And for a few seconds all that comes through the door is dark, cool silence. Then Reena appears and says through the screen, "We'll be there in a few minutes. Leave us be now, won't you?"

Tammy nods and starts scurrying down the path, and I chase after her, saying, "You're Tammy, right?"

"Right," she says, then eyes me like I'm some renegade ragweed. "Why do you ask?"

"Just wondering," I tried on a smile and said, "Is it always like this around here?"

She starts hopping along again. "You mean does someone get murdered around here every day? No."

"But is there always so much drama around here? I heard about Opal getting kicked out and—"

"No! Okay? There are your typical little spats and stuff, but nothing like this." Her eyes sharpen down on me as she says, "How'd you hear about Opal? From Dominique?"

"Well, we slept in her bed last night, so it sorta came up." I hesitate, then add, "Doesn't seem real fair, kicking a person out like that."

"Anyone will tell you Opal had it coming. Now, the bit with her contract, I can see her being miffed about. But Opal was lazy, and Opal was a hothead, so Opal pretty much got what Opal deserved."

"What do you mean about her contract? What happened with that?"

She shrugged. "Max wouldn't release her."

"But he fired her, right?"

"Yeah. She told me he said he'd 'invested,' and he wasn't about to let her out of what she owed him."

"So where'd she go?"

She turned on me. "You're starting to sound like those cops in there, you know that? It's not like I was her best friend or anything, so why are you grilling me?" She frowned and bounced her way up the steps, saying, "I heard she was working at the Peppermint Peacock down on Hollywood—all the more reason to walk the straight and narrow around here, if you ask me."

"What do you mean? What's the Peppermint Peacock?"

She turns and studies me, then her nose gives a mighty, circular twitch, like it's trying to unscrew itself right off her face. She zooms in on me and says, "It's where girls who think they're gonna make it go right before they start walking Sunset. You get the picture? Now, if you'll excuse me, I've got to use the bathroom and report to Max, 'cause I have no interest in winding up there." She punches in the code, then asks, "Are you coming inside?"

"Uh, not right now." I nod at the keypad and say, "Is the code the same as yesterday? We don't want to be locked out or anything."

"Yeah, it's the same."

"Well, how often do they change it?"

"How should I know? It's been the same for...for months! Now would you go interrogate someone else?"

The minute she's inside, I grab Marissa by both shoulders and shake her. "It was Opal! It had to be!"

"And you're happy about that?"

"Yes!"

She looks at me like I'm waltzing barefoot on barnacles. *"Why?"*

"Because...because!" I race down the walkway calling, "C'mon!"

"Where? Sammy, wait up! Why don't you just go in and tell Max? Or the police?"

I whisper, "Because...I don't have any proof, and...I don't want them asking me a bunch of nosy questions."

One look at me, and she knows I'm holding out.

"Sammy, tell me what is going on in that head of yours! You've been acting bipolar all day, and it's not just from being around you-know-who. Now tell me what it is!"

I hesitated, then dragged her way off the pathway and around the corner of the house. And when I was sure no one could possibly hear me, I yanked her behind a giant fern and whispered, "Three-thirty A.M. I hear banging through the wall. Three-thirty-*five* A.M. my mother comes sneaking back into the room."

She gaped at me, then said, "You think your *mother* killed LeBrandi?"

So I give her my Desperate Diva theory along with all kinds of supporting evidence, and what does she do?

She laughs. Out loud, head back, tears streaming out of her eyes, *howling*.

"Shh! Marissa, stop it! *Stop* it!"

"You stop! Oh, please...your *mother*? *Suffocate* someone? She has trouble swatting flies! Sammy, I've seen her try. She's timid, she flinches, she's got no *swing*. I hate to be the one to break it to you, but your mother's got the killer instincts of a butterfly."

A butterfly?

Marissa was right about one thing, though—my

mother couldn't kill flies. But that wasn't because she didn't want them dead. No, it was because of bug blood. Bug blood grosses her out. Worse than regular blood, even. It's the combination of guts and blood. She just can't take it.

She was, however, perfectly happy to catch one under a glass and let it die that way.

By suffocation.

A rattly, scraping noise above us shook me from my thoughts. And when I looked up to see what it was, there's Max, coming onto a second-floor balcony. I nudge Marissa, then put my finger to my lips and point.

Marissa crouches a little farther into the fern, and we both hold our breath, but Max doesn't seem to be looking for us. He just holds the rail with both hands and looks out past the trees and into the distance—like he's at the helm of a boat, taking in deep breaths of salt air. Then he puts his hands up toward the sky and mouths a few words before he drops his arms and goes back inside.

The minute he's gone, I scoot out from beneath the fern and say, "Let's go."

"Where are we going?"

I drag her along to the walkway. "Cosmo's Curios... and then maybe up the street to the Peppermint Peacock. Tammy said it's *on* Hollywood, not *in* Hollywood, so it's got to be close by, right?"

She chased after me. "The Peppermint Peacock? There's no *way* we should go there!"

It was my turn to laugh. "We've already had the night tour of Sunset. It can't be any worse than that, right?"

Marissa squeezed her eyes shut and whimpered, "Haven't we been through enough for one day?" But I could tell from the way she said it that she wasn't going to be left behind.

Peppermint Peacock, ho!

TEN

Bumming a ride wasn't the hard part. Hali came storming out of the cottage in jeans, sandals, and a T-shirt, ranting over her shoulder, "Tell them I've gone to get the dry cleaning. Tell them we're out of coffee. Tell them I quit! I don't care what you tell them, I'm getting out of here, and not you or that Nazi or the whole LAPD is going to stop me!"

She flew down the walkway and around back, and we raced to catch her. "Hali! Hali, wait up!"

Her braids whipped the air as her head snapped around. "What do you two want?"

"Um . . . do you know where Hollywood Boulevard is?"

She kept walking. "Of course I know where Hollywood Boulevard is!"

"Do you think maybe you can give us a ride?"

"Why would I want to give you a ride?"

I ran along beside her. "I don't know. Maybe it's near the dry cleaners?"

She kept right on walking.

"Please? We want to, you know, get a souvenir."

She scowled at me, then marched the rest of the way to a small garage and pulled up the door. Inside was a battered yellow Volkswagen Bug with faded stickers all along the bumper and a rainbow of ribbons on the antenna. "Squeeze in," she says as she yanks open the driver's door. "And don't even think about doggin' my driving."

Marissa started to climb in back, but I said, "Uh...I've got to run inside and get my money. Can you pick me up out front?"

"Look, I want to get *out* of here!"

"I know, I know. Just go up the street a little ways and wait. It'll only take me a minute."

She closes her eyes and shakes her head. "If you're not out there in—"

"I'll hurry!" I say, and then go charging toward the house.

I got back inside the mansion, no problem. But as I tiptoed through Little Egypt to the fountain, I couldn't really hear if people were around or not because of the sound of running water. So I ducked behind the fountain for a second and checked to the right toward the stairwell, then left to the dining hall and kitchen. When I was sure the coast was clear, I hurried across the intersection toward the front door.

So there I am, slinking along like a sneak thief in the Smithsonian, thinking I'm actually going to make it to the reception room without running into anyone, when all of a sudden the fading sound of streaming water is slashed by Max's voice.

I dive behind one of the big stone urns by the reception room door, and through the arc along the back of the urn I can see Max come out of the room, followed by a policeman who's saying, "The information collected earlier is not enough, Mr. Mueller. I'm sorry it's such an inconvenience for you, but each and every person who was here last night is going to have to be detained for questioning."

I tucked my high-tops back as far as I could, then hugged my knees, held my breath, and tried to disappear behind the urn.

Max nods and says, "Well, they all should be assembled by now."

"I'm curious, Mr. Mueller. Whose decision was it to strip the bedding?"

Max says, "I'm so sorry that happened. We felt it would be less traumatic on the woman who usually sleeps in that room. You have to understand, we had *no* idea."

"So it was your decision, then?"

Their footsteps are clip-clopping away from me, but right before their voices fade I can hear Max say, "Uh... well, my sister and I agreed that it would be a good idea."

"Your sister?"

"I believe you met Inga earlier. The one with the bandages?"

When they were far enough away, I scurried around the urn and into the reception room. Max's office door was closed tight, and there was no one else in the room, so I went straight to work.

First I yanked Claire's picture off the wall. Then I snagged a black-and-white photo from the bottom corner of the same wall and put it where Claire's had been. The man in the photo didn't look a thing like Claire, but at least there wasn't a gaping hole announcing to the world that Claire's mug had been lifted.

I could hear the sputter of Hali's Volkswagen outside, and when I looked out the window, sure enough, there went Hali and Marissa, up the street, past two empty squad cars, and out of sight.

I took a quick peek down the hallway, then zipped over to the large black binder that Marissa and I had gone through earlier.

I slipped out LeBrandi's photo, then Opal's, and at the last minute I decided I should take one more.

Dominique Windsor's.

I closed the binder, then stacked the head shots on top of Claire's photo and tucked them under my sweatshirt, inside the waistband of my jeans. When I was sure they were secure, I checked that the coast was clear, then slipped out the front door.

I was planning to cut across the lawn and hightail it up to Hali, only as I'm going down the steps, I notice another car cruising up the street. And even though it's not a police car, something about it tells me to duck out of view.

So I dive behind a hedge that runs along the front of the house and watch. And sure enough, the car pulls in and parks right behind the two squad cars. Then a man steps out. A man with Crisco hair and a spare tire big enough to fit an eighteen-wheeler.

And for a second there my heart comes screeching to a halt, because this man looks just like the one and only Officer Borsch, come *way* out of his jurisdiction to chew me out.

Part of what threw me was that I'd never seen Officer Borsch dressed in anything but a uniform before, so I didn't exactly know what that *looked* like. And seeing this guy out in the street, hiking his tan slacks up around his beef-belted radial, tucking in the back of his short-sleeved shirt as he checks out the house, well, he doesn't look as menacing as Officer Borsch usually does. He looks more like a scruffy Tweedledee who's chucked his bow tie somewhere on the road from Wonderland.

Still, the last thing I want is to be spotted. I've got questions to ask, and I sure don't want to waste my time answering someone else's. So as Tweedledee heads toward the door, I scoot along between the house and the hedge, past the reception room window, until I'm a safe distance away from the front door.

The picture frame is cutting into me pretty good, but I'm forcing myself to squat there, quiet as a rock. Then all of a sudden, right behind me, a fan comes on, *vroom!*

I stumble back and blink at the blur of a small fan whipping around behind a grid the size of a heating duct, and by the time my heart's stuffed back in my chest, Tweedledee is almost to the porch.

And it's strange. It's like all my senses are on red alert. Everything looks real *clear*—like it's magnified, only not any bigger. The pebbles on my palms feel like glass, the air has a woody sort of sweet smell to it, and even though that fan is only a purr, it seems to be screaming in my ears.

That's when I see Tweedledee step up to the porch and can tell that he's definitely not Officer Borsch. I mean, he's *whistling*. And even though part of me is dying to know if he's Gil Borsch's twin brother, the minute he's inside I turn around and scurry along the house and out of there.

When I get to a break in the hedge, I look both ways, then charge across the lawn and up the street to where Hali's Bug is idling.

Hali's watching the rearview mirror like a hawk, and even when I open up the passenger door, she doesn't look my way. She just keeps staring straight into that mirror.

I try to sit down without gouging myself on the picture frame or giving away the fact that I'm packing pinched photos. I tell her, "Sorry it took so long," but to my surprise, Hali's not mad. She says, "You did good," and keeps her eyes glued to the mirror, shifting her gaze back and forth between the police parade parked down the road and the mansion's front door.

Now, with her eyes up and open like they are, and with the light from outside kind of bouncing in and shining on them, I catch a glimpse of something in the mirror that I hadn't noticed before. I lean sideways for a better look in the mirror, and sure enough, her eyes are green. Not brown like her mother's. *Green.*

She grinds the Bug into gear, looks straight at me, and says, "That was a detective, did you know that?"

I'm still leaning sideways, but now I'm looking right at her. And what comes out of my mouth? Not Yeah, that's what I figured, or Yeah, for a minute there I thought he was this cop I know back home, or even Yeah . . . and why are you so charged up about it?

No, what comes out of my mouth is, "Are those contacts?"

She stares at me a minute, then snorts and gives the Bug the gas. "You and every guy who's ever asked me out." She shakes her head, muttering, "They're mine, and they're blind."

"Blind? What do you mean?"

"Never mind. No, they're not contacts!" She pulls the gearshift into second. "Wish they were."

Marissa pipes up from the backseat, "Do you know where we're going?"

Hali snickers and throws the car into third. "That would help. What block of Hollywood Boulevard?"

I say, "Sixty-six hundred? The address is sixty-six thirteen."

"What's there, anyway?"

"Oh, just this store we heard about."

"How long's it gonna take?"

"Uh, I don't know...not too long."

"Long enough for me to get a latte somewhere?" She had it floored, the little Bug heart fluttering along as fast as it could. "I could even go pick up the stupid dry cleaning, I suppose."

I flashed Marissa a relieved look and said, "Yeah. That'd be fine."

Hali downshifted into second, then rolled right through a stop sign.

And that was pretty much the way she powered through traffic, zigzagging around cars, beeping at pedestrians, grumbling about incompetent airheads and bank-boy yahoos, breaking every traffic law on the books—plus a few that lawmakers probably haven't even thought to write up.

And I was just thinking that Hali's little rumba through town made wobbling around on Marissa's handlebars seem like graceful ballet when she squeals around a corner and says, "Okay. This is the sixty-six-hundred block of Hollywood. What's the place?"

"Oh, just drop us anywhere. Right here's fine."

She spots 6613 at the same time I do, then slows down and cranes her neck at the dirty black security shutters covering the store's windows. "Cosmo's Curios...who told you about this place?"

"Uh..." I look up and down the street at all the shop windows, covered in the same black diamonds of steel. "Dominique did."

"Dominique? I can't see that china doll shopping down *here*."

"Yeah, well..."

She saved me from myself, interrupting with, "Sorry. I know she's your aunt and all, but if you're looking to buy souvenirs, I can drop you somewhere a whole lot better than this."

"No, that's okay. We'll be fine."

She looks straight at me and says, "You really are from Kansas, aren't you?"

I tried to laugh, but it came out stalled and stuttery. "Are you making fun of us?"

At this point we're double-parked, holding up traffic. And while cars are zooming past us, honking and cursing, she stays put, looking at me and then Marissa. Finally she points outside and shakes her head. "Look around, lamb-chops. You see what's out there? Derelicts, deadbeats, and drug dealers." She turns back to me suddenly, her eyes wide. Like she's trapped face to face with a carnivorous koala. "You're not here to *score*, are you?"

"Score?" I couldn't believe my ears. "You mean buy *drugs*?"

She's still looking at me like I file my canines into wicked little points.

"No!"

It takes her a second, but finally she lets out a big sigh. "Wow. For a minute there..." She smiles at me, and I smile back at her, and then all of a sudden her face falls.

"What?" I ask her, but I already know. She's looking right at my sweatshirt.

A bus swerves past us, blaring its horn, but Hali doesn't budge. She squints at me and asks, "What'chu got under there, girl?" and I can tell by the look in her eye that no little lie is going to get me out of this.

I am busted.

Busted big time.

ELEVEN

Hali didn't wait for me to try and explain. She tore at my sweatshirt until Claire's picture and the head shots were uncovered, then she snatched them from me and said, "You tricked me into bringing you down here so you could pawn *these*?"

"No! I just have to *show* them to him."

"Him? Who's him?"

"I don't know...Cosmo! Or whoever runs the place."

She looked in the rearview mirror as she ground into first gear, and my head whipped backward as she peeled back into traffic. At the first intersection she ran a red light turning right, then bounced up a narrow driveway plastered with ONE WAY and DO NOT ENTER signs. She squeaked to a stop, nose to nose with a parked delivery truck, then yanked up the brake and turned on me. "I am sick to death of being lied to! Mama told me you were hiding something. She said she could see it in your eyes. I told her it was her voodoo imagination again, but she was sure, really *sure*, that you were lying."

"I did *not* lie to her!"

"You expect me to believe that after the way you tricked me into being your little Tinsel Town Taxi? And for what? So you could pawn some stupid photographs? Like anyone's going to give you a nickel for those."

"If you would please just listen ..."

She turns her back on me, looking out the driver's door window. And for a second I thought this might be her listening position, so I'm about to start explaining at least part of what I'm doing with the pictures when all of a sudden she whips around and looks me straight in the eye. "Where in Kansas?"

"What?"

"Where in Kansas are you from?"

Uh-oh. I blinked at her, then tried to put up a convincing scowl. "What's *that* matter? Would you let me explain about the pictures?"

"What city? I want to know. Now!"

"Wichita." It was the only city I could think of. I glanced at Marissa, who was crammed in the back with her eyes pinched closed, praying for deliverance. Hali had turned back to the window, so I tried, "Look, I don't blame you for being mad at me, but—"

She whips around again. "Where in Wichita? What street?"

"What *street*? Hali, would you please let me tell you why I've got—"

She leans in closer, her eyes blazing. "Just tell me this— do you like living in a capital city?"

"A capital—"

"Answer me!"

If my brain hadn't been so tied up trying to get out of the mess I was in, I'd have said, I hate Kansas—all of it, or something else vague like that. But I *wasn't* quick enough. "Sure," I said. "It's great. Now—"

The side of her fist slammed against the steering wheel. "She was right!" She turned back to me, her eyes like cold, hard emeralds. "The capital of Kansas is Topeka, and you're nothing but a punk liar! Get out of my car!"

"No, Hali, wait!" I grabbed the picture of Claire and tapped on the glass. "See this brooch? We found it in LeBrandi's dresser. It was hidden in a sock along with a scrap of paper that had 77CURIO written on it. We figured out that it was a phone number, and when we called it we got connected to Cosmo's Curios."

Our eyes were locked together, but I could see the hardness in hers being chipped away by curiosity. "What were you doing nosing through LeBrandi's dresser?"

So I told her about searching around for something to break into the other room with, and how the brooch jabbed me through the sock.

"So where is it now? You got it on you somewhere? Is that what you're here to pawn?"

"No! We put it back in her sock drawer!"

"Then what are you doing here?"

"We're here because *all* the jewels are missing!" I point them out on Claire's picture. "The necklace, the ring, and the brooch."

"What? Pedal back now, girlie. How do you know all this? Who told you so?"

"I was in Max's office this morning when he discovered they were gone. He called them the Honeymoon Jewels, and he got mad. *Really* mad. And then he said something about Opal."

"Opal? What's she got to do with this?"

113

"She's the one who stole them—at least that's what Max seems to think. And what I think is that LeBrandi—being Opal's roommate and all—found out she was going to pawn them and blackmailed a piece from her."

Hali mutters, "Just her sort of MO," then adds, "But why are you so bent on getting yourself raveled up in it? So you found the brooch; it's not like *you* stole it."

"I . . . we . . . well, it's real important, okay?"

Hali's expression made it clear—this was not going to cut it. She picks up the other three head shots and flips through them, murmuring, "LeBrandi, Opal, and Dominique." She hesitates, then looks over her shoulder at Marissa—who's still praying for deliverance—and back to me. "You two are trying to protect Dominique somehow, aren't you?"

I hesitated, then my head bobbed. Barely, but it bobbed.

"Which brings us back to you being from Kansas."

Looking at her seemed painful. Blinding.

"That was Dominique's idea, wasn't it? You don't seem blond enough to say you're from some state you've probably never even visited. What's the deal? What are you hiding? What's *she* hiding?"

By now my heart's going *ba-boom, ba-boom, ba-BOOM*, because I know I've got to find some way to stop her, and I can't for the life of me think of a thing to say. It's like I'm lie-shy. All the ones I've told have somehow come back to bite me, and I'm scared to try another.

And I'm telling myself that if I do lie to her about it, she'll probably see right through me and blab everything to the others anyway, but if I tell her the truth, well, I might as well forget about ever patching things up with my mother. She would never forgive me.

So there I am, caught in my mother's Dungeon of Deception, staring down at my high-tops, not knowing how to escape, when a little voice from the backseat says, "You're the one who's hiding something, Hali."

Hali whips around to look at Marissa. "Don't you start messing with me, girl."

"Well, it's true! You've got some terrible secret, and it's killing you to keep it."

I jerked around because I couldn't believe my ears, but Hali did more than jerk. She cried, "Shut your mouth!"

Marissa's voice stays low. Calm. "Look at you, Hali! You're furious with your mother, but you're still trying to keep it all inside. What's she done to make you so mad at her?"

"It's none of your stinkin' business, so just stay out of it!"

"Well, we know it has *something* to do with Max...."

"This is *none* of your business. I'll work it out on my own, in my own time, and I don't need no sneaky school-girls interfering in my pain."

While Marissa's talking to her, little picture cubes are pushing and spinning around in my brain, landing one on top of the other: *thump,* Reena's eyes, so dark and intense, looking into mine; *thunk,* the cool and cocky Hali who'd come out of the cottage to needle my mother about Max's proposal; *thwack,* the angry Hali who'd attacked her the next morning about the very same thing; *smack,* the way she'd spit out insults about Max like she was dying to be

115

fired; and then *smack, thunk, thwack,* the way she'd ignored her mother, run from her mother, *yelled* at her mother.

And looking at Hali, I realized that it was her *eyes* that kept these wobbly blocks from tumbling. They were like the crowning arch connecting the columns. *They're mine, and they're blind.* All these years she hadn't been able to see it herself. All these years she'd lived as a servant in that house without knowing.

The mortar set. And for a second I thought, No! It can't be! but the longer it sat, the firmer it cured. It had to be true. It explained everything.

I touched Hali's arm and whispered, "Max...is he your *father?*"

Her eyes got huge. Then she gripped the steering wheel with both hands and shook it so hard I thought she was going to rip it right out.

It was scary. Like raw hatred erupting from her soul. The whole car shook like we were in an earthquake, and then suddenly she collapsed onto the steering wheel, buried her head in her arms, and sobbed, "I hate him! I *hate* him!"

Marissa's looking at me with her eyes and jaw cranked completely open. She mouths, "No wonder!"

Hali comes off the wheel and wails, "Mama's going to kill me!" Then she goes back to sobbing into her arms.

I whisper, "We won't tell, Hali. I swear."

Marissa leans forward and says, "Really, Hali, we won't."

It didn't make her stop crying, and I could tell that nothing but time would. It was like being in a room with a pinched hose—we'd unkinked it, and now it was going to whip around soaking things until the pressure had gone down.

When she'd petered out to a trickle, I asked, "When did you find out?"

"Last night! After you two and Dominique left. Mama finally told me. She was so upset that Max wanted to marry Dominique that she couldn't keep it inside anymore."

"But why didn't your mom tell you before?"

"Max made her promise not to."

"Why?"

"Something about the scandal ruining his reputation in the industry." Anger rolled across Hali's face like thunder. "The stupid godforsaken industry! Everything they do is based on *appearances*. Nothing beneath the surface matters to *any* of them. It's all just how it looks."

Marissa whispers, "But I don't get it—if Max has you, he already has an heir, so why's he all of a sudden want to get married and have a baby?"

"Mama says men want sons. Or at least offspring that look like them." She snorts and says, "I don't fit either bill, now do I?" She shakes her head, and her voice starts trembling as she says, "All my life I trusted them. All my life they lied to me." Then she breaks down, crying into her hands.

I whispered, "Hali, I'm so sorry," and I was. I felt miserable for her, and in a way for me too. I mean, I couldn't help thinking about my own mother, not wanting to tell me who my father was, and me, in my heart of hearts, always having been a little afraid to pull it out of her.

117

Would it be like this for me? Where knowing was worse than not knowing?

Gently, I asked her, "So what are you going to do?"

She smeared the tears across her cheeks. "I'm going to start by moving out. It's bad enough being a servant, but to your own father? Maybe Mama's got no pride, but that's not me. I am out of there, first chance I get." She takes a deep breath, then lets it out, long and choppy. "You know, I feel better. All day I felt like I was going to explode, but now I know what I've got to do. I've got to get a move on. Ready or not, honey, I am *gone*." She gives Marissa and me half a smile and says, "So there. That's my secret. What's yours?"

I looked away. How could I tell her? My mother would *kill* me. And yet it felt so unfair not to. There was so much about what my mother had done—and was doing—to me that would make Hali feel like she wasn't alone. But what would happen if I told Hali the truth and she blabbed?

Marissa whispers, "Tell her, Sammy!"

I look at her like, Marissa, I can't!

She looks right back at me like, You have to!

I glanced from one to the other, then closed my eyes and took the first step out of Dominique's Dungeon. "Hali, I swear myself to secrecy about Max. Nobody's going to find out from me. Or Marissa—right, Marissa?"

Marissa nods and says, "I swear."

I look straight at Hali and say, "But you've got to promise that what I'm going to tell you stops with you. It has to stay inside these Bug walls."

Hali looks at me, then Marissa, then back at me. And

for a second there I'm afraid she's going to laugh at us, but then she nods, raises her right hand, and says very seriously, "I swear."

I watch her for a few seconds without saying a word.

"I do! You have my word. Why are you looking at me like that?"

"It's important, Hali."

She looks at me and says gently, "I know."

I take a deep breath and say, "Okay." Then I let it out and take the next step up. "My name *is* Sammy Keyes, I *am* related to Dominique, but..."

Hali just looks at me, waiting.

I turn to Marissa, and her eyes push me up the next step. "But she's not my aunt."

Hali searches my face for the answer, and apparently it's written all over it. She whispers, "She's your mother?"

I nod and look down.

"But...why is she...? What is she...? She can't be!"

I let out a little groan. "Oh, she is, all right." So I explained to her about my mother leaving me at Grams' so she could go off and make it as a movie star, and how she'd changed so much in a year that I felt like she was someone I didn't even know anymore.

Hali was quiet for a minute, then asked, "Her real name's Lana?"

"Yeah."

"I love that name. Way better than Dominique."

I shrug. "Yeah. Forget I told you what it was, though. You've got to keep calling her Dominique."

"So where's your dad in all of this?"

So I had to tell her about *that*. And when I'm all done, I sigh and say, "And after what I've seen you go through, I'm thinking that maybe I don't want to know who he is. Not ever."

We all sat there, quiet. And I felt strange. Like I'd climbed out of Dominique's Dungeon, only to be petrified by the light.

Finally Hali says, "Wow."

I look her right in the eye. "You swore. You can't get mad and blurt it, you can't tell Max or your mother. . . . It stays right here, no matter what."

She nods and says, "I won't break your trust," then puts her right hand up, palm out, steady, waiting.

Her hand is not there to be slapped, I can tell that much. But I'm not sure what it *is* doing there, until my left hand kind of floats up to meet it. And when I press my palm against hers and hold it there flat and still, Hali says, "You have my word."

I nod and tell her, "You've got mine, too."

It was a promise I was about to regret.

TWELVE

Marissa watched us make our little palm pact, then cleared her throat and said, "Hey, aren't you two worried about me?"

So we press palms with Marissa, laughing and promising to keep each other's secrets, and then Hali says, "Now fill me in on these pictures you stole."

"Borrowed," I corrected her. "I'm just going to go in and ask the guy some questions, then I'm going to return them before Max even knows they're gone."

"But why do you have them?"

"I want to find out if Opal's been to Cosmo's Curios."

"So what if she has? Why are you so interested?"

I take a deep breath and say, "Because I think maybe Opal is the one who killed LeBrandi."

"Opal? Hmmm...." She seemed to like the idea. "Wouldn't that be classic." She frowns at me and says, "But there's a house full of cops back at the mansion. Why not just tell one of them?"

Marissa pipes up with, "Because Sammy can't go anywhere without cutting through a briar patch, that's why."

"Marissa!"

"It's true. Here we are in Hollywood, and what am I

doing? Walking down the Avenue of the Stars? Touring celebrities' homes? Checking out a movie studio or spotting movie stars? No! I'm in the back of a beat-up Bug— excuse me, Hali, I don't mean any offense—parked in a service alley behind a pawnshop." She rolls her eyes. "If this isn't typical, I don't know what is."

Hali grins at me. "You attract trouble?"

"No!"

Marissa snickers. "She put the 'bur' in burdock."

Now, the last thing I felt like being was the new definition for one of Miss Pilson's vocabulary words. And I certainly didn't see myself as "nature's very own Velcro hooks," so I turn to Marissa and snap, "Stop that! You know why I didn't tell the police!"

Hali's eyebrows creep up. "Yeah? And why would that be?"

Before I can stop her, Marissa says, "Sammy thought her *mother* killed LeBrandi."

"Marissa!"

"Oh, please, Sammy. It's the most ridiculous thought you've ever had, and you've had some really wild ones!" She turns back to Hali. "Her mom got up to take some aspirin at the same time Sammy heard something banging around next door. So of course Sammy thinks her mother—who's got the muscles of a mouse—went next door to kill LeBrandi."

Hali shakes her head at me. "Why?"

My little backseat mouthpiece answers for me. "'Cause Sammy's mom is desperate to get the part of Jewel because it'll get her out of marrying Max."

Hali bit the inside of one cheek, then the other. "It's got a certain desperate logic to it."

I was glaring at Marissa, but it was no use. She just shakes her head at me and says, "Sammy, it's the stupidest thing I've ever heard. She may have changed, but not *that* much! Now can we please go in there and show that guy the pictures? I'm getting claustrophobic back here!"

Hali opens her door to let Marissa out, saying, "You want me to come in the shop with you?"

I shake my head. "Nah. That's okay."

Marissa squeezes out, and Hali says, "I don't really think you should go in there solo."

I grab the pictures and get out, too. "Don't you think that would look kinda, you know, suspicious, having you escort us?"

Hali checks around and decides that for an illegal parking spot, this one'll work just fine. She says, "Well, I'm at least gonna walk you up there," and when we round the corner onto Hollywood Boulevard, she adds, "How about I give you five and then come in?"

I shrug and say, "Ignore us, though, okay?"

She grins at me. "You're pretty pro for a kid, Burdock."

The dirty look I gave her was completely wasted. She was way too busy laughing it up with Marissa to notice.

Near Cosmo's Curios I rearranged the photos so the head shots were upside down on Claire's picture, then put them in the crook of one arm like a schoolbook.

Hali hangs back and whispers, "See you in five. Don't get yourself killed in the meantime."

We nod, then head past the last set of barred windows and whoosh right through Cosmo's steel door.

It felt like we'd walked through a portal into a different world. Outside we were looking at a jail cell, but inside, Cosmo's was like a high-end jewelry store that had been dropped inside a gallery of exotic pieces of art.

I nudge Marissa and nod across the store at the row of spotless glass showcases. "Maybe the necklace and ring are up there!"

Marissa glances at the jewelry cases and the white velvet vanity stools in front of them, then clasps her hands behind her back and pretends to inspect a shiny brass Aladdin lamp. She fakes a smile and says between her teeth, "We're not exactly dressed for success, Sammy. Don't start snooping, okay? Just ask!"

"Sorry, girls. That one's genie got away." The voice was deep and gruff but friendly. Like a big brown bear chuckling over his own joke. The man came from behind the counter and approached us, saying, "Is it three wishes you're after? Or can I help you with something real?"

He *was* big, but dressed just right for velvet cushions. Black slacks, high-gloss shoes, starched white shirt with cuff links, and a blousy purple tie. The only thing that gave away that he was playing a part was his hair. It was black, really thick, and greased back. Which would have gone with the rest of him just fine, except there were little flecks of dust or lint or something all through it, and the wide grooves that ran from front to back looked very rough. Like he'd combed his hair with a pinecone.

I smiled and said, "Actually, I only need one wish."

"Oh?" One eyebrow went up, but the other stayed put. Like maybe he'd be better off not knowing.

"Yeah. And I was told you might be able to help."

The second eyebrow didn't budge. "How's that?"

"It's my mother."

"Your mother?"

I let out a heavy sigh and whispered, "She's got amnesia, and she's disappeared."

He looks me in the eye, and I guess in my mind there was enough truth to what I was saying to convince him. He nods and says, "And why do you think ol' Cos can help?"

"Because a guy in a store up the street said he was sure he'd seen her in this neighborhood. Would you mind looking at a few pictures?"

He shrugs and says, "Sure, why not?"

So I walk over to the jewelry cases and spread out the three head shots. "Do any of these people look familiar?"

Just then the door whooshes open and Hali comes in. Cosmo sizes up her flip-flops and toe rings and keeps half an eye on her as she starts browsing. "Why you got three different women here?" he asks me.

"Just to make sure."

He considers this, then plops a thick index finger right on Opal's nose. "This your mom?"

I let out a big sigh, then try to sound desperate. "So she was here? Did she say anything? Anything at all about me or maybe my grandmother?"

He shakes his head. "Sorry, kid."

"Did you talk to her?"

"Not about anything like that."

"My poor grandmother. She's so upset! On top of the amnesia and her disappearing, Grams is afraid my mom stole some of her jewelry." I could see him stiffen up, but there was no stopping now. I held out Claire's picture and said, "See this? This is my grandmother back when she got married, and the jewels she's wearing are family heirlooms. They're, like, centuries old. My grandmother's worried sick that my mother's pawned them for cash."

Hali had sashayed around to the jewelry counter and was about fifteen feet away from us, leaning over a case, looking very interested.

Ol' Cos puts up a stiff little smile and shakes his head. "I'm sorry. I can't help you there."

He's edging away, but I tag right along. "You probably can't tell from the picture, but the stones are red. Are you sure she didn't try to get you to buy the necklace or maybe the ring?"

He shakes his head and says, "You might try the Jewelry Connection. It's three blocks down the street. She might've gone there." He eyes Hali and whispers, "Now if you'll excuse me, I have to attend to my *paying* customers."

I can tell from the way he's acting that he's lying. He's seen that necklace, or my name's Helen Keller. So I follow him, saying, "But if she didn't try to sell them to you, then why did she come in here? Look, we're not going to call the police or anything, I just want to find her and get my grandmother's jewels back." I touch his arm and say, "Look, I know you've got them. So why don't you tell me where they are?"

Hali grins at me from across the room. "Hey, school-girls! They're right over here."

Pinecone-head looks from her to me a couple of times, then says, "What is this?"

Hali smiles, sits right down on one of his velvety stools, and crosses her legs. "It could be a bust if you want to keep on creepin' on. But if you decide to adopt a conscience and hand these baubles over, then we'll be out of here with a quick case of amnesia ourselves."

I felt like saying, Wait! No! There's a murder involved here, don't promise him that! but before I could figure out what to say, he snaps, "I paid her good money for those. How was I supposed to know they were hot?"

Hali's got no sympathy. "It's your business to know, bucko."

He whips around to face me. "Your mother's got amnesia...what a con artist!" He moves behind the counter and says to Hali, "If you think I'm just going to hand these over to you..."

Hali smiles at him and says, "Oh, you will. 'Cause you know that the wad you blew buyin' them is a lot smaller than the one you'd pay a lawyer to defend you in a court of law." She digs through her purse and pulls up a cell phone. "Your destiny's just a nine-one-one away."

He doesn't budge, so she pushes a button on her phone. *Beep.* "Nine..."

"Now, listen to me!"

She pushes again. "One..."

He lets out a chain of cusswords long enough to circle the block, but he opens the case and throws the jewels at us. "Get out of here, you hear me? Get out of here!"

We scamper up the street, around the corner, and back to the Bug, and the minute we're safe inside, Hali whoops and puts out her hands for us to slap. "You two were *smooth*! Amnesia...what a trip! I can't believe it—he just handed them over!" She holds the necklace out and whispers, "This thing must be worth a pretty penny."

I snatch it from her and say, "Don't even think about it. It belongs to Max."

She scowls and says, "Like he doesn't owe me *something*? What are you going to do? Just hand it back to him on a silver platter?"

"I don't know how or when I'm going to give it back, but I am going to give it back." I wiggle my hand at her. "Now hand over the ring."

She says, "Aw, man!" but she digs it out of her purse and gives it to me. "Like I'd want to have anything that was *Claire's* anyway." She cranks on the motor, muttering, "Poor Mama."

I hand the jewels over the seat to Marissa and ask, "Because he never married her?"

"Because," she said, flipping a U-turn, "Mama's lived in Claire's shadow all these years. He told her he could never marry again. Ha!"

"Why did she keep working for him?"

Hali squealed onto the street. "Get this—because she *loves* him. Can you believe that? Says she always has. She thought one day he'd do the right thing."

After Hali had merged into traffic I said, "You know, I wasn't really expecting to get the jewels back. I just wanted to find out if Opal really stole them, before I went and talked to her."

"To Opal? How you gonna do that?"

I gave her an apologetic smile. "We were hoping that maybe the Tinsel Town Taxi would be running that way?"

She scowled at me so long I thought she was going to rear-end the car in front of us. "And where might 'that way' be?"

I tried to make it sound light and fun. "Ever heard of the Peppermint Peacock?"

One look at her face and I knew that she had.

THIRTEEN

The Peppermint Peacock made the Heavenly Hotel look like a charming little bed-and-breakfast.

Hali tucked the Bug into a loading zone across the street while Marissa and I gawked at the dirty brick building with GIRLS-GIRLS-GIRLS slashed in lavender and pink across it.

The building is solid brick, so there are no windows to go snooping in, and you can't even see the front door because it's set way back from the sidewalk. The brick walls curve into a kind of tunnel that leads under a turquoise PEPPERMINT PEACOCK awning straight into darkness.

Hali lets the car idle and says, "No action there this time of day."

It did look dead, but I didn't want to give up yet. "Tammy made it sound like Opal *lives* here."

"Really? Maybe in one of those rooms upstairs?" Hali shakes her head and mutters, "She could've done better than that."

I lean clear across Hali to see what she's talking about. Sure enough, planted on the building like a top hat on a red rhinoceros are two floors finished in stucco. Dirty white stucco with streaks of rust running from the corners of the windows. And the windows are all cloudy. Like the glass has been washed with acid.

Marissa whispers, "I think we're in a little deep here, Sammy."

No kidding.

But I felt a little braver for having Hali around, so I said, "You want to cruise around back? There's got to be some other way in and out."

Hali grinds into gear, then cuts through traffic. "I'm game if you are."

There was another way in. Actually, two. We putted along an alley lined with garbage cans on one side and a graffitied cinder-block wall on the other, and when we got to the red brick of the Peppermint Peacock we saw a set of oily cement steps going down into a basement and a zigzag of rickety fire-escape stairs leading up to the floors above.

There's no place to park without blocking the alley, so Hali winds up going onto the side street, saying, "We could come back after they open if you want to."

Marissa says, "Why don't we just call?"

I didn't want to do either of those things. I wanted to see Opal. Now. "You guys can wait here. I'll just go knock on that basement door and see if anyone answers. Then maybe I'll try around front."

Hali rolls her eyes. "Right, Burdock. Like I'm gonna let you do that."

"Look, I just want to find out if she's here or not."

Marissa mutters, "And you can't do that by calling?"

We sat there in limbo for a minute, then finally Hali

pops up a low curb, drives along the sidewalk for a few yards, and squeezes the Bug onto a patch of dirt next to a dilapidated fence. She sighs and says, "Okay. Let's go knock."

I smile at her and say, "Thanks!" and even though Marissa does grumble something about the glitz and glamour of Garbage Boulevard, she gets out of the car and follows us down the alley.

When we're about thirty feet from the building, we see a man's head, then his shoulders, then the rest of him bob up the basement steps. His skin's dark like Hali's, and he's wearing a white apron loosely tied over a T-shirt and black jeans, and in each hand is a Hefty sack, heavy with garbage.

He swings the sacks into a garbage can, and as we get closer I can see that his hair is woven with gray and that his eyes look cloudy. Like the windows overhead.

He completely ignores us. And for a minute I thought maybe his eyes were so bad that he couldn't really see us. But as he heads back down the steps, Hali says, "Excuse me?" and he stops, turns, and stares at us. And that's when it hits me—these aren't eyes that can't see. They're eyes that don't *want* to see.

He doesn't say a word. He just stands there, two steps down, his gaze fixed on Hali.

Hali hesitates, then says, "We're here to see our friend Opal. She up?"

His head jerks enough to mean Follow me, then down he goes, through the basement door.

We hurry after him, and the minute we're inside, he

clangs the door closed and rotates a metal latch, locking the door. The ceiling is low, with ductwork and plumbing running on the brick walls and overhead, and there's only one bare bulb for lighting. Straight ahead are wooden stairs leading up to a doorway. He goes up, and so do we.

Now, when Tammy had mentioned the Peppermint Peacock, I'd thought that it was a funny name. A colorful name. Bright. Snappy. Kind of, I don't know, *tangy*. But stepping through the doorway at the top of the stairs and into the main room of the Peppermint Peacock, I saw there was nothing bright or snappy about it. It was a cave with black booths and grimy maroon carpet, and the air was damp and sour with stagnant smoke and body odor and beer. It felt suffocating. Like being caught in the grip of a giant sweaty armpit.

Hali says, "There she is," and nods across the room at Opal, sitting alone at the bar, cupping a mug of coffee in her hands. Her hair's clipped back in a tangle of ratty curls, and she's staring off into space. "I suppose you want me to hang back?"

"No, you can come. That's probably better. But can you let me tell her about LeBrandi?"

She shrugs. "Sure."

The three of us approach the bar, and I can see Opal snap out of her thoughts and start watching us in the reflection of a giant mirror on the other side of the bar. And you can tell that when she recognizes Hali, she can't quite believe it's her. First she blinks into the mirror, then she turns on her stool and almost smiles. "Hali?"

"In the flesh, girl."

"But..." She eyes us and says, "You taken up baby-sitting?"

"Don't be frosty, now. We just got here."

Opal looks around and says, "This ain't exactly a place to take kids."

"You got it backward, snowflake. They're the ones escorting me."

Opal blinks at her a minute, then looks at us. "Is that so?"

I nod at her, and she smiles at me. Like I'm some dumb little kitten who's come to the counter for milk. She slaps the stool next to her and says, "Well, tell me what's brought you to this fine establishment. Auntie Opal's all ears."

I sit down and watch her face very carefully as I say, "Actually, we're here on account of LeBrandi."

Her eyebrows go way up. "LeBrandi? *She* told you to look me up? For what?"

She didn't fidget. Or look away. She just stared at me, waiting for an answer.

Very quietly I said, "We're here because LeBrandi's dead."

Her face fell. Just bottomed out. Then her eyes got wider and wider, and she looked from Hali to Marissa and then back to me. "*Dead?* How can that be?"

"She was murdered."

"*Murdered?* When? By who?"

I kept my eyes right on her. "We figured by you."

That popped her to her feet. She pointed to herself and cried, "By *me*?" Then she shakes her head and says, "What are you *talking* about?"

Now, either she's a much better actress than my mother gave her credit for, or she doesn't know a thing about LeBrandi. So I decide to find out what she looks like when she *is* lying. "Why don't you tell us about the jewels?"

"The..." Her face clams up. Presto! It's calm and flat. Colorless. Like a pancake that's been cooked on a cooling griddle. "What jewels?"

I motion to Marissa, who pulls them out of her jeans and hands them to her, saying, "These jewels."

Opal doesn't take them, and even though she knows the jig is up, she tries, "Whose are those?"

I shrug and say, "Well, Cosmo thought they were *his,* but we set him straight."

Her pancake pose finally cracks. "Who *are* you? Shouldn't you be giving me the right to remain silent and all of that?"

Hali says, "They're kids, Opal, not cops."

Opal squints at us and sits back down. "Well, they're sure acting like cops. Who *are* they?"

Hali shrugs. "Just a couple of kids with a vested inter-est." She waits for Opal to respond, and when she doesn't, Hali says, "So...?"

"So I pawned the jewels. So what! Max wouldn't rip up my contract, and I'm sorry, but the man should *not* get fifty percent of any job I land in the next eight years. It's just not right! If he's not going to play fair, he's going to have to pay somehow, and the only thing I could find were those stupid jewels." She frowns at Hali and says, "Which, by the way, weren't worth it. First I thought Max noticed that I'd snagged them, then when I survived that, LeBrandi caught me stashing them and blackmailed a piece out of me. And after all that, all I got was enough to pay two months' rent in this place."

"Wait a minute," I say. "Max takes fifty percent?"

She gives me a lopsided scowl. "That's right. He makes you and he takes you."

"Everybody signs over fifty percent?"

"That's right, babe."

"Even after you leave?"

"Half of anything you do while you're there and up to eight years after you leave is his, and babe, it's iron-clad. He's had lawsuits with some high rollers, and every time he's come out on top." She shakes her head. "His setup's a shiny little lure, and we all take it, hook, line, and sinker."

Hali says, "So you were looking for your contract and you found the jewels?"

"That's right. He was busy firing me when some big honcho dropped in, and while he was schmoozing with him in the reception room, I was ripping through his desk, thinking that if I could just find my contract, I'd be free from that overbearing jerk once and for all. But all I found was that stupid jewelry." She rakes back some loose strands of hair. "So what now? You got handcuffs in your back pocket or something?"

"Very funny," I said. "So when's the last time you saw LeBrandi?"

It's like she'd forgotten LeBrandi was dead. "Man, that's a bummer about LeBrandi. The last time I saw her? The day I left. We had a fight about the brooch, I told her where she could shove it, and that was that. I think the woman's a backbiting leech and a liar, but I didn't hate her enough to kill her." She rolls her eyes and chuckles. "Now, if Max turns up dead, look me up."

Hali says, "Mama saw LeBrandi come in after curfew last night. Any ideas?"

"She was always sneaking around after curfew, Hali. And if Max wasn't so uptight about boyfriends, he'd have fewer fillies jumpin' the fence."

I thought about this a minute, then said, "Did she have *a* boyfriend, or was she, you know, dating different people?"

She laughed, "Oh, she was steady...like the San Andreas Fault." Then she added, "Look, LeBrandi'd keep me up all night jawin' about some new guy; then she'd drop him two days later. Beats me who her latest was. If you ask me, Max had way more grounds to can LeBrandi than he had to can me. What I want to know is, how'd you wind up at Cosmo's?"

So I tell her about the paper in the sock, and when I'm done, she shakes her head and says, "See? She ripped that off from me, too! I do all the research, and she just goes and snakes it out of my desk. Like she couldn't find her *own* contact?" She snickers and says, "That sums up LeBrandi right there. She's a snake." She hesitates. "Uh...*was* a snake."

Nobody said anything for a minute; then Hali looked at me like, Well? and really, as much as I'd wanted to believe that Opal had killed her roommate, I could tell she hadn't. My theory was dust, and that took me right back to a place I didn't want to go.

I shrugged and said, "I guess that's it."

"So what now?" Opal asked. "You gonna hand those back over to Max?"

"Well, they *are* his...."

"Yeah," she grumbles. "And so's my life." She took a gulp of cold coffee, her face pinching up as she swallowed. "Get out of here, would you? I don't need the reminder."

So we said good-bye and filed back down the steps to the landing below. The man we'd met in the alley passed us along the stairs on his way up, carrying a shredded sponge mop and a pail. As he moved past me, he didn't look at me—he looked right through me.

And as we let ourselves out the basement door and climbed up the steps to the alley, I couldn't help wondering again if those eyes of his were blind.

Or if that's just what happens to eyes that have seen too much.

The back of the Bug was fine with me. And while Hali hopped curbs and violated traffic, I sat curled up, looking out the window at nothing. If it wasn't Opal, then who? I hated sliding back into dark thoughts about my mother, but I couldn't help it. She'd changed so much. And maybe Lana Keyes, Big Daddy waitress, was too grossed out by the *potential* of goopy guts to hurt a fly, but Dominique Windsor, actress at large, seemed ruthless. Determined.

Unstoppable.

Besides, there were no goopy guts involved here. It was
a tidy, spotless little murder.

And I was seriously slipping into the darkness of Dominique's Dungeon again when Marissa says from the front seat, "Oh, please."

I turn from the window and blink at her. "What?"

"She did not do it, Sammy. You've got to get that out of your head!"

I didn't argue with her. I just looked down.

"It—was—some—one—else," she says, like she's counting to a preschooler.

"But who?" I whisper. "And why?"

"That's why we have police, Sammy. Paid professionals who know how to figure these things out."

"But—"

"But nothing! There are what—fifteen? sixteen?—a *lot* of people living in that house. And you've eliminated *one* as a suspect. What about the rest of them? You don't know anything about them. Any one of them could have had a reason to kill LeBrandi, and hel-lo...*you're* not going to be able to figure it out! Just let the police handle it, would you?"

"Okay, okay!"

She faced forward for all of three seconds, then whipped back around and said, "Stop it! You're killing yourself over nothing. She did *not* do it!"

I tried to hide from Marissa by looking back out the window. I couldn't just drop the thoughts twisting and tangling in my head. It's like my brain was a giant knot, and no matter where I tugged on it, the knot wouldn't budge. It just got tighter.

And I couldn't figure out what was worse, having a murderer for a mother or suspecting my mother of murder.

So while Hali tooled around town, pointing out tourist traps and movie star hangouts for Marissa, I looked out the window at nothing, pushing and pulling on this gigantic knot in my head.

And even after Hali had picked up some groceries and the dry cleaning, even after she and Marissa went into Java Joint so Hali could finally get her latte, there I was, scrunched in the back of this beat-up Bug, brooding and moody, picking at that knot.

Finally I started getting antsy. Hali and Marissa had been inside Java Joint for a long time, and I was feeling suffocated by the smell of green onions and cilantro steaming up out of the grocery sack, and by the sterile plastic dry-cleaning bags lying across my lap.

And all of a sudden I wanted to bust out of there and run home. I wanted to get away from Hollywood. Away from my mother.

Away from the giant knot strangling my brain.

I missed Grams. I missed Hudson. I was so homesick I even missed Officer Borsch.

And thinking of Officer Borsch made me flash back to his secret twin Tweedledee and how seeing him appear at Max's mansion had spooked me. And in the middle of *that* flashback, it hit me how it was the second time that day that I'd been spooked by people who could have passed as twins.

And thinking about the first time—about seeing LeBrandi, dead in my mother's bed—suddenly made a spot in that knot in my brain give way. It didn't just slip, it *snapped*. And like a tiny hole snagged in a skintight stocking, all of a sudden it ran, unraveling into a gash as broad and fast as the Sunset Strip.

At first I couldn't move. Then I couldn't not move. I wrestled myself out of the back of the Bug, my heart pounding so hard I was shaking.

I had to find Hali and Marissa and get back to Max's house. Now.

It was a matter of life and death.

FOURTEEN

Getting Marissa to the car was like dragging a bloodhound from the chase. She'd seen a star. And even though it wasn't anyone I'd ever heard of, Hali sat at the counter drinking her latte and confirmed it was true.

Neither of them seemed to believe that getting back to the mansion was a matter of life and death. Hali just shook latte foam into her mouth while Marissa talked right over me, saying, "Do you think I should ask him? Do you think it would be rude?"

Hali says, "Oh, go on. He's about done."

Marissa grabs a Java Joint napkin and asks Hali, "Do you have a pen?"

Hali digs one out of her purse and nods across the room with her nose. "Better hop to it. He's beatin' a path."

So there I am, trying to talk about life and death while my best friend deserts me for a tube twinkler's autograph and Hali laps up coffee foam from the depths of a cardboard cup.

"Hali," I beg her, "we've got to go back. *Now.*"

She checks the inside of her cup and shakes it out one last time. "I hear you, I hear you." She dumps the cup in the trash and says, "So let's go."

Marissa joins us back at the Bug, looking all disgruntled. She plops down in the front seat and says, "He doesn't sign napkins."

Hali fires up the Bug with a grin. "Give him a couple of years. He'll be falling all over himself to sign your *trash*."

I sat in the backseat, quiet. And hurt. I mean, I knew that I'd dragged them all around town on a wild-peacock chase, but still, they didn't have to ignore me like that. But sitting there in the back of Hali's Bug, scrunched in on all sides, I couldn't really blame them for not listening. At least not Marissa. I mean, it was true—I'd been a maniac. All day. A raving, panicked maniac.

Sure I'd been upset, dealing with my mother and the thought of her snagging me a dinosaur dad. And having all that on my mind, well, it's no wonder I'd just been sucked in. But still, if I'd had the brains to stop and take a deep breath early in the day, I'd have thought of it right off, and I wouldn't have had to take the Tinsel Town Taxi to Cosmo's or the Peppermint Peacock. I'd have stayed right at Max's.

Right next to my mother.

All that caffeine Hali'd had seemed to be having the reverse effect on her. Here I wanted to be moving, and what was she doing?

Coming to a complete stop at a red light.

And what I couldn't figure out was why. Why now? I mean, there were at least three different illegal maneuvers she could be making to get through the light—and then one sort of iffy one that involved the ramp of a delivery truck—but she was just *sitting* there.

Finally she looks at me in the rearview mirror and says, "Quit squirming, I'll get you there."

"Hali, you don't understand...."

"Yeah, yeah, I know—life and death."

The light changed, and she went back to driving, but my eyes were stuck on the rearview mirror, seeing a mirage of her eyes. And all of a sudden I start having the worst panic attack of my life. I can't breathe right, I can't seem to *see* right, and in no time my hands are shaking and it feels like I'm covered with wool. Itchy, sweaty, scratchy wool.

Hali eases into a gas station and says, "It'll only be a minute" as she swings her door shut.

The second she's outside, I shoot forward in my seat and whisper, "Marissa! Marissa, you've got to listen to me!"

"What, Sammy? You are acting so weird! I gotta tell you, it's kind of embarrassing."

"Marissa, just listen. Please, just listen!"

She turns to face me. "Okay, okay! What?"

"I was wrong. I was all wrong about Opal."

"Yeah. Didn't you decide that a couple of hours ago?"

"*Please,* Marissa!"

"Okay. I'm sorry. Go on."

"And I was a *moron* for not thinking of this sooner, but you know, there were sleeping pills and everyone thought LeBrandi had OD'd, so I got off on the wrong track and—"

"Would you please just tell me what you're all panicked about, Sammy?"

I take a deep breath and say, "Opal didn't kill LeBrandi."

"Right...."

"Nobody killed LeBrandi."

"*What?*"

I lean in closer and whisper, "At least they didn't mean to."

"Now you think it was an accident?"

"No! What I think is that whoever killed LeBrandi meant to kill someone else. Someone who looks enough like LeBrandi to be mistaken for her—especially in the dark. Someone who *should've* been sleeping in that bed last night."

Gradually Marissa's jaw drops down and her eyes bug out. She whispers, "Your mother?"

"Exactly."

Now Marissa tries to take a mental step back from what I'm saying, but it's not an easy thing to do. It makes too much sense. Finally she says, "But...but why?"

"Exactly. Why would someone want my mother out of the way? Well, LeBrandi would—for the same reasons my mother would've wanted LeBrandi out of the way—but obviously it wasn't her." I lower my voice even farther. "Then there are all the people who don't want my mother to marry Max."

It took no time for Marissa to make the connection. She puts a hand in front of her mouth and whispers, "Oh... my...god! You think it's Hali?"

We both sneak a peek at Hali, who's screwing the gas cap back on. "Maybe, but more likely Reena or Inga."

"Inga? How do you figure that?"

"Well, look. If Max is worth a bundle—which obviously he is—and if he never told Inga that Hali is his daughter—which, from their conversation this morning, I'd say he didn't—then Inga has probably been expecting to inherit his fortune. Enter my mother, whom Max has decided to start a family with, and *poof!* that pretty little purse of his is snatched right out of Inga's hands."

Marissa keeps an eye on Hali as she walks over to the station's building, and whispers, "Wow!"

"But what all this *means* is that whoever thought they were killing my mother last night didn't get the job done. My mother is still a problem."

"Are you saying you think they're going to try it again? Sammy, there are cops all over the place trying to figure out who killed LeBrandi. Who'd be crazy enough to try it again?"

"Maybe they won't. I don't know. I just can't take the chance. We've got to get back and talk to my mother and maybe Max."

"Max? Why him? What about the police?"

"If I tell the police, then I have to break my promise to Hali—otherwise what I'm telling them won't make sense."

"But what if it was *Hali* who tried to kill your mother?"

"What if it's *not*? I mean, you were right—that house is full of people we don't know anything about—and if it's *not* Hali and I break my pact with her, then..."

Hali pushes through the gas station door with a quart of oil in her hand. Marissa watches her approach the Bug and nods. "Then she can break her pact with you."

I rested my head against the seat back. "I was crazy to tell her. Cra-zy!"

Hali calls through the window, "You two okay? I think I'm low a quart—it'll only be a minute."

She pops the hood behind us, and I whisper to Marissa, "I need to find out if Inga knew."

"That Max proposed?"

"Yeah. 'Cause if she *didn't,* then my prime suspects would have to be either Hali or her mother."

"Or...," Marissa whispers, "both."

Hali slams the hood and dumps the empty oil jug in the trash. I lean back a little and say, "I don't know about that.... They're not even talking to each other!"

Marissa sits forward as Hali comes around to the driver's door. "Yeah, well, maybe that's why!"

Hali plops into her seat, whips her seat belt on, and says, "Okay, now we're ready to jam." She fires up the Bug, lets the thing idle a minute, then throws it into gear and lays rubber getting out of the parking lot. "Did you hear it pinging before? God, this thing just eats oil, but hey, it beats shelling out my savings on a new one." She looks at me in the rearview mirror. "You okay back there?"

I nod and try to change the subject. "Don't you think Max would, you know, buy you a new car?"

"You mean blackmail one out of him?" She laughs and says, "You've got a super-sized naughty streak on you, girl."

"No, I didn't mean blackmail! I meant just ask."

She didn't say anything else. Didn't mention life and death or what a freak I'd been at Java Joint. All she did was

147

shake her head and chuckle. The whole way home. And then, when we pulled into the driveway and parked inside the cottage garage, she grins at us and says, "Thanks, girls. I've got myself a whole new perspective on my situation."

I buried the picture of Claire and the head shots inside a grocery sack, and we helped Hali carry in the dry cleaning and food. And as we let down the garage door, she started humming.

Humming.

And she kept right on humming as she punched the code into the kitchen's back-door panel, thumped a bag of groceries on a counter, and went over to the laundry room door. I had a grocery sack, too, so I put it next to hers on the counter, but I guess I was taking too long, because she says, "C'mon, Burdock. The dry cleaning goes in here."

I catch up to Hali and Marissa, saying, "Quit with the Burdock, would you?"

Hali grins. "Aw, it's cute. Suits you."

I grumble, "Thanks a lot."

So Hali pushes through the laundry room door, and all of a sudden we're like a rush-hour pileup. Hali screeches to a halt, Marissa plows right into her, and I bump *smack!* into Marissa.

And the reason we're all piled up is because standing there, blocking the road, is someone none of us is ready to see.

FIFTEEN

Hali must've decided that since there was no going around him, she'd put the pedal to the metal and go right through him. She gives him a sour look and says, "Hello... *Dad*."

For a minute he just stares at her through his tortoise-shell glasses; then he nods very slowly and says, "This would explain your mother's disappearance." He eyes Marissa and me while he asks Hali, "Who else have you told?"

"Oh, aren't you precious. Nineteen years of deception, and all you're worried about is who else knows? Well, the answer, my pathetic padre, is nobody. These girls do, but they're highly motivated not to talk." She turns to us. "Isn't that right?"

Now, believe me, at this point I am sweating it out pretty good. I mean, she's driving this conversation like she drives her Bug, and any minute she's going to take a wrong turn and wipe us all out.

"Isn't that right?" she asks me again.

I swallow hard and nod.

Hali slaps back a braid that's fallen across her face. "And what's this about Mama?"

"She's nowhere to be found. We thought she might be with you, but obviously that's not the case." He sighs and says, "I'm sorry things happened this way. Truly, I am. But right now Detective Doyle is anxious to speak with you, and I think it'd be a good idea if you'd go in there and dissuade his suspicions regarding you."

Hali points to herself. "Me? He thinks *I* killed LeBrandi?"

"Your exit at their arrival did not exactly put you in a favorable light, Hali."

"I went to get the dry cleaning!"

"Go explain that to Detective Doyle. He's in the dining hall. I believe he's finished interviewing everyone else."

Hali grumbles a bit, but she takes off, and when she's gone Max looks at Marissa and me and says, "Dominique's been quite worried about the two of you, and I know she'll be greatly relieved to see you. *However,* this situation with Hali is personal and it's private, and I would greatly appreciate your not discussing it with Dominique."

"But . . . it *is* her business to know, don't you think?" I look him right in the eye and try to forget the irony. "Wouldn't *you* want to know if the person you were thinking about marrying had a secret child somewhere?"

He freezes. "She's told you about my proposal?"

"Well, we could tell something was up, so we kind of talked it out of her."

He closes his eyes and says, "Oh, heaven, what a mess."

All of a sudden I realize that this is my chance. Maybe my only chance. I take a deep breath and say, "Mr. Mueller, there's something else that I really have to discuss with you, but not here. Can we go into your office?"

"My office? Why?"

"Because I . . . I can't talk about it here."

He snaps, "Why not?"

Now, I could've talked about it right then and there, but I didn't know how else I'd ever get into Max's office. I mean, it was easy to see that something, somewhere, was going to give, and that my mother's whole world was about to come crashing down around her. And even though I hadn't really done anything to get her into the mess she was in—well, except for that little mistake of confiding in a girl who might've been trying to kill her I still felt like I had to at least try to get her out of it. Because I was beginning to understand that if my mother did get kicked out of Max Mueller's agency, she'd never work again. Not as an actress, anyway. Not with the way Max's contract sentenced her to his little financial prison for eight years. If my mother thought she was old now, she'd be Fraulein Fossil by the time her contract with him ran out.

So I wanted to get inside the office again. And this time I wanted to look at more than just the weird decor. There had to be a filing cabinet. Somewhere. And even though I knew I wouldn't be able to get my hands on her contract with Max standing right there, maybe—just maybe—I could do something about it later.

So when Mighty Max tells me he doesn't have time to go to his office, I signal Marissa, who digs up the ring and hands it over to him.

At first he doesn't take it. Then he turns red, then completely white. "Where did you get this? Do you have the other pieces?"

"Like I said, we can't talk about it here. Can we please go to your office?"

He blinks twice behind those glasses, then marches off. And while we trail after him, I whisper my plan to Marissa. I can tell she thinks I'm losing it again, but she can also tell that it's very important to me. She hisses, "If this lands us in jail . . ."

I try to kid her with "Maybe there'll be some drunk and disorderly movie stars in the cell next to us," but she just hits me in the arm.

When we get to Max's office, he unlocks the deadbolt, whisks us in, and says, "So. Here we are." He sits on the edge of his desk and unfolds his hand, showing us the ring. "Now. Where did you get this, and do you know where the brooch and necklace are?"

His eyes are looking glossy and hard. But in the center there's a soft spot, and to me, they don't look stern and fierce like he wants them to. They look like two kiwi-flavored Tootsie Pops under glass.

"Well?" he demands.

"Well," I say, "actually, it's sorta hard to talk about—and there's a lot *to* talk about—but since I know you're worried about your Honeymoon Jewels, I'll start at the end and work back, okay?"

The crunchy candy outside starts to crack. "Yes. Please." He puts a hand toward two carved ebony chairs. "Would you be more comfortable sitting?"

Marissa takes a seat, but I start moving around a little, saying, "No, actually—"

Marissa pipes up with "Actually, Sammy has trouble talking and sitting. Actually, she has trouble thinking and sitting, or eating and sitting, or..."

I pull a face at her and say, "He gets the idea, Marissa," but when I'm sure Max can't see, I wink at her so she knows *I* know she's doing me a favor. Then I say, "Yes. I know where the necklace and brooch are, and yes, you'll get them both back today."

He springs up from the corner of his desk and says, "But how did you find them? Who had them? Where are they now?"

"Like I said, it's pretty complicated, and we'll tell you the whole story, but first, I'm confused about a couple of things. You called these the Honeymoon Jewels. Is that because you're planning to give them to Dominique?"

He blinks at me a minute, then sighs and says, "From your vantage point, I'm sure I appear to be a real cad." Then he looks up toward the ceiling and proceeds to talk about good intentions and human frailties, and how he hopes he'll make fewer mistakes the next time around.

Now, while he's musing about his mountain of mistakes, I'm checking out furniture, lifting table skirts, moving slowly away from him and Marissa to the other side of the room. And I'm in the middle of finding a whole lot of nothing when he swivels on his desk to face me and says, "So yes, I was planning to present them as a token of everlasting love."

I scratch my neck and signal Marissa to start snooping. "Who knew this?"

"No one, really. I had only recently taken them out of . . . of storage."

"You didn't tell Reena? Or Inga?"

He frowns. "Inga knew nothing of the jewels, and discussing a gift of this kind with Reena would have been most insensitive."

"But they both knew you wanted to marry Dominique?"

"Yes. I tried my best to explain it to Reena, but she didn't grasp the concept."

So Inga did know! My heart was kicking and bucking, but I tried to hold the reins tight. "The concept?"

He looks at me and sighs. "Yes. I'm afraid it's something that's beyond Reena's grasp, and at this point it's too late for me to do anything about that."

"But what concept?"

"The concept of Claire. Now please. You were telling me about the jewels?"

I still didn't understand what he meant, but I had to concentrate on keeping his focus away from Marissa. I mean, I was afraid she wouldn't do anything, but there she is across the room, moving around like Super Snoop. It's amazing—she's not biting a thumbnail or doing the McKenze dance. She's being nervy. Very nervy. It's like she's whipped on a mask and double-S cape.

So I start maneuvering myself around the room in such a way that Max's back is always to Marissa. And while she's busy sliding open his desk drawers and checking inside boxes, I'm telling Max the story, handling his knickknacks and artifacts just enough to make him nervous so he won't take his eyes off me.

I'm dragging the story out, too, telling the tiniest little details about the brooch and how we'd figured out Cosmo's phone number, and about going to the curio shop and confronting Opal at the Peppermint Peacock.

Finally he interrupts me, saying, "She admitted it?"

I'm pretending to be interested in the big hieroglyphic shapes that are woven into the tapestry that's hanging on the wall, kind of fingering them as I say, "Well, she couldn't exactly deny it...," when all of a sudden I get this vague, heady feeling of déjà vu. And that's when I realize that something—the tapestry? I'm not sure—*smells* familiar. So I sniff. And it's coming back to me, but not quite, so I stick my nose right into his woolly woven heirloom and take a good hearty whiff.

Well, I guess he didn't appreciate me Dustbusting his tapestry because he comes over, takes me by the shoulders, and steers me into a chair, saying, "You have no idea of the value of some of these items. Please, try not to touch, or *sniff*, anything else, would you?"

Marissa's already slid back into her chair, twitching and shaking a little beside me as she recovers from her adventure as Super Snoop. She shakes her head just enough so I know she wasn't able to find anything, and really, I can't think of an excuse to stall any longer. So I signal Marissa to give him the necklace, and when she does I say, "The brooch is in LeBrandi's dresser. In a pair of olive green socks." Then I stand up and say, "You've got the jewels back now, so...well, I hope you don't do anything to Opal. I know she was wrong to steal them—which is why we're giving them back to you—but she was upset about, you know, about how she was fired and everything. And besides, she didn't kill LeBrandi."

"How can you say that? You've just built her up to be the perfect suspect!"

"I know, but she didn't do it. I could tell."

He frowns at me and crosses his arms. "You could tell."

"Well, yeah. And besides, I don't think whoever killed LeBrandi was trying to kill LeBrandi."

His frown digs in a little deeper. "You don't."

"No. I think they were trying to kill my"—I caught myself in the nick of time—"aunt."

He throws his head back and laughs, then tries to compose himself. "Oh, my dear girl. Why on earth do you say that?"

So I explain my theory to him. And pretty much I just give it to him in black and white. No sidetracks, no details—just the facts, ma'am. Then I shut up and wait.

And does he laugh at me or tell me I've got an overly active imagination? Does he tell me it's preposterous or implausible or just plain dumb?

No.

He says, "Well, now. This is serious." Then he nods and says, "I'd better discuss these new developments with Officer Doyle. I'm sure he'll want to talk to you, but in the meantime, why don't you go upstairs and rest? You girls have had quite a day, and frankly, you look worn. I'll tell Dominique that you're fine." He hesitates, then says, "You will let me be the one to tell her about...things, won't you?"

"Uh...that depends. When are you planning to do that?"

"I've arranged a special dinner for the two of us tonight after LeBrandi's farewell service."

"Her farewell service? When's that? And you're going to a romantic dinner afterward? Excuse me, but isn't that kind of...cold?"

"Young lady, if LeBrandi's death has taught me anything, it's that we must celebrate life. Every moment of it. So yes, I'll...I'll tell your aunt all truths tonight. And the farewell service for LeBrandi is just an in-house memorial to help us all deal with her passing." He eyes me. "So, can you wait that long? It just wouldn't be right for Dominique to learn such delicate information from someone else."

I nod and ask, "Where is she, anyway?"

"She's with Inga, trying on a gown."

"With *Inga*?"

"Yes. Why do you look so alarmed?"

"Because...oh, please!" I head out of his office. "Where are they? I need to see her. Right now!"

Just then Inga walks into the reception room, her bandages looking a little droopy around the eyes and tattered around the knuckles. She says, "Did I hear my name?"

I look right into her yellow eyes and whisper, "Where's...where's Dominique?"

Tiger Eyes blinks at me with a strange sort of detachment. Like she's not sure if I'm a morsel worth munching. "She's changing clothes," she says, then turns to Max and

157

smiles. "The dress fits beautifully—like it was made for her."

He lets out a contented sigh, then asks, "And the shoes?"

"Perfectly. And now, if you don't mind, I'm going out to work in the garden. I found that policeman most unnerving."

"Of course, of course. You go on. It'll do you good."

"And you should take a swim, Maxi. You've not looked too well lately." She stretches up to kiss him on the cheek, then turns and leaves without glancing back.

After she's gone, Max seems to pull himself out of a heavy thought. He locks up his office, then says, "If you'll wait right here, I'll tell Dominique to come see you." He hesitates on his way out. "I implore you, though—don't mention the situation with Hali to her. Or the jewels—I don't want what's happened to tarnish their surprise."

My stomach flutters a bit as I ask, "Well, what if...what if she doesn't accept them?"

"Oh, she will," he says, then leaves the room.

The minute he's gone, Marissa whispers, "He's, like, head over heels for her."

I plop down on the couch, groaning, "What a mess. What a monumental mess!" And what I'm thinking while I'm shaking my head is Why? Why couldn't she just have been herself instead of this stupid Dominique person? So what if she was a little bit older? So what if she had a kid? Why was she so afraid of being who she was? I mean, if she had just stuck to being Lana Keyes, someone, somewhere, would've liked her for who she was and what she could do, and she wouldn't be tangled in this web of lies, with a tortoise-eyed geezer moving in from one end and a murdering maniac creeping in from another.

While I'm busy brooding about maniacs and geezers, Marissa's looking at something on the wall. She interrupts my thoughts with "He's going to have to pull all this stuff down if he marries your mom."

"Shh! And she is *not* going to marry him!"

"You wait and see. I'll bet she does."

"Marissa! Are you trying to kill me over here?"

She shrugs and says, "Love can be pretty persuasive," then nods at what she's been looking at on the wall. "It's so sad."

I get up and say, "What is that?"

"It's that newspaper article your mom was telling us about last night. What a tragedy." She shakes her head. "Some valentine."

"What do you mean, some valentine?"

"Here, look. She died on Valentine's Day."

It *was* sad—from the headline RISING STAR DIES, to the story of Claire being run off the road at dawn by a delivery truck, to famous movie people calling her a "dramatic diva" and an "unparalleled talent," to the closing paragraph about Claire being survived by "her grief-stricken husband, the renowned film producer Maximilian Mueller." And then there was the last line, which seemed to drop the final curtain: "The couple had no children."

Even behind glass, the article had turned brown from age. It looked brittle and old, and the photo they'd printed of Claire had become sort of hazy.

Marissa whispers, "Can you see him ever taking this stuff down or gutting his office?"

I look straight at her and say, "He won't have to, because she's not going to marry him!"

Marissa keeps right on whacking nails into my coffin, saying, "I mean, if it were me, I'd make him get rid of *all* Claire's stuff. You can't live like that! And this Egyptian stuff, too. What is up with all of that?" She plops down on the couch, then slaps the front cover of the Cleopatra coffee-table book. "Enough's enough, already! It's like living in a museum. I'd gut it and start over. This place should be Southwest or Spanish or Barcelona. Yeah! Barcelona would look great in here. You know, those cool couches that are kind of curved, with one arm up higher than the other and..."

Well. While Marissa's busy deciding that Early Bullfighter would be the perfect substitute decor for Señor Mueller's abode, my eyes are stuck on that Cleopatra book jacket. And it's not the picture of Cleopatra that I'm staring at. It's the title.

Beneath the word *Cleopatra* are hieroglyphic symbols. Nine of them. Under the *C* is a triangle—like a pyramid that's been cut from the tip straight down to the base. Under the *L* there's some kind of lion or cat or something, crouched down on all fours. And every one of the letters in *Cleopatra* has its own symbol. Well, except for the *A*'s. They both have the same symbol—a profile of a standing bird.

And I probably wouldn't have paid any attention to the hieroglyphics at all, except that I had just seen most of these symbols on the tapestry in Max's office.

I closed my eyes and tried to remember the order of the big shapes woven into the cloth. On top there was a triangle, and under it was a lion, then a bird. . . .

I opened my eyes and looked back at the book. It began just like the tapestry, with a triangle and a lion. The next symbol under the title—the one under the *E*—was a robe, just like the bottom symbol of the tapestry.

Once I made the connection, it didn't take me long to piece together what was written down the length of the tapestry in Max's office.

C, L, A . . . R, E.

The only letter I couldn't match was *I*.

And really, I shouldn't have been surprised, but for some reason piecing together Claire's name sent chills running all through me. And as I whispered, "Marissa!" and explained what I'd deciphered, those chills didn't go away. How could somebody live surrounded by the pain of what had happened so many years ago? How could somebody haunt himself this way?

And why *why* would he fall in love again now?

SIXTEEN

When my mother came bursting into the reception room, she had a ruby red dress slung over one arm, a pair of matching sequined shoes clutched in the other hand, and a forehead so full of wrinkles it was crying out for a steam iron.

"Where did you *go*? I couldn't believe you'd just *leave* like that!" She flung the dress and shoes on the chair, then smothered me in a hug.

All of a sudden I was eight years old again, home late from school after being sidetracked by a lizard. "I'm sorry." I cleared my throat and pulled away. "It took a lot longer than I thought it would."

"What did? Where have you been?"

So I rewound to when she'd sent Marissa and me to put the brooch back and told her all about finding the number in LeBrandi's sock and the Cosmo connection and how we'd talked to Opal at the Peppermint Peacock. And I was just about to tell her how I was sure that someone was trying to kill *her*, not LeBrandi, when she interrupts me with, "But why? Why did you *do* all that?"

I sputtered and stuttered and wound up saying a whole lot of nothing.

"Samantha! You're keeping something from me—what is it?"

"I...I...it's really not..."

"Samantha!" She looks at Marissa. "What is going on?"

So Marissa leans in and whispers, "She was trying to prove that it was Opal who killed LeBrandi, not you."

"*Me?*" She turns to me. "You thought *I* killed LeBrandi?"

I cringed and shrugged.

"But why?"

"Because..." It suddenly seemed too convoluted and lame to explain, so I just threw my hands in the air and plopped down in a chair by the window.

Marissa says to my mother, "Because she thought you were desperate for the part of Jewel. You know, so you could get out of this whole mess with Max?"

My mother squints at me. "So I'm going to *kill* my competition? Is that it?"

I sit forward a little and say, "Well, you were also gone when I heard that banging next door...which is probably when she was getting killed. And you didn't want me to say anything about it, remember?"

My mother checks out the doorway to see if anybody's in the entry hall. Then she pulls the door closed and whispers, "It's a good thing you didn't, too. Apparently the coroner's determined her time of death to be around three-thirty, but, Samantha, that was just very bad luck on my part—it doesn't mean I *killed* her. Besides, Tammy was in the bathroom, too, so we have each other for alibis if it ever comes up."

163

I slump back into the chair and cross my arms. "So what you're saying is, it's not something you bothered to mention when the police took your statement."

She sits on the arm of my chair and says, "Tammy and I agreed that it would be better not to mention it. Samantha, why would I voluntarily put myself in hot water?"

I sit up and look her square in the eye. "Because it's the truth, and by skating around it, it makes it look like you're trying to hide something. And yeah, I went a little crazy and thought—really thought—that you'd killed LeBrandi, but that was because I don't even know who you are anymore! Do you know how many *lies* you've got going on here?" I start ticking off the things she's told me. "Your name, your age—your whole identity! Fake driver's license, fake newspaper articles, fake acting credits—"

"Shh! Samantha, stop it! Yes, I know...but *murder*?"

I open my eyes at her real big. "Why not? You said you weren't going to let anything stop you!"

She puts her hands in front of her face and just shakes her head. Finally I take a deep breath and say, "What's important right now, though, is why I *don't* think you killed LeBrandi."

She peeks at me through her fingers and waits.

"Well, it's kind of hard for someone to suffocate themselves."

Her hands whip off her face. "Samantha, I am *not* in the mood for puzzles!"

"What I'm saying is, I think that whoever killed LeBrandi thought they were killing *you*."

Good thing she was sitting down. And while she turned

pale as a polar bear, I told her my mistaken-identity theory, and how the more I thought about it, the more sure I was that there was *some*body in the house who wanted her dead.

"But *who?*" she whispered.

"Exactly, Mom. That's what we've got to figure out. So you've got to tell me—who could possibly be that mad at you? Have you done anything to any of the people in this house to make them mad enough to kill you?"

"No!"

"Don't just say that... *think!*"

She thought a minute, then gave me a completely bewildered look. "I can't think of *any*thing!"

I sigh and say, "Well, I can."

"You can? Tell me!"

"I think that whoever killed LeBrandi is someone who doesn't want Max to get married again."

"But I'm not going to marry him! I *can't* marry him!"

I jump up and start pacing around. "No one knows that! And *he* thinks you're going to say yes tonight." I lean in and say, "The guy is bonkers in love with you, you know."

She whimpers, "But why? I haven't given him any reason to fall in love with me. I'm not flirtatious, I'm not interested in his collections or travels.... I've focused solely and completely on my acting!"

"Well, it's too late. He is. And I think the only way out of this is to tell him the truth. The *whole* truth."

She starts following me around. "But then...Samantha, you don't understand. I really believe that if I tell him, he'll be so angry that I deceived him that he'll pull the plug." She lets out a heavy sigh and says, "And then I'll never work again—his contract is—"

"I know, I know. Opal told me all about it."

"There you go! You see?" Her face completely crinkles up, and just when it looks like it's going to shatter into a million pieces, she starts sobbing. "It's all over. The whole thing's shot. All that work, all that time . . . I was so close, and now I'll never know. Why does he want an answer tonight? Why couldn't he wait until . . . you know . . . later?"

I lean in and whisper, "I know you're concerned about your career, but hel-lo? Somebody tried to kill you? Wouldn't it be better to stand up right now and say, Hey! Everybody, listen up! I'm not gonna marry Max, so you can put your knives and guns and pillows away now."

She sniffs at me through her tears. "Oh, Samantha . . ."

"I'm serious! There's a lunatic out there who wants the future Mrs. Mighty Max out of the picture, and the sooner you tell the world the truth, the longer you will live."

She wipes away a tear and says, "But who? Who doesn't want me to marry Max?"

"Well, who else knows he's asked you? You told LeBrandi about it, right? Did you tell anyone else?"

"No." My mother looks down. "But apparently *she* did." She hesitates, then looks up at me. "Tammy knows."

I threw my hands in the air. "Which probably means that everyone knows! So pretend it *is* everyone, okay? *Everyone*. And the sooner you tell Max you're not going to marry him, the better off you'll be."

She sighs and says, "Okay, but it would be completely classless to take a megaphone and announce it, Samantha. I'll tell him at dinner."

"Talk about classless! Someone did just *die* around here, and he's wanting to go out to some swanky dinner tonight? Can't you just tell him you're not up for it?"

"I already tried that, but he's insisting that LeBrandi's death is all the more reason to celebrate life."

"No matter how *you* feel about it, huh?"

We were quiet for a minute, then my mother sighs and says, "I have to, Samantha. He finagled reservations at Trouvet's in Venice and—"

"You're flying to Italy for dinner?!"

"No! Venice down by the water. Near Marina del Rey? Never mind. It doesn't matter. The point is, Trouvet's is booked solid for nearly a year. It's impossible to get late-date reservations there unless you're a big-name celebrity, so I'm pretty sure Max shelled out a substantial bribe to get us in. He's arranged for a limo, and he's ordered in that gorgeous vintage dress and those shoes." She picked up the red sequined shoes and held them out for me to admire. "Have you ever seen anything like them?"

I couldn't help it. I blurted, "Yeah—on Dorothy!" and I was on the verge of saying something snide about her skipping along the yellow brick road when she scolds, "Samantha!"

So I bite my tongue and say, "Sorry. But I would never embarrass my feet that way."

She frowns at me but then forgets about the shoes and holds the dress up to her body. "Amazing, isn't it? I only

wish they'd cleaned it better. It smells...I don't know...
peculiar." She holds the skirt out for me to whiff. "Do you
think perfume would cover this?"

Now, really, I couldn't care less. How could she stand
there discussing the cover-up power of perfume when
someone wanted to *kill* her?

Then I took a whiff.

It was like lightning shooting up my nose and into my
brain. It was the same scent I'd smelled on the tapestry in
Max's office—in his shrine to his dead wife.

In a flash I knew how Max had managed to get that
dress delivered on a Saturday on such short notice.

It had been stored here all along.

And in a flash I knew why he'd been so pleased to find
out that the dress fit and why he wanted her to wear it.

His other wife must have worn it the night she'd agreed
to marry him.

My heart was racing. The whole situation seemed to have
an unstoppable momentum—like a destiny I couldn't
change. If I didn't do something to stop it, my mother was
going to be the new Claire. Max was probably too far gone
to even care if she wasn't who she said she was.

"Samantha?" It was my mother's voice, distant and soft.
"Samantha, what's wrong?"

I snapped out of it and decided I had to try something,
anything, to stop this. Even if it meant breaking my pact
with Hali. "There's...there's something I've got to tell
you."

"Oh?"

"The trouble is, if I tell you and someone finds out,

then everyone else is probably going to find out about *you*."

"About me? What about me?"

I just looked at her.

"Samantha!" she squealed. "You didn't!" Then she whispered, "Who? Who did you tell?"

I tried to sound confident. "Hali. Only Hali."

"*Hali*? She's on the verge of a mental *break*down, and you tell *Hali*?"

"There's a reason she's been acting like that, Mom! Now, will you please just listen?"

My mother tosses the dress across the chair I'd been sitting in and flops into another. And as she's landing, she throws a forearm up to her forehead and whimpers, "I don't believe this!"

So while she's being all dramatic over there in an armchair, I tell her the story about Hali's eyes and how we figured out that she was Max's daughter, and how upset Hali was to find out who her father was, and how of course, after all of that, I had to tell her the truth about me.

When I'm all done, I've got her attention, all right. She is sitting bolt upright with her eyes *wide* open. And I'm really expecting her to say something like, His *daughter*? or That *scoundrel*! but instead she jumps up and cries, "You did not *have* to tell her. You *chose* to tell her. Samantha, I *trusted* you!"

Fire seemed to stab through my heart. This is the thanks I got for choosing her over Hali? "Yeah?" I said. "Well, so did Hali! I swore to her that I wouldn't tell anybody, and the only reason I told you was so you'd be able to turn things back on Max—so you could buy yourself a little time! He *says* he's going to tell you over dinner tonight, but you know what? I don't believe him. He's so bent on getting you to say yes that I can just see him conveniently forgetting to tell you until after you say yes."

"I am *not* going to say yes!"

I plop down in the chair that's got the stupid red dress draped over the back of it and say, "Yeah, well, he seems to think you are, and so does Marissa. Huh, Marissa?"

My mother and I both look at her, but all she does is put both hands up and take two steps back. "Don't bring me into this!"

I shove the dress aside, saying, "This whole thing's *insane*! Do you realize—"

"Careful with that dress!" she says.

"Oh, please!" I take it off the back of the chair, and I'm about to toss it at her and say, Here! Take your precious dress, when the smell from it wafts up my nose.

It snapped in my brain like a wet towel. Yes, I'd smelled that smell in Max's office, but *before* that I'd smelled it somewhere else. And even though I hadn't been able to re-member where when I'd been Dustbusting Max's tapestry, now I knew.

I flipped around in my chair and looked out the win-dow, then jumped out of the chair and checked along the window wall, all along the floor.

My mother whispers, "What are you *doing*?"

"I've . . . I've got to go outside. I . . . I'll be right back!"

I raced out of the reception room and through the front door, propped the front door open a crack with the floor mat, then ducked behind the hedge like I'd done hiding from Tweedledee. I scooted along the house and peeked in the window, and there was my mother, talking to Marissa real intently.

I figured that the distance from the far edge of the reception room window to Max's office wall was about six feet. So I took two pretty big strides, then drew a line in the dirt with the heel of my high-top. Then I closed my eyes and tried to picture Max's office. It felt like it was only about ten feet deep, but with all that furniture crowded inside, it might have been more. Maybe fifteen. At the most.

So I took five more giant strides, then made another mark in the dirt and looked back at the wall between me and the reception room window. Smack-dab in the middle was the fan vent that had spooked me so badly when I'd been scooting away from Tweedledee, and right above it was a big square window with a heavy beige curtain over it.

It was definitely within the walls of Max's office, yet I hadn't seen a window or heard a fan when I'd been snooping around with Marissa.

I got down on my knees by the fan, but I didn't even have to sniff. That same woody, sweet smell was being blown right up my nose.

I stood up and tried to peek inside the window past the edge of the curtain, but it seemed to be tucked in and around something at the sides. I couldn't see past it at all.

Then I looked up and saw that above the curtain rod were a bunch of evenly spaced black rods. I looked closer, and then down, past the curtain's hem, and that's when I realized that right on the other side of the beige curtain, on the inside of the house, were burglar bars.

Burglar bars.

On the *inside*.

Suddenly I knew why Max's office seemed so small. It *was* small. He had converted part of it into a secret room. A secret room where he could store his valuables.

Valuables like Claire's jewels and her sentimental gowns.

And, if I was lucky, something worth a lot more to me than those.

SEVENTEEN

It was like a five-million-to-one shot. How was I going to break into Max's office, anyway? I mean, maybe I can pop a privacy lock with a pin, but that wasn't going to get me anywhere with a Schlage deadbolt. No, it would definitely take a key, and Max wore the stupid thing around his neck.

Still, I couldn't shove the thought completely out of my brain. To me it wasn't just any key. It was the key to my mother's freedom—and somehow it felt like the key to mine, too.

Not that getting my hands on her contract with Max would bring her back home. If anything, it would keep her in Hollywood longer. Maybe forever. But at least I had to *try* to stop this avalanche of mistakes from completely crushing her.

From crushing us.

When I got back inside, I closed the reception room door tight and told my mom and Marissa what I'd discovered about the secret room in Max's office. "That's where he keeps the contracts, Mom. It must be!"

"Oh, Samantha, how can you be so sure? He could keep them anywhere. Besides, what are you thinking? That you can just climb through that window and steal them?"

"That would be a really great idea, but it won't work because he's got burglar bars inside."

"*Inside?*" Marissa asks.

"Yeah. I could see them around the curtain. None of the other windows have them, and he probably didn't want it to look conspicuous."

My mother looks over her shoulder and, even though the door's closed, she whispers, "This talk is making me very, *very* nervous." She grabs the dress and ruby slippers and says, "I'm going to go upstairs and I'm going to pretend we never had this discussion, you hear me?" She opens the door and adds, "And I expect the two of you to do the same!"

No one can kill a conversation quicker than my mother. No blood, no guts, it's just over.

As the three of us made our way upstairs, we ran into Tammy on her way down. Tammy says hi and gives my mother a wink that she thinks we don't see. Then she stops and says, "Oh, by the way, Dominique, they've cordoned off your room, so if you want to change before LeBrandi's service you can borrow from me."

My mother grabs her by the arm and says, "Cordoned off? You mean I can't go in there? For anything?"

Tammy wrinkles her nose like she's going to sneeze but doesn't. "That's right. Police tape is slapped all over it."

"Can't I even go in there for some new underwear?"

"Are they worth going to jail for?"

"But—"

174   "The crew this morning made assumptions, and honey,

from what I overheard earlier, some heads are going to roll downtown. Meanwhile, you can't get your underwear." She leans in cautiously, like she's transporting plutonium. "It's a murder," she whispers, "remember? And Dominique, they think it's one of *us*. God, everywhere I go now, I'm looking over my shoulder!"

Watching Tammy talk was one of the weirdest things I'd ever seen. She was spastic—like an actress with a short circuit. And every time she opened her mouth, out came a different voice. A different character. The only thing they all had in common was a twitchy nose.

And as I watched her hop down the stairs, it hit me how none of those characters seemed to care about *LeBrandi*. As a matter of fact, no one around here did. Not really. It was all other stuff they were worried about. Like jewels and clothes and *underwear*.

And it was a strange feeling to wonder if her being dead bothered me more than anyone at Max's. I mean, I seemed to think about it more than anyone else, and I didn't even know LeBrandi.

Well, not as an alive person, anyway.

So I just kind of followed along behind Marissa and my mom, up the stairs and down the hall, thinking that if LeBrandi could pop up from the dead, she'd be pretty disappointed to see how everyone was acting.

Then we came to my mother's room. And I think that's when it finally hit my mother that this was *her* room, and the body that had been hauled away could very well have been *her* body.

She stares at the wide bands of yellow-and-black police

tape for a minute, then turns to me and whispers, "Don't go."

"Go where?"

"Home. I know I said you had to, and I know we've been spatting, but...would you stay? I'm sure it'll be fine with Max, given the circumstances...."

It was out before I could stop it. "Why? So I can be your bodyguard?"

To my surprise, she didn't snap back. Instead she said, "No, I just..." She shook her head and walked over to LeBrandi's room, saying, "I just don't want you to leave...like this."

LeBrandi's room was wide open. And empty. Well, except for one banged-up backpack and a pummeled pink suitcase. They were sitting on the bed Marissa and I had slept in. Everything else, and I mean *everything* else, was gone. The closet was empty, the dresser was empty...and with the bedding stripped and the sun slashing lines on the wall through the blinds, the room looked like some sort of weird prison cell.

My mother just stands in the middle of the room for a minute, then lays the red dress carefully across LeBrandi's bed and says, "I'm going to ask for a different room. I don't care if it's the laundry room, I can't sleep here."

The afternoon sun's beating in, and the room's a little sweatbox. So I turn the window crank fast, saying, "It may be kind of creepy in here, but actually, this is probably the safest place for you to be."

Now, while I'm cranking open the window, I notice Max walking along the pathway to the swimming pool. He's carrying a white towel and is wrapped in a heavy white terry-cloth robe. When he gets to the deep end of the pool, he slips his glasses off his nose and into his pocket, then pulls off the robe and drapes it across a chaise lounge.

My mother's saying something to me, but I'm not paying attention. I've got my eye on Max as he heads for the front of the deep end, and let me tell you, my heart is starting to hammer. This might be my chance.

The chance I thought I'd never get.

But I hadn't seen him take off his chain, and I couldn't really see from across the courtyard whether or not he was wearing it. If only I had Grams' binoculars!

He's standing there in the direct sun, getting ready to dive, and I'm staring, focusing as hard as I can. Then, at the last second, I try a trick that Hudson taught me when he was explaining about pinhole cameras. I pinch my thumbs and index fingers together so there's a tiny diamond of space in the middle of them. Then I hold it up to my eye like a telescope and focus on Max. On his chest.

He pushes off to dive into the pool, and it's like slow motion to me. Him lifting from the ground, arcing into the water, going in with barely a splash. And when I take my hands away, I'm sure—there had been no glitter of gold in the sun.

I didn't know how I was going to sneak down there without freaking out my mother, but I had to get down to the pool. Now.

So I come away from the window with my blood pumping, scrambling for an excuse—any excuse—but my mother's gone.

"Where'd she go?" I ask Marissa.

Marissa laughs and says, "I knew you didn't hear her. She told you she was going to Tammy's to borrow some things, and you said, Uh-huh."

"I did?"

"Uh-huh."

"Well, look!" I drag her over to the window and whisper, "Max is swimming."

"So?"

"So he's not wearing his chain. At least I think he's not."

"His chain? Why do you care if he's wearing his chain or not?"

"Because of the *key* on it. . . ."

"Sammy, no! It isn't worth it. Besides, your mother signed the contract, it was her choice, it's *legal,* and hello, Sammy? What you're talking about is completely *il*legal. Besides, he probably has copies somewhere. Like at a bank or something."

"Then why the Fort Knox security? Maybe most people would, but I don't think *he* does. He's too much of a control freak!"

"But still . . ."

"Please, Marissa. Look at it this way—right now it's like he *owns* her. She didn't violate her contract, she didn't skip classes or break curfew or do any of the things Opal did. She just had the horrible luck of having him fall in love with her. And after tonight—assuming she tells him no— she won't be able to stay here. How can she stay here? But she can't afford to leave, either. Fifty percent of everything goes to him for the next eight years! Do you think he's going to just rip up her contract and let her go? Do you think that's fair? Do you have any idea what that's going to do to her? It'd be like you never playing softball again. And I don't want her coming home if she's going to be all bitter and resentful. It would be worse than having her be a bubblehead down here! Please, Marissa, *please*. It's my only chance."

Marissa frowns at me long and hard, then grumbles, "So what do you want me to do?"

I practically hugged her in two. Then I let go and asked, "Where are your house keys?"

"In my suitcase."

"Are any of them Schlage keys?"

"Schlage? How am I supposed to know?"

"They say right on them."

So she pops open her suitcase and digs through a mountain of clothes until she finds her keys. And I guess I shouldn't have been surprised to find a Schlage among them, but still, I was jazzed. I pulled it off the ring and said, "Let's go!"

"But wait! Why do you need my key? How am I going to get in my house?"

I couldn't stop to answer. I had to get down there. Fast.

Marissa comes chasing down the stairs after me. "Sammy, wait! What are you going to do?"

I whisper, "I'm going to exchange keys, all right? Now, shh!"

She was not happy with me. Not at all. But she stayed with me as I zigzagged through the ferns and palms, keeping an eye out for Hali or anyone else who might be walking around. And before you know it, there we are, huddled in the shrubbery not more than ten feet from Max's chaise lounge.

Trouble is, those last ten feet seem impossible. So exposed. Marissa whispers, "He'll see you, Sammy."

I try to sound all confident as I say, "He's underwater. Besides, he's not wearing his glasses. If he does see me, I'll be just a blur." And really, I can't wait around forever. I mean, he's going great guns now, but who knows how many laps this guy can do?

So the minute he flips over to start a new lap, I take one last look around and decide it's now or never. I scurry into the sun and across the deck, and twenty seconds later, I knew I'd been wrong. The key wasn't in his robe. Only his glasses were.

I double-check, then drop the robe and dive back into the shrubs with Marissa. She whispers, "Did you get it?"

"It's not there."

"Are you sure?"

"Positive."

"Well, I didn't see it on him, either."

I look up to the second-story bedroom windows to see if anyone's spotted us. Then I check over my shoulder toward Hali and Reena's cottage, and then off the other way toward Inga's garden. Except for Max swishing through the water, the place seems completely dead.

I grabbed Marissa's arm and said, "C'mon."

Marissa was so glad to get away from the pool that she didn't even question me. Not until I cut off the pathway and charged past some ferns and banana palms and around the corner of the main house, that is. "Where are you going now?" she whispers, then sees me looking up at Max's balcony door.

It was cracked open.

"Sammy, no! You can't be serious."

I knew it was crazy. I knew *I* was crazy. Or really close to it, anyway. But there it was, an opening into Max's suite, begging me to at least try.

I got to the base of a jacaranda tree that grew beside the balcony, and tried to shimmy up the trunk, but I couldn't. It was too slick, and the first branch was too far up. I turned to Marissa and whispered, "Give me a boost, would you?"

"Sammy, it barely reaches. That branch can't hold you!"

"It has to. Now give me a boost."

So she laced her hands together, I stepped in, and she floated me up to the first branch.

Piece of cake.

But the higher I got, the more this little voice kept telling me that she was right. The branches were naked, scrawny little twigs. They'd never hold me.

Still, I inched out, farther and farther, glancing down at Marissa from time to time. She seemed miles away. And so did the balcony.

I tried to keep my weight back as far as I could as I stretched my arm for the railing, but it was no good. I had to get out farther. Four more inches. Five more. I was bending down more than I was going out, but I was close. So close.

Finally I just pushed forward and grabbed for the rail, and there it was, in my hand! But I heard the branch crack, felt it give, and suddenly there was no going back. I pushed against it with all my might and managed to catch the rail with my other hand before the branch collapsed from beneath me.

Marissa got out of the way, but the branch didn't crash to the ground; it just hung there like a limp, broken arm.

I swung myself over the rail and motioned Marissa to clear away. She couldn't help me down—there was no going back the way I'd come.

The screen door was locked, but it was easy to jimmy. Pull up, wiggle, jiggle, *snap*. Hudson says they only keep honest people out, and he's right. Screen door locks are a joke.

Now, you may not believe this, but I don't break into people's houses very often. Actually, I've done it once before, and let me tell you, it's creepy. Scary. The truth is, it makes you feel icky all over. Like there's nothing you want more in the world than a shower.

And being in Max's suite, well, that's exactly how I felt. And no, I didn't stop and take a shower—I just wanted to get that key and get out of there.

The first place I checked was his dresser top. No jewelry at all. I went into the walk-in closet. Nothing on the dressing table.

Then I found the bathroom, and on the counter under the lid of an oblong obsidian dish were his watch and a bracelet.

And one gold chain with a shiny Schlage key on it.

I looped the key off the chain and slipped Marissa's key on. And since Marissa's wasn't quite as shiny as Max's, I took a towel and buffed it out until it shone. Then I put everything back the way I'd found it, tucked Max's key in my pocket, and headed for the door.

The door. Well. It was a lot easier than the branch, but as it turns out, not any less dangerous, because as I'm closing it behind me I hear Marissa's voice coming up the stairwell, loud and clear. "No, really! Didn't you see that cat?"

Then there's Inga's voice, shrill and harsh. "I know what I saw and didn't see. There was no cat. Now get out of my way!"

I couldn't go forward—I'd run right into them. I couldn't go back into Max's suite—I'd be trapped inside and Inga'd catch me red-handed. And even though there was some furniture in the hallway between them and me, it wasn't enough to conceal me. I'd be like a parrot trying to hide in the snow.

Then I looked to my right and it hit me. There was another way down.

If only I could reach it in time.

EIGHTEEN

Personally, I wouldn't recommend a laundry chute as a means of transportation. It's fast, it's painful, and it's way smaller than it looks. But it was the only escape hatch around, and believe me, with Marissa and the Mummy getting closer by the second, I climbed in and dropped, like Alice on her way to Wonderland.

And when I landed with a mighty *thump* at the bottom and dragged myself out, who's standing there staring at me?

Not the Plaid Rabbit.

Not Tweedledee.

No, it's the Mad Hali.

Now, let me tell you, she is not serving up tea. She takes one look at me and starts pouring cusswords instead. And when she's all done letting me know just how badly I scared her, she yanks me up by the arm and says, "You got no business clownin' around like that!"

"Hali, shh! I'm sorry. I wasn't clowning around. I was—"

"You were what?"

Just then Max walks in, robe wrapped tight around him, glasses wedged in place. And I try not to look stupid,

184

scared, or guilty, but seeing as how I'm feeling all three, that's not an easy thing to do.

And it's strange. It feels like we're all connected by some force, yet separated by it, too. Like we've each got the negative pole of an invisible magnet pointed at the other guy, keeping us a safe distance away as we move around the room.

Max tosses his towel on a heap of dirty laundry and says, "LeBrandi's farewell service starts in half an hour." He looks back and forth between us. "You haven't forgotten that, have you?"

Hali won't even look at him, but I manage to say, "Half an hour? I...I should have the beds made up by then." He gives me a puzzled look, so I add, "The beds in...you know, everything was stripped?"

"Oh, yes. Thank you for taking care of that." He turns to Hali and says, "I expect you there, too." Then he adds, "Have you found your mother?"

She whips around to face him. "What do you care?"

He closes his eyes and makes it to three before opening them again. Very quietly he says, "Don't be flip, young lady," then pushes out through the swinging doors.

Hali calls after him, "I hope you don't expect *me* to rustle up chow! Or to do any more stupid laundry around here. Hey! Who do you think's gonna wash this towel? You think I am? Well, you can just servant *this*!"

She lets the door close, then turns to me. "So you slid down here for some sheets. Likely story."

"Look, Hali, Inga was after me. It was my only way out."

She sort of prowls around me, studying me, her eyes sharp and focused. Like she doesn't know whether to trust *me*, either. "Inga, huh? Well, why was she after you?"

"Because I...because she thinks I...Hali, it looks like we're going to stay here another night, so I really do have to make up the beds...."

She flips open the washers we'd filled that morning. "Then you'd better get a move on dryin' these suckers." She sneers at me and says, "Looks to me like you're back to being a punk liar. And this after I snuck those photos back into the reception room for you."

All of a sudden I feel awful. Just beat up with guilt. Why had I told my mother? Why hadn't I just let Max tell her? He would, he said he would! I'd betrayed Hali's trust, and for what? How had I become sucked into this world of lies and suspicions and backstabbings? How had I become part of this mess?

With a shiver I realized that in less than twenty-four hours I'd managed to get myself hopelessly tangled in a giant web of deceit, and all my flapping around was just making things worse.

I really didn't know what to do anymore. So I whispered, "Hali, I thought you were going to lose it earlier. You're so upset about Max and your mom that I thought..."

"I was gonna blurt something I shouldn't?"

"Yeah."

"Well, I didn't, did I?"

"No, but you came close. And I don't know what your angle is anymore. Are you moving out? Are you black-mailing him?"

She hops up on a washer and heaves a sigh. "I don't know. I can't find Mama, and that's all I care about right now. I've checked at Uncle Manny's, the neighbors'... everyone I can think of. No one's heard from her. And I'm starting to worry that maybe she, you know, *did* something to herself."

I go up to her and say, "Hali, she'll come back." Then very softly I add, "Unless she's the one who killed LeBrandi."

Those braids go whipping around. "What? *Mama?* She is the gentlest, kindest creature on earth!"

Just then Marissa comes blasting in. She takes one look at me, holds her heart, and slides down the wall, saying, "Inga...ohmygod, Sammy.. She..."

I give her a watch-what-you-say warning with my eyes and interrupt her with "I know. I heard."

She jerks her head toward the laundry chute and says, "Did you...?"

"Yeah. And it really hurt."

Marissa says, "Not as bad as Inga's pitchfork would've."

"Her *pitch*fork?"

"Yeah. It's not full-sized—I think it's some kind of gardening tool—but it could puncture your ribs pretty good!"

A mummy with a pitchfork. I was almost sorry I'd missed it.

I got busy moving sheets from a washer into a dryer and told Marissa, "Hali's real upset because Reena hasn't come back yet. And Max says we're supposed to be at that service for LeBrandi. It starts in like twenty minutes, so we'd better get going."

Hali must've been really worried about her mother, because she didn't ask any more questions. She just sat on the washer hugging her knees to her chest, her head down so her braids hung like a beaded curtain in front of her jeans. I whispered, "See you in a little while" as we made for the door, and her beads clicked together softly, but I couldn't tell if they were going up and down or side to side.

The minute we were alone, I flashed Marissa the key.

"Is that mine?"

I shook my head, but I didn't feel like grinning. I felt like some kind of stupid ground squirrel playing chicken with Old Faithful. I knew the geyser was about to blow, but I kept scurrying around it, coming in closer and closer. And even though I'd been nearly burned the last time, I had to charge in one last time. Just had to.

Marissa whispers, "So when?"

"When they've gone to dinner. How did you get away from Inga?"

"*Max* got her away from me. We ran into him on the stairs, and he thought she'd gone nuts. Said you couldn't be in his room when he'd just seen you in the laundry room. Inga knows, though, Sammy. She *knows*. And what about that branch? How do you explain that? I sure couldn't!"

"Maybe we won't have to. Nothing's missing. I left everything the way I found it. . . . Look, we have to go to that service. Max practically commanded us to go, so if we don't show up, it's going to look really suspicious."

Marissa and I hurried toward the stairs, and on our way up, a group of gussied-up women was coming down. And from the way they were whispering back and forth so intensely, they reminded me of a bunch of eighth-graders who had been sent to the principal's office.

When they saw us coming up, they zipped their lips and plastered on smiles, and we were almost past them when I stopped and asked, "Which one's Tammy's room?"

A woman who looked as if she'd shampooed with black ink said, "Right across the hall from the phone cubby." She gives my jeans and sweatshirt the once-over and says, "Max isn't making you go to the service?"

"Yeah, we'll be there...."

She pops an eyebrow up and says, "It's not black tie, but you could've done better than that."

As they disappeared around the corner, I grumbled to Marissa, "What's it matter? She's *dead*."

"It's a way to show respect, Sammy, and it's not going to kill you to wear a dress."

"Oh, please. I've got places to sneak to and people to hide from. You expect me to do that in a dress?"

"Just wear it and change back later, okay? Trust me, you're going to feel like a bumpkin in high-tops."

I scowled at her. "Never."

My mother was doing fine, dressed to the nines for a funeral. She and Tammy were both in black with gold accents, but the funny thing was, they didn't look anything the same. My mother had slicked what little hair she had completely back, and Tammy's was ratted and sprayed from here to Kingdom Comb.

189

Okay, so maybe it's just funeral protocol to put on fancy clothes and give your hair the ol' 220-volt treatment. I don't get it, and I don't like it, and if I die, I sure don't want people saying good-bye to me in high heels and hair spray, but I was through arguing. I had too much else to worry about.

My mother says, "Girls, we're already running late." She cringes at what I'm wearing and says, "Do you have anything more presentable with you?"

Marissa tugs me along by the arm, saying, "I brought a couple of dresses. We'll be down in a flash."

So Marissa's dragging me off in one direction while my mother and the Ratted Rabbit scurry off in the other, and then I realize that we don't know where to go. So I call out, "Where's the service?"

My mother calls back, "In the Great Room. Past the dining hall, around the corner, double doors on the right."

Marissa and I go into our barren barracks, lay out the elephant-trunk arsenal, and pick our weapons. And actually, Marissa could've done a lot worse. The dress she'd brought for me was a little too pouffy in the skirt, but it did have a pocket where I could stash the key, and since the top was like a fancy elasticized T-shirt, it didn't want to migrate or flap open the way some dresses do. She'd even brought me a pair of shoes that were a whole lot better than some I've worn. For one thing, they were flats; for another, they were a little bit big, so they didn't really bite me anywhere.

Marissa says, "Royal blue is your color, you know that? You look great."

I looked at myself in the mirror and frowned. "I don't know if it's a funeral color, though."

"Beggars can't be choosers. So zip me up, would you?"

I helped her into her little black-and-violet velvet jobbie, and after we raked a brush through our hair, off we went, mere privates in the ranks of the respectably dressed.

The Great Room looked like an enormous Egyptian den. The windows were swagged with miles of earthy-colored chiffon, there were small clusters of armchairs and coffee tables, and I think the giant tasseled pillows thrown here and there were supposed to be like high-class beanbags or something. There were cat sculptures everywhere, and then stone urns and pyramid shaped lamps and even a four-foot brass *camel*.

In the heart of the room was a black marble fireplace. Actually, it was more like a fire pit. It was up off the floor, with a ledge around it that you could sit on, but then it was just open. No glass, no screen. Just sort of a fancy campfire pit with a giant suspended hood that vented out through the ceiling.

A bunch of chairs had been arranged around one side of the fireplace, and as we got closer, it became clear that this was no party. Everyone but Max was seated with their hands in their laps, dead quiet, waiting.

Max checks his watch and says, "I think we should begin. Girls, if you'll take the two seats right there?"

The chairs he's pointing to are on the edge, off to one side, and as we scoot into them, my mother gives us a nervous little wave from her seat on the opposite side of the grouping. Inga is sitting right beside her, looking extra stiff, and as she glances our way, I can see she's also extra angry.

Marissa whispers, "She's not going to let you get away with it, Sammy. God, look at her!"

I couldn't. Those eyes of hers burned like acid. I turned away and started trying to figure out who was missing. Knowing Max, he'd take roll by putting out the exact number of seats. I whispered to Marissa, "Hali's not here."

"Neither's her mother."

"But everyone else *is*."

"So?"

"So I'm thinking..."

"Oh, Sammy, no. Please. You want to flush out the killer? You want to stand up and make a scene like you know who did it, and then—"

"That's a great idea!" I whispered back.

"Stop! Sammy, you can*not* be serious! This is not some TV mystery of the week!"

"You're the one who brought it up!"

Max cleared his throat and gave us a reprimanding look, then clasped his hands at his chest. And it looked for all the world like he was going to start things off with a prayer, but instead he takes a deep breath, looks from one side of the group to the other, and says, "It's been a rough day, hasn't it? From the moment Dominique discovered LeBrandi to now. It's been rough. On all of us."

They're all sitting as stiff as their hair, listening to Max but still kind of eyeing the people around them. Max makes some long apology about the grueling police interrogations

192

everyone's had to endure, but I'm not quite tuned in to him because my brain is running away with Marissa's idea, trying to figure out how to use it.

Then Max says, "I do have an announcement that I hope will make you rest a little easier, though. It's shocking, but still, a welcome resolution to the suspicion that has shrouded our home since this morning." He looks across the group and says, "Officer Doyle has arrested Opal Novak for LeBrandi's murder."

All at once the tension snaps. Everyone gasps or cries out and then starts talking a million miles an hour to someone next to her. I jump up and say, "No! Opal didn't do it! I *told* you she didn't do it! She...she..."

It's as if I hit the mute button. Everyone's quiet, and they're all staring at me. And I realize that I didn't have to come up with a way to put Marissa's idea in motion— Max had done it for me. So as everyone's staring at me, I look around at them, searching for a face that looks nervous or angry or scared. But what's out there?

The biggest bunch of doe eyes you've ever seen.

Well, except for ol' Tiger Eyes. She jumps up and says, "You sit down! You are completely out of line!"

Then my mother starts frantically motioning for me to shut up and sit down, and then Tammy joins in, too, waving at me to sit down. And before I can say anything else, everyone starts talking again, and Marissa yanks me back to my seat, hissing, "Don't argue with him! You're going to give yourself away!"

Max calls, "Ladies! Ladies! If I may *please* have your attention!"

When everyone settles down, he says, "I realize there are still a lot of unanswered questions, and our young guest is right—Opal has not been convicted." He looks at me sort of sternly and says, "But, young lady, the police have been working nonstop on this case and know much, *much* more about it than you do. I'm sure they have more than enough evidence to support their decision, or they wouldn't have taken Opal into custody."

He stands up tall, then clasps his hands again and says, "For now, though, I think it's important for us all to take a deep breath, put our questions aside, and give thanks. Thanks for the time we've spent together. Thanks for the positive influences we've had on each other, and thanks to LeBrandi for having graced us with her beauty, her style, and her talent.

"It's also a time to open our minds—to rejoice. LeBrandi transcends us. She is no longer bound by her earthly shackles, her human frailties or dependencies. LeBrandi is free to start again.

"And as she is free, you too must free yourselves of the sadness that comes with her passing. She is not sad, nor should you be! She has met her destiny and has moved on. So, too, must you." Max spread his arms up and out—like Father Mayhew does when he's talking to God—only Max never mentioned the Pearly Gates or the everlasting fire of Satan's Kingdom. It was like he was explaining some new religion.

"LeBrandi's life has doubled. She will live on in our hearts and minds, and yet she has already begun her new life. On a plane above us, higher and broader, clearer and wiser, her soul is rejoicing in its new beginning. Rejoice with her, for someday you too will be on a higher plane and know more fully your fate, your destiny, your purpose. Like the rain and the snow and the dunes of the earth, we come and go, and come again." Max's eyes were shining. Intense. And he seemed so convinced by his own words that he was glowing. Absolutely glowing.

And to tell you the truth, even though I was still upset about Opal being arrested, I couldn't help but be swept up by what he was saying. It made me feel sort of—I don't know—*floaty*. Like my whole body was lifting out of my chair.

I think Marissa was feeling a little dazed, too, because she leaned over and whispered, "Wow. He ought to be a preacher or something."

When Max was done, he asked for volunteers to get up and share some special stories about LeBrandi. And it's kind of strange—I know my mother got up and said some stuff about them auditioning together, and Tammy stood up and talked for a really long time about them shopping for avocados—but other than that, I don't remember much. I wasn't feeling right. Not sick. Just kind of disconnected. Like my mind and body were in different places.

And then, when the service was over, Max gets back up and says, "As a farewell feast, I've ordered in LeBrandi's favorites: pizza and pasta and feta salad from Portello's, chocolate raspberry cheesecake from Toppers, and an assortment of D'Fleur wines. The food is due to arrive"— he checks his watch—"momentarily. So spend some time together remembering LeBrandi and rejoicing in the life we shared with her. Tonight there are to be no diets, no workouts, no studies...and no regrets."

This announcement seems to surprise all the women in the room, and as Max heads for the door, a brunette in front of us says, "Wow. Someone ought to die around here more often."

I almost cried, *What?* I mean, it wasn't just that it was an ugly comment. It was an ugly comment made by a very pretty person. How could someone so attractive on the outside be so callous on the inside? I looked around the room at the other women, and I wondered—behind their doe eyes and their beautiful masks of makeup, were they all so cold? Did they all have secrets they were hiding? Did they all have résumés of lies?

Opal hadn't killed LeBrandi, I was sure of it. But I was becoming less and less sure that I was ever going to be able to figure out who had.

And after everyone started to file out of the Great Room, I thought that maybe what I should do was go upstairs and call the police myself. I mean, why hadn't they come back to talk to me? It just didn't make any sense. It was almost like Marissa and I weren't even there—which at first was good, but now it felt wrong. Completely wrong.

And I might actually have done it if I hadn't stuck my hand in my pocket and run into Max's key. What was I thinking?

I had places to sneak into. . . .

Laws to break. . . .

This was *no* time to call the police!

NINETEEN

I made myself focus on what *did* make sense. And what I kept coming back to was that once my mother finally told Max that she wasn't going to marry him, she could tell everyone else, and then if whoever had killed LeBrandi was really after *her*, well, at least my mother wouldn't be in danger anymore.

And since there were people everywhere, and since my mother was being driven to dinner at a busy restaurant in a limo and she wouldn't be alone—even with Max—and since I had this key burning a hole in my pocket, I told myself I'd talk to the police *after* I got my hands on my mother's contract. Sure, I wanted LeBrandi's killer caught, but I was at a dead end on that for now. In the meantime, at least I could try to salvage what was left of my mother's career.

Marissa, on the other hand, wasn't big on chasing down my mother's contract. She'd experienced Tiger Eyes up close and personal and didn't want to risk getting anywhere near her again.

We went back to the bedroom so we could talk, and the minute the door was closed, Marissa said, "Inga is out there somewhere, watching, and believe me, she is not going to let you get away with it. She is going to get you, Sammy!"

"*Get* me? Look, Marissa. Once we're in Max's office, we can lock the door and *stay* in there, safe and sound, until we find the contract. Then all I have to do is burn the thing and we're done. We could go to the Great Room and toss it in the fire! How's she going to *get* us?"

Marissa grumbles, "With that pitchfork." Then she gets right in my face and says, "You haven't seen that thing, Sammy. I thought she was going to stick it up my nose and skewer my brains!"

"You don't have to come, you know. Or you can just stand guard while I—"

"No! Remember what happened the last time you left me behind? That was probably more dangerous than being *with* you!"

"Then just stay here."

Now, I guess while we were arguing, my mother was down in Tammy's room changing her clothes, because all of a sudden there she is, in sequined shoes and that ruby red dress, wearing white gloves and carrying a little white beaded clutch bag.

Marissa gasps, "You look beautiful!"

She did, too. And something about that seemed completely wrong. I closed the door and said, "Wouldn't it be better to look really *ugly* when you go to turn a guy down? I mean, at least that way he's not, you know, totally devastated."

My mother gives me a little smile. A sweet, loving little smile. Then she kisses my forehead and says, "It's Trouvet's, Sunshine. You can't do ugly at Trouvet's."

"Well, maybe tone it down a little? Paint some bags under your eyes or something?"

She sits down beside me on the bed and says, "I've thought a lot about what you went through today and what we said to each other, and I want you to know that I'm sorry." She shakes her head. "That you thought *I* killed LeBrandi..." She looks at me and whispers, "I haven't been a very good role model for you lately, have I?"

I folded my hands in my lap, and after a minute of staring at them, I whispered, "I think I understand things better than I used to, but..." I looked up at her. "Would it kill you to just be you?"

She lets out a sigh and says, "There was a time when I thought it would."

Just then there's a knock on the door. Not just a *knock-knock-knock*, more a *rat-a-tat-tat!* My mother calls, "Who is it?"

Even through the door, there's no mistaking Inga's voice. "Dominique, the limousine is here. Are the girls in there with you?"

"Yes, and I'll be right down." She turns to me and says softly, "Now, Samantha, don't worry, and don't wait up. Tomorrow I'd like to spend some time with you coming up with a plan. I appreciate very much what you told me about Hali, because now I realize that I don't have to tell Max *any*thing tonight."

Oh, great. I'd put myself right back to square one.

She could tell what I was thinking. "Samantha, it took me a little while to get into this mess, and it's going to take a little while to get out of it. I *am* planning to distance myself from him, and I *do* think a move is in order, but it's going to take some time to do it right." She pats my knee and smiles. "Monday I'm going to do everything—short of *killing* somebody—to land the part of Jewel, and after that I'll know what our options are. In the meantime, please just tell me that you don't hate me or think I'm a despicable person. It all kind of got away from me, but I will do my very best to pull it back together."

You know, it's funny. Until that moment, my mother had always been my mother. Just my mother. But at that moment, sitting there on that bare mattress with her hand on my knee, I realized that she was much more than just my mother.

She was also a person.

And the reason it struck me the way it did was because for the first time in my life, she wasn't treating me as a daughter.

She was talking to me like a friend.

There are times when I'm at a total loss for what to say. Not very often, but there are times. This was definitely one of those, and since my mother was getting all teary-eyed, I guess she thought it was time to get the show on the road. She got up, gave me a quick kiss on the fore-head, and said, "You two have a good time stuffing your-selves on Portello's pizza and chocolate raspberry cheesecake. I'll see you in the morning."

As soon as the door closed, Marissa said, "Well. I'd say you've made some pretty good progress here."

I pushed away a tear, and all I could really say was, "Huh. I guess so." I mean, I'd been so caught up in everything else that I hadn't really been spending much time thinking about why I'd come to Hollywood in the first place.

I let out a big sigh and leaned back on the bed, but my hand landed on something prickly, so I yanked up and turned around. And there on the bed behind me was my mother's beaded clutch bag.

I grabbed it and ran to the door, but when I pulled the door open I came to a screeching halt, because blocking the doorway was one of the scariest things I'd ever seen.

A yellow-eyed mummy with a pitchfork.

"Hey!" I cried. "What are you doing?"

"You're not going anywhere," Inga says, and holds the fork two inches from my chest.

"What do you mean I'm not going anywhere? You can't—"

"Oh, yes I can," she whispers, and jabs that fork right at me.

Now, Marissa's right—this is not a pitchfork for throwing around full-on bales of hay. It's like a little kid's pitchfork for throwing around piles of, I don't know, dandelions. And I'm not about to let a yellow-eyed mummy with her pint-sized pitchfork stop me from leaving the room. So I say, "Look, Inga, you've got no right to—"

She snaps, "I've got *orders* to."

"Orders?" I go to grab the handle and swing the fork aside, but the Weed Warrior jabs me with it instead. Right in the stomach. I yelp and look down, and suddenly blood spreads out in little circles across Marissa's dress.

"Yes," she says. "From my brother. He finally believes

me. Now get back in the room and stay there until he comes home and decides what to do with you."

Part of me was furious. I couldn't believe she had actually jabbed me with that thing. I wanted to plow right through her no matter how badly it hurt me.

But part of me was guilty, too. I knew she had a reason for holding me in the room. To her, I was an evil, lying thief.

Then Marissa yanked on my arm to get me back inside, so guilt won out. I closed the door, pulled up the dress, and looked at my wounds.

They weren't bad, really. Just two little holes and a red spot where the third prong hadn't quite drawn blood.

Marissa says, "I can't believe she did that!" She marches to the door, whips it open, and says, "We need Band-Aids and some disinfectant! Now!"

Inga jabs the fork in Marissa's direction, and that's all it takes. Marissa squeals and slams the door, then pushes the lock in and shouts, "You maniac!" in Inga's direction. She comes back into the room, zips open her suitcase, and says, "When all else fails, use a sock."

We put some pressure on the punctures, and when the bleeding had pretty much stopped we wedged a clean sock inside the top of my dress, where the stretchy fabric held it in place just fine. And while we're straightening out my dress, it dawns on me that we're stuck. Really stuck. I go over to the window and look down. There's nothing to grab on to, no tree anywhere nearby to climb down, and even *I* wouldn't jump. We're up way too high.

Marissa stands next to me and whispers, "He must've tried to get into his office before they left. You think?"

"Maybe. God, I wish we had a rope! We could tie it to the window crank and rappel down."

"Or even sheets. Like in the movies?"

Yeah. I would've gone for sheets. But there was nothing, absolutely nothing, on the beds or in the closet. Then I had an idea. "Hey! What if we tied all your clothes together and made a rope?"

"I didn't bring *that* much stuff!"

"Okay...I know! How about we throw the mattresses out the window?"

"And *jump*?"

"Yeah!"

"Sammy, that's crazy! What if you miss?"

"I'm not planning to miss."

'Course, I hadn't planned on having a yellow-eyed weed-whacking mummy lock me in a room, either.

I snap my fingers and say, "How about we take all the clothes we have, tie them together, *and* throw the mattresses out the window?"

Marissa looks out through the window and then back at me. "I'd say your chances would be about fifty-fifty."

"Good enough for me."

"Seriously?"

"Hey, if I'm going to get in trouble for stealing a key, at least I want to *use* it."

"But—"

"You want to be trapped in here all night by the Pitchfork Patrol?"

"No...."

"Then come on!"

Mattresses are heavier than they look. Way heavier. And I've always thought of them as being quiet, flat, *sedentary* items, but try to push one out a window sometime and you'll see—they're really rebellious bales of angry cotton.

Anyway, by the time we'd gotten one of them wedged in the window, we were both panting and sweating. We wrestled it along, grunting, "Push this way" and "It's hung up over here" and "Shh!" back and forth to each other until finally, *finally,* we've got it pushed halfway through the window. Then, with one more shove, gravity takes over.

Now, this was no feather bed, and let me tell you, it didn't even pretend to fly. It dropped like a rock and landed with a *thwack! ka-thunk!* and *crunch!* as it took out part of a shrub.

So it was loud. Real loud. And after a minute of holding our breaths, waiting to see if anyone was going to show up outside, we pulled ourselves *in*side and I whispered, "Do you think she heard?"

"I don't know."

"Do you want to do the other one?"

Marissa shook her head. "No way."

I head for the door, whispering, "I want to make sure Inga didn't hear," and when I peek outside, there she is, sitting in a chair with a pitchfork across her lap, blocking the doorway. Her eyes sharpen, so I say, "Won't you let us out? We *really* have to use the bathroom."

She just sneers through her gauze and says, "You're going to have to hold it."

I locked the door before I closed it so she wouldn't hear

it click. Then I hurried back inside and said, "Let's get going!"

We tied together all the clothes we could find. And really, I wanted to *wear* my jeans and sweatshirt, but they were some of the sturdiest clothes we had—ones I knew wouldn't tear once I started climbing down—so I was stuck in a dress.

You'd think a pair of jeans and a sweatshirt would stretch out to make a pretty good length of clothes, but by the time you've got a knot that you're sure won't slip, all you've really got is the knot. But Marissa had done a great job of overpacking, and we just kept on knotting everything together, starting with the sturdiest and working our way down to the flimsiest.

Then we tested every section. Really *yanked* on every section. And when we were sure it wasn't going to slip on us, we went to tie it to the window crank. Trouble is, I couldn't get a decent knot on the crank. It was too small, and the jeans leg kept slipping off.

So I unlaced my high-tops, doubled up the laces, and wrapped them tight around the knot to keep it from slipping. And when I was sure it was going to hold, I said, "Ready?"

Marissa nods, then stops me. "What are we going to do afterward? Climb back up?"

I look down at the mattress and then back at her. "Actually, I don't think we can stay here."

Marissa digs through her purse, saying, "I don't know if I've got enough money for a hotel...."

And that's when I remember my mother's clutch bag. I

go over and open it, thinking that she won't mind if I borrow some money from her. In the long run, anyway. So I click the purse open, and inside there's a lipstick and a small wallet. I pop open the wallet, and the first thing I see is my mother. And even though it's a mug shot—and not a very good one—I stop and look at it a second because, well, it's my mother.

The way she used to look.

And then it hits me that this is her phony ID. It looks real. Very real. But the name is Dominique Windsor, and the address is one I'd never heard of. And even though the information on her eyes and height and weight is all accurate, she's got a brand-new date of birth. February fourteenth.

"Does she have any money?"

"Huh? Oh." I dig through the wallet. "Fifty-...three dollars." I fold it up, then put it in the pocket with Max's key and say, "Ready?"

She wasn't, I could tell, but she said, "Ready," anyway. So I grabbed the top of our clothes ladder, gave it one last tug, then climbed out the window and into the night.

TWENTY

The clothes ladder held together just fine. And even though I heard something rip a little as I got near the bottom of it, I didn't worry about it. I just pushed off from the wall, let go, and landed with a nice soft *thud* on the mattress.

Marissa whispers out the window, "You okay?"

I roll up and off the mattress, then stand beside it and motion her to come down.

Instead, she disappears. And when she pops back in the window a minute later, she says, "Catch" and tosses something down that looks like a black brick on a string.

What she should've done was toss it onto the mattress. And really, I don't know how it slipped through my fingers—maybe it was the lack of light, or maybe I'm just not used to fielding flying objects without my catcher's mitt—but one second it's hurtling right at me, and the next, well, Marissa's purse lands *crack!* on the ground right in front of me.

"Oh, no!" she whispers from the windowsill. "Did it break?"

"It didn't sound too good," I whisper back up to her. "I'm sorry! I didn't know what it was!"

"Does that mean you couldn't *catch* it?"

"I'm sorry! What's in it?"

"The phone!"

Oops. Well, there was nothing I could do about that now. What I could do something about, though, was the fact that we were standing around in party dresses with a mattress on the ground and a rope of knotted clothes dangling from a window, arguing. "Marissa, you've got to come down. Now!"

Marissa is unstoppable at certain things, like video games and softball. But then there are things Marissa McKenze is not good at. Like cooking—even toast is beyond her. And giving people a ride on her handlebars—she looks like she can handle it, always *says* she can handle it, and you really believe that she is *going* to handle it . . . until you find yourself paving the road with epidermis. Then you realize it's a lot like the toast—once again, you've been burned.

And I knew that Marissa wasn't big on heights. Or climbing fences. And believe me, being in a party dress doesn't exactly boost your confidence when rappelling tall buildings with a clothes rope, but this was not the time to worry about underwear showing. This was a time to move.

Fast.

So finally, as she's hanging on to the top knot like a kitten in a tree, looking down at me, whimpering, "I can't . . . I don't think I can . . . How did you—" I say, "Marissa! She's in there! I saw the pitchfork! Quick!" and you've never seen someone fly down a building faster. She pushes off and lands on the mattress, and the first thing she does is look up at the window. "Where? Where is she?"

I help her up, saying, "Sorry. But you were stuck, you know?"

She snatches her purse from me. "You mean she's *not* up there?"

"Nope."

She shoves me down on the mattress. "Give me a heart attack, why don't you?"

"I'm sorry, but I didn't have time to call the fire department!" I get up, grab her by the wrist, and say, "Come on!"

We hurried to the back door, where I made the sign of the cross at the Altar of Stucco, and we let ourselves right back into the house we'd just snuck out of. Then we tiptoed through Little Egypt, past the fountain, and ducked into the reception room. And really, after you've been attacked by a mummy, after you've hurled a mattress out a window, after you've climbed a tree to break into one room and climbed down a clothes ladder to escape from another, using a *key* to get into someone's office doesn't seem very risky. I had it in and the deadbolt turned back before Marissa could finish saying, "Are you sure we want to do this?"

Once we were inside, I flipped on the light and shut the door, and then *click*, I locked us in, safe and sound.

The tapestry was a lot heavier than it looked and I had trouble pulling it off the wall, but in seconds I knew I was right. "Marissa, look! There's a door!"

"But it's got a deadbolt, too!"

"It'll use the same key, don't you think? He only wears the one."

I guess leaping tall buildings in a single bound didn't have the same effect on Marissa that it had on me. She helps me hold the tapestry back so I can shove the key in the lock, but let me tell you, she is doing the McKenze dance and biting a thumbnail, and between all that squirming and gnawing she manages to say, "Sammy, this is not right. We have no business doing this. When Inga finds out we're gone—"

The deadbolt turns back with a snap. And my heart is starting to speed up a little, but I push the door open and whisper, "It's too late, Marissa. We're here, and I'm not leaving without that contract."

"But what if it's not in there?"

We're both behind the tapestry by now, and there's very little light coming in from Max's office. "It's got to be," I say, then push back on the tapestry with my foot to try to let some more light inside the secret room.

Now all I can see is a little tunnel straight ahead of me, but that's all I need. The light falls across a desk against the opposite wall, and I can tell that this desk isn't just there in storage. It's got a piano bench in front of it, a wooden mantel clock and a lamp on top of it, and a large open book with a portable phone lying sideways across it. But what really gets my heart pumping is that the desk has a drawer.

A filing drawer.

I whisper, "Hold back the tapestry until I can switch on that lamp, okay?"

She pushes it back some more and says, "I see what you mean about the smell, but I kinda like it. It's like pipe tobacco or something."

So maybe Max Mueller was a closet smoker. At this point, I didn't care. I went inside, turned on the lamp, and got straight to work. And the minute I yanked open the file drawer, I knew I was in the right place. "Marissa!" I hissed. "I found the files!"

I pawed straight for the end of the alphabet, and when I found the W's, there was only one manila folder inside. A big fat one with DOMINIQUE WINDSOR typed along the tab.

I held up the file and cried, "Eureka!"

Now, what I was expecting was for Marissa to squirm around and say, "Great, now let's go!" but what I get instead is a quiet little "Oh, good." And she's not even looking at me or at what I'm doing. No, she's fawning over a rack of evening dresses. She touches a white one with ostrich feathers and murmurs, "Man, aren't these something?"

So okay, if she's got time to ogle ostrich, I've got time to make sure my mother's contract is one of the things in the folder. I start to lay the folder open on the desk, but as I'm doing that I realize that the book on the desk is a phone book and that the section it's open to is PHYSI-CIANS. And right there, staring up at me, is the section heading for OBSTETRICS & GYNECOLOGY.

Baby doctors.

I stopped cold. Something about the thought of Max calling baby doctors made me feel creepy. Did this have something to do with him wanting to marry my mother after all?

I really couldn't tell much of anything from looking in the phone book. There were so many listings. And there *were* other sections—he could've been looking up any one of them. But all of a sudden I wanted to know—just had to know—which doctor Max had called from inside the security of his little vault.

Then it hit me. The phone. I picked it up and looked at the keypad, and sure enough, there was the button I was looking for.

Redial.

So I pressed it, and waited through five rings, my heart whacking away, faster and faster.

A woman answered, "Good evening, Dr. Kundaria's exchange."

"Oh, sorry," I said. "Wrong number." I hit the off button and searched the yellow pages, muttering, "Kundaria...Kundaria...Kundaria..."

Marissa takes a break from ogling to say, "What are you doing?"

"Kundaria...here it is!"

"Here what is?"

"The doctor Max called."

"Sammy, *what* are you talking about?"

"Max called someone from here. A doctor. I thought it was a baby doctor, but it's not. This Dr. Kundaria guy does hematology and oncology...." I turn to her. "What's that?"

Marissa comes over and looks at the phone book, then points to the section heading. "Oncology—Cancer."

Cancer? I stared at the heading a second, then looked up at Marissa. "You think Max has cancer?"

She shrugs. "I don't know. Maybe that's why he's so hot to marry your mother, you think?"

"Because he's got *cancer*?"

"The whole mortality thing . . . you know."

Well, no. I didn't know. And it didn't make a whole lot of sense to me, but I almost didn't care. I had my mother's file, and that's what really mattered. And I was going to switch the light off so we could get out of there when Marissa says, "You've got to check this dress out, Sammy. It's metal. Like mail—you know, that knights used for armor?"

"Marissa, I don't care about—"

She grabs me by the arm and yanks. "Would you just look?" she says, then forces me to pick up the skirt of a metal dress. "Heavy, huh? It'd be like wearing an anchor!"

Now, I'd been so intent on getting my mother's file that I hadn't been paying much attention to anything else. But standing there with a metal dress in my hands, I saw that beyond the dresses was darkness. Deep, cool darkness. Then I remembered the fan that I'd seen outside. I could hear it purring, but I couldn't see it. Where was it? And the burglar-barred window? Where was that?

The dresses completely filled a pole that ran from one end of the room to the other, and a lot of them went clear to the floor, even though the pole was mounted pretty high. It was like a dense curtain of clothes—a curtain I wedged apart and stepped through. I bumped into something hard, but I couldn't really see anything because the only light coming through was a glowing strip above the clothes.

"Sammy, where'd you go?"

"Back here."

Marissa muscles apart some dresses and says, "Back where? God, Sammy, why? You've got the folder, let's just go!"

But the light that came streaking through the little opening that Marissa had made flashed across something that I couldn't quite believe I had seen. "Do that again, Marissa."

"Do what?"

"Well, come through so I can see. You're blocking the light."

So she stepped through. And when the light tunneled in behind her, we both let out a gasp.

We weren't alone in Max's secret room.

TWENTY-ONE

We stood there for what felt like an hour, just staring. Finally Marissa croaked, "Maybe he just didn't have room for it out in the foyer. Maybe it's, you know, just in storage. Maybe it was too big and just didn't *go* anywhere."

One look at me and she knew I wasn't buying.

"Sammy, he collects the stuff. If this thing's real, it's probably worth a small fortune. Maybe it's—"

"Marissa. It's a sarcophagus."

"Exactly. And that's probably *all* it is."

Neither of us budged. We just stood there in the quiet hum of the secret room's fan, staring at the massive stone coffin lying on the heavy table in front of us. And the longer I stood there looking at the protruding feet, the chiseled face, and the mysterious hieroglyphics, the more certain I became that this was exactly what I wanted it not to be.

I spotted a pack of matches sitting beside a large candle at the foot of the sarcophagus, so I picked it up and struck a match. This actually lit the room up quite a bit, and now I could see other candles on stone pedestals in the corners of the room, and a few more on a console table at the head of the sarcophagus. I went around and lit most of them, and pretty soon the room was glowing and flickering with long shadows. That's when I noticed incense sticks laid across small flat bowls between candles on the console table. I sniffed one, and sure enough, it had that same smell, woody and sweet.

"Sammy, this is not a good idea. We've got no business—"

"He wants to marry my mom, Marissa—think about it."

"C'mon, it's not *that* weird. I mean, think about all the other stuff he's got around his house. So maybe the guy owns a mummy. So what?"

I just blinked at her, not knowing what to say.

She pulls a face at me, like *I'm* the one not understanding something. "What? Don't look at me like that! There are weirder things in the world than owning a mummy, Sammy. And, unlike what we're doing at the moment, owning a mummy is probably not against the law."

"Marissa," I whispered, "this is not just any mummy."

She shakes her head. "What are you talking about?"

I stare at her a second, not believing she's not thinking what I'm thinking. Finally I ask her, "What does the tapestry hanging outside the door say?"

"What does the...What does *that* matter?"

"Whose dresses are those?"

"Dresses?" She was blocked. Seriously blocked.

I tap the stone coffin. "Whose *body* do you suppose is in here?"

When she finally clicks into what I'm thinking, she lets out a wimpy little laugh and says, "No way."

I lean across the table toward her. "This ain't a storage

locker, Marissa. Look! The candles, the incense . . . the visiting chair!"

Her eyes quiver as she looks at mine. "It can't be!"

"It is, Marissa." I put my hands on the head of the sarcophagus and say, "Now, are you going to help me prove it or not?"

"No! Are you crazy? I'm not going to open that thing up!"

"Marissa, please. I have to know."

"*Why?* What good's that going to do you?"

"Will you just take that end and lift?"

"No!"

"Okay, fine. I'll do it myself."

"Sammy!"

The lid made a grinding sound as I slid it across the base, and once I had a lip to lift with, I pulled up to test the weight of it.

"Sammy! What if you break it?"

"It's not as heavy as it looks, but it's hung up down there. Lift it up, would you?"

"I can't believe you're doing this. I really can't believe you're doing this. I am so *not* into this. Who wants to see a dead body? It's probably going to smell. It's probably going to give me nightmares for the rest of my life. Between this and Inga and her stupid pitchfork, I'm never going to sleep again. Ever. And if you think—"

Now, while she's cranking out complaints, she's also lifting the foot end of the sarcophagus lid. And as we clear the base and set the lid on the floor, she interrupts herself to say, "Oh my god—it's . . . beautiful!"

She wasn't saying this about a mummy, believe me. No, what was inside the stone coffin was a smaller coffin, this time made of wood. It was carved from head to toe in the shape of an Egyptian pharaoh, with large inky oval eyes and a serpent-wrapped headdress. The arms were crossed on the chest so that one hand lay peacefully over the other, and from the waist section down, there was a spiraling pattern of green, blue, and gold. Tons of gold. The whole thing was glowing with gold. And it wasn't just gold from a can, either. Nothing about this looked sprayed. The green was like liquid jade, the blue looked almost electric, and the gold was leafed. Heavily leafed.

But it didn't look like it'd been pulled from the ruins of some ancient civilization. It wasn't cracked or chipped anywhere, the paint wasn't flaking—it just lay there, glowing up at us.

And even though it looked Egyptian to me, there was something tying it to the here and now. Something that made me know that this wasn't just some valuable artifact stored here because it "didn't go" anywhere else. Besides the blue and green and gold, there was another color.

Red.

An oval, surrounded by a band of gold, sat at the base of the neck. And scooping around it was an arc of carved beads, also red. And the last bit of red was right up on top, on the ring finger of those peaceful hands, resting on the chest.

I whisper to Marissa, "It's her, all right."

"You don't know that. How can you know that? It's probably empty. It's probably here because—"

"Marissa! It's here because it's Claire, and this"—I motioned around the room—"is her tomb!"

I thought Marissa was going to break down and cry. "It *can't* be! It's like against the law, isn't it?"

"Oh, I'm sure it's against the law, but believe me—she's in there." I point to the spots of red decorating the coffin and say, "You know what these are, right?"

She whimpers, "The Honeymoon Jewels?"

"That's right."

"But why?" She shakes her head and shivers. "I can't believe anyone would *do* that. I mean, don't they soak mummies in salt and take out their organs and stuff before they wrap them up? Do you think he did that? Do you think he did it *himself*?"

"Marissa, I don't know. I don't know how to make a mummy. All I know is that having the body of your dead wife stored in a secret room in your office is beyond weird—it's crazy."

"Well, maybe not. I mean, people have little urns of ashes on their mantels and nobody thinks anything of that...."

I couldn't believe what I was hearing. "You pick the strangest times to be sensible, you know that?"

"Well, you *don't* know. Maybe that's all this is. Maybe it's just ashes in there."

She was right about one thing—I didn't know. And I wouldn't know—not for sure, anyway—until I took the next step. "You think it's just ashes in there?" I put my hands around the headdress part of the coffin and said, "Okay. Lift."

She steps back. "No way I'm gonna do that."

"Why not? If it's just ashes, what are you afraid of?"

She shivers again and says, "I don't know. It's just not right. It's like digging up someone's grave."

"This isn't like digging up someone's grave!" I said, but even to me, the words sounded hollow. Like there was nothing behind them to support them.

We looked at each other for a minute, and finally I whispered, "Marissa, I have to know. Don't you? I mean, maybe you're right. Maybe it's empty. Maybe all of this is my stupid imagination again. Or maybe there are just ashes inside. But if it is her *mummy* in there, don't you think that's something we should, you know, *know*?" She just stares at me, so I cut to the facts. "Marissa, the guy is having dinner with my mother as we speak. He wants to make her his second wife. I think that gives me license to look at what he did to his first one, don't you?"

She holds her breath for a minute, then puts her hands on the foot of the coffin and closes her eyes. "Tell me what's in there, 'cause I'm not looking."

I get ahold of the headdress and say, "Got a grip?"

She nods, but her eyes stay closed.

"Okay…lift!"

The lid came up and off, and when I saw what was really inside I just stood there, stock-still.

Marissa's holding up the foot end of the coffin with her eyes clamped shut, and she's dancing. First just a twitch, then a wiggle, then a full-on side-to-side jiggle. "Sammy, what's in there?"

I whisper, "It's Claire."

220

She freezes for a second, then asks, "In what *form?*"

I inch around the table, getting the full weight of the lid so I can set it on the floor. "In mummy form."

She shivers and says, "Are you serious?"

"Yeah. You can let go."

"What are you doing?"

"I'm putting it down."

"On the *floor?*"

"Just for a minute."

"*Why?*"

"Marissa, you've got to see this."

She hesitates, then pops an eye open for a split second. And that's all it takes. She shrieks, "Aaaah!" then whispers, "Was that a *mask?*"

"If you'd open your eyes, you'd see."

She says, "I don't *want* to see!" but a few seconds later her eyes are fluttering open and she's gaping at the contents of Claire's coffin.

Except for the mask, it wasn't creepy. Not really. It was just a bunch of yellowed bandages, wrapped from head to toe. And all around the body were little knickknacks. Some of them were Egyptian-looking—like the little figurines with human bodies and strange animal heads, a copper-and-blue beetle, and a sandstone relief of a woman with wings for arms.

But there were also normal things inside—like photographs and crystals, a little music box with Claire's name etched on a brass plate, a few necklaces and bracelets, and peacock feathers. A whole bouquet of peacock feathers.

And if it had been just a mummy surrounded by little

sentimental knickknacks, that would've been one thing. But the mask that was positioned over the head made the whole thing seem real. It was made of plaster of Paris, and you could tell—this was not a work of art. It had been cast from the original.

From Claire's face.

The eyes were black and brilliant green, but they were all that was painted. The rest of the mask was chalky white.

And glued around the edges was hair.

Real hair.

It was the mask that made me shiver. It was the mask that drove home the fact that this was a *coffin*. I whispered, "Let's close it up. I've seen enough. More than enough!"

We had the lids put back on and the candles blown out in no time. And as we're stepping through Claire's old wardrobe, Marissa says, "He's had her in there for twenty-five years. Twenty-five years—I can't even imagine. Talk about not letting go! What's going to happen to her when he dies? You think he wants to be buried together with her or something? And how can he even think about marrying your mom with his first wife still . . . around?"

I wanted out of there. Fast. The whole thing was really starting to give me the creeps. I went over to the desk to grab my mother's file, and as I was reaching to switch off the lamp, I saw the yellow pages, still flipped open to PHYSICIANS.

This weird kind of *cold* spot stabbed me right in the middle of my chest, and then panic—icy, breathless panic—came over me. And suddenly I'm light-headed, and I can't breathe. I mean, I'm gasping for air and shaking, and I've got to sit down. Just have to sit down.

Marissa takes one look at me shivering on the bench and says, "Sammy? Sammy, what's wrong?"

I pant and whimper, "Twenty-five years. She's been dead for twenty-five years . . ."

"Yeah . . . so . . . ?"

"She died on Valentine's Day twenty-five years ago."

"Sammy, stop it! You're scaring me!"

"Oh, Marissa!" Tears start running down my cheeks. Just pouring down my cheeks. "Marissa, my mother's driver's license . . ."

Marissa takes me by the shoulders and shakes me. "Stop it! Sammy, you're freaking out! What are you talking about?"

"He thinks she's her!"

"*Who's* her?"

"My mother! Oh, Marissa!" I look up at her and push out what I'm thinking in hard, painful gasps. "She was . . . she was *born* on February fourteenth. *Twenty-five* years ago!"

"*Who* was?"

"Dominique Windsor!"

"So?"

"He thinks she's her!"

"How can she be her?"

"Her soul came back, into the body of Dominique Windsor!"

"Sammy, that's crazy!"

223

Thoughts were shooting through my brain, exploding in my skull. "I kept asking myself, Why now? Well, he's *dying*, that's why now! And if he dies without her, he'll lose her again! He'll be reincarnated and she'll still be here, getting older and older. They're out of sync, and the only way they can be together is if they start over together. At the same time!"

"But your mother's *not* twenty-five."

"He doesn't know that!"

"So what's he going to do? *Kill* her?"

I looked up at her and whispered, "He tried that. Last night."

Marissa put her hands in front of her mouth. "Oh... my...god...!"

I grabbed the phone and said, "We've got to call the police!"

And I'm in the middle of dialing 911 when Marissa says, "What are you going to *tell* them?"

I looked at her, then back at the phone. She was right. It would take too long to explain it—too long to convince anyone I wasn't a teenage lunatic. We were way better off getting a ride from Hali.

So we fly out of the tomb and through the tapestry, unlock Max's office door, and charge through it.

Trouble is, there's a mummy with a pitchfork standing in our way.

TWENTY-TWO

"You criminals!" she cries. "You thankless, sinful criminals! What have you stolen? What is that?" Her pitchfork is positively shaking as she pins us back with it. It's like she's harnessed three bolts of rusty lightning that she can't quite contain. And I'm inching back, trying to decide how to explain to her just exactly what *is* going on, but really, there's no talking to a yellow-eyed mummy with a spastic pitchfork.

So I pass my mother's files off to Marissa and say, "Run!" Then, before I can talk myself out of it, I whip my arm over the top of the pitchfork prongs, and this time I manage to grab the base of the handle and twist the fork down and away from my body. And I know she thinks I'm just an evil juvenile delinquent, and I know she's fighting for what she thinks is justice and honor and truth, because let me tell you, it is making her *strong*.

Either that or digging up dandelions gives you a really good workout.

Anyway, we're twisting and struggling with each other, and I'm saying, "Inga! Claire's body's in there...in a coffin...he made her into a mummy! He's crazy!" and she's fighting back, crying, "How dare you!" and, "You liar!" and, "You belong in *jail!*"

Finally I manage to twist around so my back is toward the reception room doorway. I try one last time. "Go in there and *look*. Behind the tapestry there's a secret room. She's in there! Behind the clothes." Then I fling my end of the pitchfork to the side as hard as I can and run.

I guess the Pitchfork Mummy didn't want to compare wrap jobs with her sister-in-law, because she comes flying after me, screaming, "Come back here! You! You come back here!"

Like *that's* really something I'm going to do.

No, I beat it out of Little Egypt, through the back door, down the path, and straight into Hali's cottage. And I'm checking all the rooms, rasping out, "Hali? Reena? Marissa?" only no Hali, no Reena, and no Marissa.

And I'm in their kitchen area when I spot Inga, cupping her hand against the screen door, looking for me. And I can tell that she's not sure if I'm inside or not, because if she *was* sure, she'd be inside turning me into Sammy kabob.

There's a door at the back end of the kitchen, and I don't know where it goes, but I'm taking it. I mean, maybe it's safer to stay inside, but I'm trying to do more than get away from the Pitchfork Mummy—I'm trying to save my mother's life.

I squeeze out the back door and find myself in a narrow dirt corridor between the cottage and the garage. And when I close the kitchen door, I realize that I hear voices. Whispering voices.

I sneak along the wall of the garage and peek around the corner, and there's Marissa, holding on to Hali's arm, talking a hundred miles an hour.

I come out from behind the garage and nearly give them both a heart attack. Hali recovers first. She points to Marissa and asks me, "What *is* she babbling about?"

"Hali, please—you've got to take us out to Venice, *now!*" I look over my shoulder. "Inga's after us with a pitchfork."

"With a *pitch*fork?"

Just then I hear the back door to the cottage clap closed. I grab Hali and whisper, "Is your mom around?"

"No."

"Then that's Inga, sniffing us down."

Hali's around the garage with the door pulled up in two seconds flat. Marissa takes the front while I dive past the driver's seat into the back, and Hali's got the Bug fired up before the car doors are done slamming.

And we're just backing out of the garage when *smack!* there comes the garage door, swinging down on Hali's Bug. Inga's holding it down while she looks through the opening, so Hali rolls her window down and yells, "Out of my way, Inga, I'm coming through!"

"You, Hali! You're the ringleader! I should've known!"

The ringleader? I couldn't believe my ears. Like we're a band of robbers, out to lift the silver.

Hali revved up the motor and let out the clutch, calling, "Out of the way, Inga!"

Inga tried, but even her hoeing muscles couldn't keep a lid on the Mighty Bug. Hali let out the clutch and rammed right into the door, tearing it out of Inga's grasp.

Does that stop the Pitchfork Mummy? No way. She picks up her oversized fork and *jab! jab! jab!* she tries stabbing right through the moving tires. And while she's jabbing, she's crying, "You think you can get away? Over...my... dead...body!"

Hali must've figured, Why not? She's wrapped and ready, let's get her a coffin! because she practically plowed her over, peeling out of there.

And even after we were out of her reach, even after we were down the drive and out onto the street, Inga kept on coming, waving that pitchfork in the air, crying, "Come back! Come back, you hear me? Come back!"

Hali watches her in the rearview mirror and shakes her head. "Auntie Inga." She throws me a look in the mirror and mutters, "And you think you've got trouble with *your* relatives."

When we were a safe distance from the house, Hali says, "Okay. Marissa here tried to explain to me what's going on, but to tell you the truth, it sounded a little...how do we say...crazy?"

I'm leaning forward between the front seats, nodding. "That about sums it up."

"Well, could you take it from the top? Sloooowly?" She comes to a complete halt at a stop sign and says, "And *why* are we going out to Venice?"

"Because...because...we've got to go to a restaurant there."

"A restaurant? Look, I don't have my wallet and I'm shoeless, so I don't know that this is something we should be doing, Burdock." She frowns at me and says, "Does this restaurant have a name?"

I can see her right foot pressing down on the brake pedal.

Nothing but toe rings. I cringe and say, "Trouvet's?"

"Are you serious? There's no way they're gonna let me in!"

"Hali," I say, shaking her seat, "*floor* it! There's no time for this!"

She gives it the gun and says, "Okay, okay—I'm flyin'!" She grinds into second gear and says, "Now tell it to me from the top. Something about cancer and reincarnation?" She shakes her head. "You girls are so lucky you got me, 'cause anyone else would've had you wrapped in little white jackets by now."

I didn't know how she'd react to hearing about Max. In one day he'd gone from employer to father, and now I was going to break it to her that he was dying and a *murderer*? A hammer to the head might've been less painful.

But what choice did I have? I needed her to get me to Trouvet's, *fast*, and I knew that if I stalled, she would, too.

So I told her. I started at the beginning, because I knew it just wouldn't make sense to her if I started at the end. And after I'd explained about all my mother's lies, all about me wanting to get her contract and figuring out that Max had a secret room, and after I'd confessed about stealing Max's key and escaping from Inga through the window, I told her about what we'd found in the secret room—about the open phone book and hitting Redial; about the dresses and what we'd discovered behind them. And when I got to the part about opening the sarcophagus, Hali's green eyes were cranked wide open and all she could say was "Tell me this isn't going where I think it's going."

"She's in there, Hali. She's been, uh... mummified."

"Are you sure it's her and not one of his . . . you know . . . collector's pieces?"

"There's a little music box inside with her name on it."

"Oh, god. This is too sick. He's had her in there all these years?"

"Twenty-five, to be exact, and why that matters is, that's how old Dominique Windsor is."

She squints at me. "Again?"

So I explain to her about the death day/birthday and tell her some of the things he'd said at LeBrandi's service. And when I'm all done, she just sits there, hands clamped to the wheel, eyes straight ahead, her Bug whining along at eighty miles an hour. I whisper, "He says it's their destiny to be together. He called her Claire when he proposed. He says your mom doesn't understand the 'concept of Claire.' Hali, the concept of Claire is that her soul is recycled—reincarnated—ongoing. And he thinks Claire has come back to him as Dominique Windsor."

She kept staring straight ahead, the speedometer needle pushing past eighty-five.

"Hali, he killed LeBrandi by mistake—he meant to kill my mother. And the reason he's doing this is because he's got cancer; he's dying. And if he dies and she lives, he'll lose her again. But if he kills her, he'll start their souls over again. Together."

Marissa whispers, "But wouldn't he have to kill himself then, too? Cancer can take years!"

"Maybe he was going to. Maybe he *is* going to." I lean in a little farther and say, "Hali, are you all right? You're going awfully fast."

230

She jogged around a car in the fast lane like it was standing still. "I'm just trying to get you there."

"Then you believe me? You believe *it*?"

"Oh, it's crazy, but in my heart I know you're right. All my life I've heard him say, 'In my next life . . .' Even I say it. I just never knew he believed it like *this*." She barreled along in silence for a while; then suddenly we're scooting across three lanes at once, taking an off-ramp. "I think we should call the police. I'd use my cell phone, but it's back at home with my shoes and my wallet."

"I want to call the police, too, but first can we get to my mother?"

"We're almost there."

So we're whipping through the streets of Venice, going against traffic, honking and swerving and in general acting like the Getaway Girls, when Hali spots a police car at an intersection. And she starts to slow down, but suddenly she grins and says, "Who needs a phone?" She lays on the horn, blasts into the intersection, and spins that Bug around in a complete three-sixty, right in front of the cop.

Well, heigh-de-ho and away we go, with a Venice squad car in hot pursuit. Hali whips down the street, saying, "I bet that boy's on the radio, callin' all cars!" Then she zips into the red zone in front of a long arched awning, screeches to a stop, and says, "Out-out-out! I'll catch up with you later."

There are sirens in the distance, all right, and as we shoot out of the Bug and up Trouvet's red-carpet walkway, I look over my shoulder, and there's Hali, with her hands in the air, being confronted by two policemen.

Now, if you come from a town like Santa Martina and you're dropped at a place like Trouvet's, you can't help but feel like, well, like pigeon poop on a parasol. But we managed to get past the doorman—probably because he was so busy checking out the commotion Hali was causing that he just *whooshed* the door open without thinking—and in we went.

But then I felt like a pigeon *inside* a parasol. I tried not to flutter around too much, but it seemed like everyone was looking at us. The entry area was pretty big, with large, Roman-looking pillars all around. To the left people were getting or checking their coats; through some pillars to the right was the bar area, purring with laughter and voices; and straight ahead was a podium.

The podium was like a big oak roadblock, and the heavy gold rope that stretched from it to a brass O-ring in a Roman pillar conveyed way more than any PLEASE WAIT TO BE SEATED sign could. It said HOLD IT RIGHT THERE, BUDDY and WHO DO YOU THINK YOU ARE? and MILK DRINKERS GO HOME, all in one simple swoop of gold velvet.

Behind the podium, checking his seating charts, signaling his staff with finger snaps and commanding waves, was the tuxedoed maître d'. And maybe I should've just gone up and asked to be let in, but I could tell he wasn't in the mood to listen. Not at less than six bucks a syllable, anyway.

So we put our noses up and our chins out and tried to look adequately snotty as we ducked behind a pillar to make a plan.

Marissa says, "Sammy, maybe we should rethink this. Obviously nobody's being murdered here. Maybe we just let our imagination, you know, get away from us?"

I look her straight in the eye. "The coffin, Marissa. Remember the coffin. Did you *imagine* the mummy?"

"No, but look, Sammy. Nothing's going to happen here! This is a public place."

Now, ever since we'd whisked through the door, I'd had the same feeling. And to tell you the truth, I was kind of embarrassed. I mean, I was so sure my mother's life was in danger that I'd put everyone else in danger, trying to save her: us, rattling along in Hali's Bug at ninety miles an hour; Hali, out there getting ticketed or arrested, or who knows what; even Inga. Crazy Inga. Pitchfork or not, we could've really hurt her.

Marissa points across the way and whispers, "I think you can see down into the restaurant from there. You want to try and spot her?"

So that's what we do, and sure enough, there's a great view of the restaurant from about a half level up. The ceiling in the dining area is very high, and it's dripping with chandeliers, and the tables are all laid out in heavy white linens and crystal, separated from each other by white marble pillars topped with plants. Ferns, ivy, big droopy crawly plants.

And smack-dab in the middle of all these tables and crystal and big droopy crawly plants is my mother. I grab Marissa's arm and point. "There! There she is!"

Marissa smiles and says, "See? She's fine." Then she grabs *my* arm and points. "Over there! Isn't that Jason

Stone? It is! And look! There's Suzette Andron! Wow! Sammy! Over there! Ohmygod, it's Cole Canyon!"

Now, while Marissa's going goo-goo over some guy whose name sounds like a mining town, I'm watching my mother. And at first I'm relieved because, well, there she is, sitting at a table out in public, doing just fine. Their dinner plates look mostly empty, and she's holding a glass of wine a few inches off the table, her head moving from side to side as she's listening to Max.

But then my heart stops because I realize that she's wearing the Honeymoon Jewels.

Max lifts his wineglass and waits until my mother lifts hers. They make some kind of toast, although my mother seems pretty wobbly about it. Her glass barely comes out, but she does take a sip. And when she takes another, he lifts his again and downs what's left in it.

And I'm starting to get mad at my mother, because what does she think she's doing, toasting and drinking wine with those jewels on, anyway?

And then her glass drops. Just *clink!* it falls right out of her hand and disappears onto the floor. Max reaches across the table and grabs her hand, and he's looking into her eyes, talking to her. Her head's still moving, but it's not nodding in conversation, it's kind of rolling around slowly. Like she's having trouble holding it up.

Now, I know society has rules about things. You don't climb over walls and jump into restaurants. Especially not in a pouffy dress so you flash the world your underwear. But in emergencies, well, sometimes you have to break the rules.

This was one of those times. Definitely one of those

times. My mother wasn't drunk. She was drugged. And when I figured out what was going on, I cried, *"Nooooo!"* and went flying over the banister into the restaurant.

The couple I landed, well, *on*, must've thought I was a teenage terrorist, because they fell away shrieking while I got my balance and charged for my mother. And the second I get to my mother's table, I grab Max by his coat front and say, "What did you give her?"

He looks at me and smiles, his head wobbling like it's held up by jelly. Then he rasps, "Don't try to stop us. It is our destiny!"

"What did you give her?"

"It's too late! This time I have made no mistakes. This time I showed the gods proper ceremony!" He looks to the ceiling and rasps, "Osiris! Horus! Hathor! Sobek, Anubis, Thoth! Surely you are now pleased!"

I yell, *"Call nine-one-one! Somebody, please!* CALL AN AMBULANCE!" Then I grab my mother by her shoulders and shake. "Mom! Hang on! Please hang on!"

Her eyelids are halfway down as she slurs, "He thinks... I'm... Claire... he thinks..."

"Mom! Wake up! Mom, he's poisoned you.... Mom!"

By now I'm surrounded by people trying to figure out what's going on. And as I see Max's face contort into a grotesque smile and his head start to wobble all around, all I can think is that it's too late—no ambulance could possibly get there in time.

So I yank my mother's head back and try to get her to throw up by putting the end of her spoon down her throat. She gags and coughs, but nothing comes up.

The maître d' shoves through the crowd, saying, "What is going on here?"

Then I remember. Coffee. Coffee and salt.

So I charge through the people gathered around and find a cup of coffee on somebody else's table. I whip back to my mother's table, screw off the saltshaker top, and dump the contents in. I stir and test the temperature. Too hot. Way too hot.

So I scoop out a few chunks of ice from my mother's water glass, put them in the coffee, and stir.

The maître d' is trying to talk to Max, but he's just sitting there with that stupid, grotesque grin on his face, slurring, "You cannot change . . . our destiny. . . ."

I put my arm around my mother, hold her head steady, and say, "Drink. Mom, you've got to drink this. Max poisoned you!"

She looks at me, her eyes dull and closing.

Marissa pushes through to me and says, "I called nine-one-one. An ambulance is on the way!"

"It'll never get here in time!" I put the cup up to my mother's mouth and start pouring. "Drink!" I shake her and cry, "DRINK!"

She does. And you can tell it tastes terrible, but I pour it in anyway and clamp her mouth closed until she swallows. Then I do it again. And again. And in the middle of her choking down salty coffee, Max crashes to the floor.

A few people scream. One shouts, "We need a doctor! Anyone here a doctor?" but no one volunteers. And everyone around seems to move in closer so they can gawk at Max, sprawled out on the floor.

Me, I'm busy holding my mother together, drowning her with coffee, when all of a sudden she pushes me away. Her eyes open wide, she licks her lips a few times while she pants like crazy, and then *presto!* Up it all comes—coffee, salt, dinner, wine. It is one ugly, chunky mixture, and it shoots everywhere.

And while the maître d' is grossing out at the state of his barfed-on suit and celebrities of the world are retreating to their own unpolluted corners for safety, my mother—who thinks it's impolite to burp or bleed or pass a little public gas—is on her knees on the floor of the fanciest restaurant known to man, puking her guts out.

TWENTY-THREE

It was Marissa who got my mother to the hospital in time. Well, her talking did, anyway. While I was concentrating on Beauty and the Barf, she was out convincing Hali's police force that we couldn't wait for an ambulance— that one of *them* had to take my mother to the hospital or they'd be held liable for "apathetic indifference to an imperiled citizen."

Apparently they all looked at her like *What?* but it must've made them nervous, because when Hali offered to blaze a trail to the hospital, one of them decided the Imperiled Citizen could ride with him.

Trouvet's let us borrow one of their silver-plated ice buckets as a receptacle, no problem—they wanted us *out* of there. So we hauled my mother out of the restaurant, and Marissa and I held her together in the back of a police car while we squealed through the streets of Venice. It was a lot like riding with Hali, only this time the wailing sirens were above us instead of behind us.

Marissa and I spent the night at the hospital, waiting. And at first when they were rushing around, poking my mother with needles and hooking up tubes and IVs and stuff, they shooed us out and made us wait in a little room down the hall. Then some police came in and cross-examined us about *everything*, and then another set of police investigators showed up and made us tell them everything again. But finally, after what seemed like forever, they let us see her.

She was asleep. Sound asleep. And even though they told me that her heart was stabilized and that she was holding her own, I was worried. What if she went into a coma? What if she stopped breathing or her heart gave out in the middle of the night? I wanted to wake her up and keep her awake all night. All week. Just to make sure.

But they showed me the heart monitor and told me it would sound an alarm if something happened and for me not to worry.

Obviously *their* moms are sturdy, sensible, non-swooning creatures. What could they possibly know about mine?

So I stayed right next to her, watching her sleep while Marissa curled up in a chair, and after a while the nurse came in and told us it was way past visiting hours and that we'd have to go.

Go? Like there was anywhere for us *to* go. We didn't have a place to stay, we hadn't seen Hali since the restaurant, and besides, I didn't want to go anywhere. I wanted to stay right there and watch her breathe.

The nurse said, "You'd at least be more comfortable in the waiting room. There's usually a free couch or two...."

Marissa got up, but I whispered, "Can't I stay? *Please?*"

"I'm sorry, dear, it's against the rules."

I could feel the tears burn their way into my eyes. I

tried to tell myself that I was just exhausted—that a snooze on the waiting-room couch would probably be a good idea.

But those tears wouldn't blink back into their ducts. And I wasn't just tired—I was afraid. Bit by bit I'd been losing her. To acting, to Hollywood, to her alter ego, Dominique, to Max...And now here she was, lying in a hospital bed with tubes dripping and monitors bleeping, and in my heart there was a panic that I'd lose the rest of her.

Maybe forever.

"*Please?* She's...she's...you know...my mother."

Marissa whispered to the nurse, "She's been through a lot. I'll go down to the waiting room, but let her stay. Just a little while?"

The nurse pinched her lips together, then whispered, "When I get off duty, you've got to leave."

I wiped off my cheeks with the back of my hand. "Thanks."

So I sat there with my chair scooted right up to the bed, watching her by the glow of instrument lights. Her chest went up and down, up and down, and she looked so very peaceful.

At some point I must've put my head down to rest, because the next thing I know I feel a hand on it, stroking my hair. And when I remember where I am and realize it's daylight out, I lift my head and there's my mother, smiling at me.

"Good morning, Sunshine," she whispers.

"Mom! You're...you're okay?"

"Dr. Burnes says I'm going to be fine."

"But...When was he here? Where are your tubes and stuff?"

"You slept through it. Frankly, I've never known you to sleep through anything, so you must've been completely exhausted. How's your neck? You looked so uncomfortable."

I just blinked at her.

"Samantha?"

"The neck's fine. But I thought you were...you know... I thought you might not...And here you are like nothing happened!"

She laughed. A sweet little quiet laugh. And after a minute of just smiling at me, she holds my hand and says, "I'm glad you're not the kind of girl who likes pink angora."

I thought about the sweater she'd given me for Christmas and shook my head. "You are?"

She takes a deep breath and whispers, "Very."

Just then a man in a long coat and stethoscope comes in. "Hello again, Lana," he says, then picks the clipboard off the bed frame and grins at me. "Good morning, Samantha, I'm Dr. Burnes. How's the neck?"

"The neck is fine. How is *she*?"

"Oh, she'll be up and out of here in no time." He flips the clipboard cover back and eyes me. "There are some pretty wild stories flying up and down the corridors about you, though."

I look at him like, Uh-oh.

He laughs. "Good things, don't worry. But tell me, where'd you pick up that salt-and-coffee purge?"

"The salt and coffee?" I looked back and forth between him and my mom. "Doesn't everybody know about that?"

My mother shakes her head. "Like everyone knows how to pick a lock?"

"It was only a privacy lock!"

Dr. Burnes laughs again and says, "Regardless. You did the right thing, and we're all very glad about that. And now you might want to go out there and say hello to your friend. She seems pretty anxious to see you."

Marissa! I could just see her, talking a gazillion miles an hour about mummies and reincarnation and the Great Pitchfork Escape. I look at my mom and say, "I better go find out how Marissa's doing, okay? She slept in the waiting room."

"You go," she says with a smile. "Go have breakfast down in the cafeteria while I get my clean bill of health."

All of a sudden I realize I'm starving. So I get up and say, "I'll be back in a little while," then zip out to find Marissa.

Good ol' Marissa. Jabbering away to some stranger about me showing off my underwear at Trouvet's. I drag her to the elevator and downstairs to the cafeteria, and that's where we spend the next hour, scarfing down hash browns and eggs, fruit cups and cranberry muffins, talking and wondering about everything that had happened.

And when there's nothing but microscopic crumbs left on our trays, we bus them and head back upstairs. And in the elevator, I say, "I wonder what happened to Hali. Do you think they arrested her? Do you think that's why we haven't seen her?"

Marissa shakes her head. "I don't know. I sure hope not."

When we get back to my mother's room, Marissa

whispers, "Can I come with you?" So we both go inside, only my mother's already got company.

Hali.

And not only does Hali look like *she's* got a kink in the neck, her eyes are bagged and puffy, and her braids look like they need, well, tightening. But she gives me a half-hearted grin and says, "Hey, Burdock. Congratulations."

My mother's looking very somber, too. She hasn't been crying or anything, but her eyebrows are all scrunched and her mouth is looking very, I don't know, *small.*

Now, maybe this was selfish of me, but I hadn't even thought about Max. Oh, sure, I'd thought about the things he'd done, but not about *him.* In my mind, he was still on the floor at Trouvet's.

And maybe I should've pumped him with salty coffee, too. But the truth is, it never even crossed my mind. "Is Max . . . ?" I couldn't bring myself to ask it.

Hali nods and lets out a heavy breath. "He didn't make it." She shrugs. "Like I should care."

My mother whispers, "She told me about Max."

I look back and forth between them. "Uh . . . everything?"

Hali waves her hand through the air. "Everything. Mama doesn't care anymore that people know, and . . ."

"You found her?"

"Yeah. Right where I should've looked in the first place—church. Anyway, we both went back to the house last night just to see . . . you know, the tomb. Mama had to see it to really believe it." She shudders and whispers, "I think he made himself crazy keeping her in there. It was . . . god, it was *creepy.* Then the cops came and cordoned the whole office off." She shakes her head. "I don't know *what* they're going to do with all of that."

My mother puts her hand on Hali's and says, "I know you don't want to hear this now, but before they bury him you've got to establish his paternity."

Hali snorts. "Like I want proof that the Mummy Man was my father?"

"Hali, have them do some blood tests."

Hali frowns and says, "What's it matter?"

"Trust me. This is something you need to do. Can I tell Dr. Burnes about it? He'll help you set things up, I'm sure of it."

Hali shrugs, but the shrug means *okay*.

Just then another visitor comes in. She's not real big to begin with, but she's wearing a gray wool suit that sort of hangs on her, making it look like *she's* the thing that had been washed too hot and dried too long. And I noticed right off that her face was an odd kind of mother-of-pearl color, but I didn't really realize who she was until her eyes landed on me. And let me tell you, she may not have been carrying the pitchfork, but I jumped anyway.

Inga gave us a closed smile, then said to me, "I've come here to say I'm sorry. *Very* sorry. I did not know that my brother was so...so troubled." Before I could say anything, she turns to my mother and says, "And *you*, Dominique— or Lana, or whatever your name is—you are even more pathetic than my brother. To think that you would forsake this girl to further a *career*. Had I a child like this at home, I would never have left."

244   Whoa! Pitchfork or not, that woman knows how to jab.

And while we're all stinging from what she said to my mother, she turns to Hali and says, "I want no part of his properties. No share in his business. There are a few sentimental things I'd like to take with me, but that is all. The rest is yours and your mother's."

Hali says, "Take with you? Where are you going?"

"Back to Austria." She shakes her head. "I knew my first month here that I should've gone back. All the ways he tried to make me fit in...it never worked. The truth is, I don't belong here. I belong with my fields and my flowers, and nothing he tried to change on the outside ever changed the way I felt on the inside." She smiles at Hali—a sad, painful smile. "I'm going home, Hali, where these scars won't matter—where people will accept me for what I am, not how I look."

Without another word, she was gone. And I just stood there feeling kind of, I don't know, *sticky*. Like my lips were glued closed and my feet were taped down, and the elastic of my dress had become a permanent part of my body.

Finally my mother whispers, "Maybe I should just take that Greyhound home with you."

From the way she was saying it, it seemed to me that she was trying it on. Seriously trying it on. Like of all the clothes on the rack, this was the one thing she could afford, and she was standing in front of the mirror telling herself that with a sash here and a necklace there, hey, it could look all right after all.

I looked at her and I knew—this was my chance. My big chance. She really would come home if I asked her to.

My heart started banging around, and suddenly I felt like

a puppy freed from the pound. Somebody wanted to take me home! And home could be a little apartment of our own. We could have a normal life—one where I wouldn't have to sneak in and out of my own house because I wasn't supposed to be living there. One where I'd have a real bed instead of a couch and a whole dresser instead of just the bottom drawer. One where I could actually have friends over and make some noise.

Her eyes were searching mine, and I almost jumped right up and said, "Yes! Please, come home!" but I couldn't. I just couldn't. I mean, she was so close—*so* close—to making her dream come true, and after everything she'd been through, after everything she'd done, I couldn't snatch it away from her at the last minute.

So instead of jumping up, I looked down and blinked at the floor. And that's when I noticed the heels of her ruby slippers peeking out from beneath the bed, and the folder I'd gotten out of Max's secret room lying near them on the floor by Hali's chair.

Hali catches me looking at the folder and hands it over, saying, "You left this in the car. I wasn't sure what you wanted with it."

I took it from her, and then with a swift kick I sent those shoes flying under the bed. I handed the folder off to my mother, saying, "I didn't practically kill myself and my friends here so you could come home and serve burgers at Big Daddy's. Here. Have a bonfire."

She takes the folder and says, "What is this?"

I smile at her, but there's a tear stinging my eye. "Your freedom."

She opens it up, and when she sees what's inside she whispers, "How did you ever find this?"

"Oh," I laugh, "piece of cake." Then I add, "Not that you really need it anymore." I grin at Hali and say, "I mean, ol' Toe Rings here would probably have just ripped it up for you, but how was I supposed to know?"

Hali says, "Hey, Burdock, watch who you're callin' names! You got no way home, you know?" Then she turns to my mother and says, "There's one more thing I gotta know. Were you really born on Valentine's Day?"

My mother shakes her head and says, "No, I wasn't. I should've just changed the year, but I was so busy changing *every*thing that I . . . well, I changed the day, too." She blushes and adds, "I wanted something easy to remember, plus I thought it would make me sound more romantic."

Hali grins and shakes her head. "Worked a little too well, didn't it?"

Marissa says, "Yeah, but to have all of this happen because of a birthdate?"

My mother frowns. "He made connections everywhere, Marissa. At Trouvet's he was telling me all the little things that made him know I was Claire."

"Like what?"

"Like the dress and the shoes fitting me so well, like me being from Montana—at that point I tried to tell him the truth, but he wouldn't listen. He said he knew I was Claire because I like a slice of *lime* in my water, and because of the way I say 'motion picture.'"

I couldn't believe my ears. "Because of the way you say 'motion picture'? How do you say 'motion picture'?"

"Apparently I say it just like Claire did—with a lot of *shuh* in it. There were other ridiculous little things like that, too. Obviously he saw what he wanted to see. He knew his time was limited, and I think that sooner or later he would've picked some reason—any reason—to believe that someone was his long-lost Claire."

We all sat there quiet for a minute; then Hali slaps her thighs and says, "So, you gonna be up to that audition tomorrow? I'd be willing to drop you curbside if you need me to."

My mother looks at me, then at the folder and back to me. Finally she whispers, "What do you think, Samantha?"

I take a deep breath, then say, "What I think is, if you don't get that part, *I'm* going to be the one who kills you!"

"Really?"

"Heck, yeah."

She looks down. "Well, you know, there's a good chance that I won't get the part." She glances up at me. "After all, they're expecting Dominique Windsor, and Dominique Windsor will not be appearing."

I just stood there, looking at her. I didn't want to ask. I didn't want to breathe. I just wanted to stand for a minute in this vacuum of hope.

She smiles at me and says, "Who *is* going to show up is Lana Keyes, proud mother of a certain thirteen-year-old who goes by the name of Sammy."

As much as I tried to stop it, my face crinkled up and my tears gave me away. Completely away. And for the first time in over a year I fell into my mother's arms and hugged her. She was back.

TWENTY-FOUR

After my mother was released from the hospital, Hali gave us all a ride back to Beverly Hills. It was my mother's first ride on the Bug Blast Express, and during one little do-si-do maneuver on the freeway I thought for sure she was going to wind up back in the hospital with a heart attack.

Hali did manage to get us home in one piece, though, and while she spent the rest of the day with her mom, Marissa and I spent the day with mine. Not that my mother helped us carry the mattress back upstairs or anything. But she did hover around giving what she thought was good advice, and really, I didn't mind. I was just glad she was up and walking around.

And while we were untying our clothes, trying to figure out which ones were totaled and which ones would bounce back, my mother was down the hall on the phone, telling all to Grams.

She came back a little red around the edges, so I knew the update hadn't flown real well at home, but all my mother would say about it was "Well. I'm glad that's done."

And after everything was reassembled, we just hung out—by the pool, in the kitchen, just sitting or walking around, talking. Of course, Tammy and the other women kept buzzing up to us, trying to get the straight scoop, but my mom did a good job of holding them off, saying she didn't want to talk about it just then.

That night we were back in Opal and LeBrandi's old beds, but I was so tired that I didn't even think about them—or Max, for that matter. I just put my head down and *click*, I was out.

Until 3:30, that is. I don't know why, but at 3:30 I woke up with a start, and when I sat up and looked over at my mother's bed, she was gone.

I sat there listening for a minute, then got up and went down the hall.

My mother wasn't in the bathroom, but there were some fuzzy cottontail slippers in a stall, so I waited, and when Tammy came out I asked her, "Have you seen my mother?"

She rewrapped one of her bunny-ear pigtails and eyed me. "We don't have a regular date down here or anything, you know."

I nodded, then got a drink from the tap and started to head out. But Tammy flicked on her faucet and said, "Check the viewing room."

"Where's that?"

"Downstairs. Basically, it's right beneath us. Can't miss it."

I thanked her and took off downstairs, and sure enough, there was a door with a VIEWING ROOM placard on it. I peek inside, and there's my mother, watching an episode of *The Lords of Willow Heights,* taking notes.

"Samantha!" she says when she sees me. "What in the world are you doing up?"

I sit down beside her. "It was 3:30. You were gone, I got worried."

She says, "I'm sorry," then laughs and adds, "I guess I should've left a note." She points her pen at the TV and proceeds to explain who's who on the soap opera she's watching and what she's looking for.

Now, to me the acting seems corny and overly dramatic, but my mother is *into* it, studying it like it's swept the Oscars or something.

Then suddenly she stops the tape and says, "I know! You can play Roullard."

"Roullard?"

"The man who brings Jewel back to Willow Heights!" She digs through her papers and says, "Here! I've got the script right here."

"But, Mom..."

"Just pretend you're Roullard and read the lines. It'll be fun!"

"How do I pretend I'm Roullard? I don't even know who Roullard is!"

She looks at me, stunned. "Don't you *ever* watch *Lords*?"

"Never."

"Well." She takes a deep breath and says, "Roullard is Jewel's older brother. Half brother, to be exact. Her mother was married earlier to a wealthy businessman who died mysteriously the night Jewel ran off with—"

"Mom!"

She blinks at me. "What?"

"Do I need to know all this?"

"Well, yes, to get into character." She was still blinking at me.

"Can't I just read the lines?"

"Hmmm...I suppose. But it would help me tremendously if you could get into character. Just a little?"

"You want me to be a man, older than you, who goes by the name of Roullard."

"Yes."

I blink at *her*.

She holds me by the shoulders and says, "Close your eyes, Samantha. Close your eyes and just imagine. Put yourself into his body, into his mind. Feel his soul. He's tortured that his sister doesn't remember him. He's torn by the knowledge that Sir Melville *must* be told that she is still alive and the suspicion that Sir Melville has fallen in love with Cassandra Salvador."

"Cassandra Salvador? Who is—" I put my hands up and whisper, "Never mind. Can you just tell me what I'm supposed to *do*?"

"Here," she says, handing me a script. "Do Roullard's lines."

For the rest of the night I tried my best to be Roullard, and let me tell you, I was terrible. Even after she took a break and showed him to me on tape, I couldn't "touch his soul" or "channel his essence" or "feel his spirit." I even really *tried* for a while, but the only thing I felt was dumb.

Finally she said, "Well, I think I'll do all right. I'm not exactly at one with her yet, but I'm close." She put her arm around me. "Thanks for the help."

I laughed, "Oh, right."

"Really, Samantha. It helped."

We ate breakfast, then took turns taking showers. And while Marissa and I packed, my mom went off somewhere to meditate—to commune with the spirit of Jewel, I suppose.

Then all of a sudden Hali was calling that it was time to leave, so we crammed into the Bug, battered pink suitcase and all, and headed out to the audition.

The first thing my mother did was pull the casting director aside and tell him the truth about who she was. And the funny thing is, he didn't seem to care. No one seemed to care. Here she went and practically killed herself trying to be someone she wasn't, and for what? She would've been way better off just being herself.

Besides, by the end of the audition, no one on the set was thinking of her as Dominique Windsor or Lana Keyes. To them she was Jewel—she absolutely knocked them out.

When it was over, we congratulated her, and after about a zillion hugs all around, we left her there, buzzing with the real Roullard and Sir Melville and some other soapy stars, happier than I've ever seen her. Then Hali blasted us down to the bus station to catch the Big Dog home, only she couldn't hang around for very long. We exchanged phone numbers and promised to stay in touch, and then she was off, saying something about needing a latte and a pair of shoes before giving up blood at the doctor's office and trying to set up a meeting with a counselor at UCLA.

So there we were, back at the Hollywood bus station, all by ourselves.

At first we waited inside, trying to ignore the people around us, but it was hard. They just sat there with their baggy eyes and sunken cheeks, holding small packages or clutching their purses, waiting. And after we'd sat there a while, too, I realized that they reminded me of the guy we'd seen at the Peppermint Peacock. Their eyes just kind of spaced off into the distance, dull and blind.

I grabbed the pink suitcase and whispered, "Let's go wait outside, okay?"

Marissa was all for that, and we wound up planting ourselves outside the back door, Marissa on her suitcase and me on a parking curb. And we're just sitting around wondering why the bus is late when all of a sudden Marissa points and cries, "Look! Over there!"

At first all I notice is the bus station parking lot wall. It's about eight feet tall and sprayed here and there with graffiti, and on top of it are rolls of razor wire. There's no way anyone would climb it, even if they were suicidal.

Then I look past the wall and razor wire to the corridors of tall buildings—cold gray cinder-block buildings with phone lines crisscrossing between them. And then above those, to the billboards of glamorous-looking people selling tight jeans and vodka and twenty-four-hour lipstick.

But beyond the wall and the barbed wire, past the buildings and ads, sticking out of the dry brown foothills in the distance, I finally see what Marissa is pointing at— blocky white letters spelling out HOLLYWOOD.

I'd never seen this view of the Hollywood Hills sign anywhere on television or in magazines, but as I stood there looking at it through all the ugly obstacles, it struck me as the right view.

The honest view.

When the bus finally arrived, we couldn't get in line fast enough. And when the bus driver saw us chomping at the bit to get on board, he grinned and said, "Goin' somewhere special?"

"Yeah," I said. "Home."

"There's no place like home," he murmured. "No place like home."

But as Marissa and I got into our seats, I could tell that something was bothering her. "What's wrong? You want the window seat?"

She shook her head, then asked real quietly, "So when do you think *Hollywood's* going to be your home?"

I crossed my arms and gave her a dark look. "There's no way I want to live in a place where everyone around you is pretending to be someone they're not. No way."

"But c'mon, Sammy. After your mom's been working a few months, don't you think she'll want you to move down here and be with her?"

I looked out the window and tried to tell myself that it was too early to start worrying about that. That between now and then, anything could happen.

Especially on a soap opera.

So I turned back to Marissa and said, "I'll ride that wave when it comes crashing in. Meantime, there's only so much worrying a person can squeeze into one weekend, and I'm full up. Aren't you?"

"Yeah," she laughed. "Full up."

A few minutes later we're on our way, bouncing out of the parking lot and onto Vine Street. And as we come to a stop at an intersection, my stomach lets out a growl. A long, loud, rumbly-tumbly growl. And even over the hum of the bus, I swear people all around us must've heard it. I know Marissa did, because her eyes pop open and she says, "Wow! Was that you?"

I blush. "Yeah. My stomach."

"You're that hungry?"

Well, all of a sudden I realize I'm starving. And what I want is something you just can't find on the corner of Hollywood and Vine. What I want is something real. Something warm and hearty and sweet. Something that'll hold a spoon straight up in a hurricane.

I nod and say, "For oatmeal."

"Oatmeal?"

"Yeah, oatmeal," I say, and settle in for the long ride home.

Have you read
SAMMY KEYES and the SEARCH for SNAKE EYES
yet?

Here's a sneak peek.

PROLOGUE

I'm embarrassed to say that I didn't see it coming. She just passed off the bag, and suddenly there I was, stuck. And even after I felt how heavy it was, I *still* didn't know what was in it. How was I supposed to know? I'd never touched one before—never even been that *close* to one before. But the minute I looked inside, I knew I was in trouble.

Serious, heart-stopping trouble.

ONE

I don't generally hang out at the mall. It's full of biting shoes, shrinking clothes, and useless knickknacks. It's also crawling with poseur kids who think it's their private stage for rehearsing public coolness. Please. I get enough of that in junior high.

But the Santa Martina mall also has a video arcade, and if you know anything about my best friend, Marissa, you know that video games are the only thing that'll make her quit talking about softball. And since we're in the middle of gearing up for the Junior Sluggers' Cup tournament, softball is *all* Marissa's had on her mind. For *weeks*. She's working up plays, she's practicing after practice, she's even talked Coach Rothhammer out of her home phone number so she can run ideas by her in the middle of the night. You have to know Ms. Rothhammer to understand the significance of this—nobody's got her number, and I mean nobody. She teaches P.E. and eighth-grade science, and she's got a reputation for being really strict and really private. Like, is she married? We don't know. Does she have kids? Dogs? Horses? Flower beds? Nobody knows. I'll bet Vice Principal Caan doesn't even know, that's how good she is at being private.

What I do know about Ms. Rothhammer is that she's the one person who wants to bring home the Junior Sluggers' Cup as much as Marissa does. Probably for different reasons—like, I know Ms. Rothhammer couldn't care less about us winning the school a party day. More likely it has to do with showing up Mr. Vince, who told her she'd never get her hands on the cup. Of course, that was last November, after our team beat his team in our school's playoffs, so maybe she's forgotten all about that.

Then again, maybe not.

Anyway, the point is, Marissa McKenze has been the Softball Czar for weeks, and the past few days it's been driving me batty. And maybe I should've just said, "Marissa, enough! There's life beyond softball!" but I *do* live in Santa Martina, a town where everyone from Heather Acosta, Princess Prevaricator, to Mayor Hibbs, Sultan of City Hall, is *into* the game. So much so that people play year-round. Rain or shine, mud or flood, people play.

So instead of telling Marissa something she'd never buy into anyhow, what I said was "Hey, you want to go to the mall and play some video games?" And since I'm *never* the one to suggest it, she said, "Are you kidding?" and off we went.

Now, I'm not big on playing myself. I don't have the quarters to spare. So while Marissa's seriously invested in the skill of electro-badguy annihilation, I'm more an observer than anything else. Sure, I'll play a few games just to keep her happy, but pretty much I'm a peanut gallery of one.

Good as she is, though, I get bored and wind up looking around at other stuff. People, mostly. And let me tell you, there are some pretty strange people in the arcade. I'm not talking about the kids, either. They just strut around, cussing and stuff, acting like they'll take you down if you look at them wrong. Like they could actually *catch* you with the way they wear their pants halfway down their butts.

No, the *adults* are strange. It's men, mostly, and mostly they look the same—scraggly hair, faded band T-shirts, dirty jeans, and work boots. They come in alone, park themselves at the gun games, and shoot. They don't look at anyone or anything else, they just shoot. And good luck cutting in if you want a turn. I've seen kids try it, and let me tell you, it's *dangerous*.

Anyway, there I was, at four in the afternoon, surrounded by the noise of electro-fire, checking out the arcade clientele, when this girl with a big red-and-white Sears bag backs right into me. Hard.

Does she say, Sorry? Or, Excuse me? Or even turn around and *look* at me?

No.

She whimpers, "Jesus! Oh, Jesus!" and drags that bag in close, between her feet. Her eyes are glued to the arcade entrance, and she's shaking. First it's just sort of a shiver, then a rumble; then she starts having her very own internal earthquake.

"What's the matter?" I ask her, but she still doesn't turn around to look at me. She just paws through her Sears bag and rearranges a yellow towel that's on top,

5

then weaves the bag's cord handles together, shaking the whole time.

I look between the two video games we're standing in front of so I can get a clear shot of the entrance, but all I see is a bunch of people milling around outside.

This girl is melting down about something, though, so I say to her, "Are you all right?"

"No! Oh Jesus, no!" She turns to me, her eyes full of terror. "What am I going to *do*? He'll kill me! He'll kill us both!"

"Who?" And I'm thinking, Whoa, now! Why would he want to kill *me*?

She doesn't answer. She just stays behind cover while she checks out the entrance.

"Do you want me to call the police?"

"No!" She turns back to me, looking even more scared than she had before. "No!"

"But—"

"Whatever you do . . ." Her shaking goes up a notch. "Oh Jesus, there he is!"

"Where?"

"Right over there!" she says, looking out into the halls of the mall. Only there are about thirty people roaming around out there. "Oh Jesus, what am I going to do? What am I going to *do*?"

"If you're that scared, why don't you let me call the police?"

She whirls around and says, "No! You hear me! They mess everything up. They put him away and now he's out! He's gonna kill me!"

"But if he's going to *kill* you . . ."

"Oh Jesus, here he comes." She looks around frantically. "Is there a back door to this place?"

I shake my head.

"How am I going to get *out* of here?" She goes back to looking outside, practically shaking herself to death.

Then I see him. I can just tell. It's the way he's walking. Slow, but, I don't know . . . *tight*. Like every step is for a reason and nothing better get in his way.

He's wearing a tight white tank T that shows off his muscles, and his hair is short on the sides, but a little longer on top and gelled forward. There's a heavy gold cross around his neck and a beeper on the waistband of his baggy jeans, and there's no doubt about it—he's headed straight for the arcade.

She slumps down at my feet. "Hide me. You've got to hide me!"

"Hide you?" I look around and say, "There's no place *to* hide!"

"Is he in?"

I look at the entrance. "He's hanging right outside."

"He'll be in. He can smell me."

"*Smell* you?" I hadn't noticed any perfume or anything on her, and the way she said it was weird.

"It's his way."

"Now he's in. He's . . . he's going down the first aisle." I squat down beside her and say, "Why don't you let me get security? Or we could get a bunch of people together and tackle him if he tries to hurt you. . . ."

She gives me a sad little smile, then closes her eyes and

7

mouths a quick prayer as she makes the sign of the cross on her chest. And that's when I notice these weird sort of slashy scars on the inside of her left arm. Not down by her wrist, up higher. One zigzags side to side and the other overlaps it a little, zigzagging up and down. And I want to ask her if the guy she's so afraid of cut up her arm, but all of a sudden she stops shaking, slides her Sears bag toward me, and says, "I'll meet you back here at . . . at seven. *Be* here, you hear me? Everything you need's in the elevator—go get it. And don't let nothing happen to him!" She grabs me by the shoulders and says, "Do not, do *not* call the cops. You hear me? Promise me!"

Everything was happening so fast. First she's scared to death of this guy; then she doesn't want anything to happen to him. And what was that about the elevator?

But her eyes were so intense. It was like they hypnotized a nod out of me. And before I could ask her any questions, she said, "If I'm not back right at seven, *wait* for me, you hear me? I *will* be back." In a flash she's gone, crawling around the corner, then darting out the door.

I look around for the guy who's stalking her, and there he is, coming my way. I do my best to act cool, but let me tell you, this guy's creepy, and the closer he gets, the more I shrink back until I'm practically hugging a video game backward.

When he's right beside me, he sniffs the air. Three times really fast, then slowly three times. And while he's sniffing, I'm noticing the tattoo on the top part of his left arm. It's the head of a cobra with eyes like *dice*. They're popping out, with the ones facing forward. Real "snake eyes." And the mouth of the snake is open—like it's in midstrike, coming right at me.

Now, the tattoo's plenty scary, but when the guy turns and looks straight at me, my knees practically buckle. I'd never seen a face like his. He had hatred for eyes. Steel for a mouth. He almost didn't look human.

And while I'm dissolving into the front of a video game, he keeps looking right at me, then sniffs the air again and heads slowly out the door.

I had chills running all through me. Hard as she ran, that girl would never get away from him. He'd hunt her down until he found her. I could just tell.

"God, Marissa, what are we going to do?" I looked over my shoulder. "Marissa?"

"What?" Her finger's just a blur, punching the shoot button.

"Don't tell me you didn't see any of that . . . ?"

"Any of what?" Her finger's flying, fast and furious.

"Marissa!"

She looks at me for a split second. "What?"

"There was a girl in here, scared to death that this creepy guy was going to kill her!"

"Hang on a minute, I've just about . . . Yeah!" She turns to me. "Okay, what?"

I shake my head at her. "You didn't see *any* of that?"

"Any of what?"

"What I just told you! About the girl and the creepy guy."

"So where are they now?"

9

"They *left*."

"So . . . ?"

"So do you think we should call the police?"

"About *what*?"

"Marissa!"

"Look, I don't know what you're talking about! I was in the middle of a game. It's noisy in here. I didn't even know you were talking to someone." She points to the Sears bag and says, "What's that?"

"She left it with me. I think she couldn't run with it. It looks kind of heavy. And I'm supposed to get some stuff of hers out of the elevator and meet her back here at seven."

Marissa squints at me. *"Why?"*

I shrug real big and say, "I don't know! That's just what she said!"

"How *do* you get yourself into these things?"

"Hey! I just asked her if she was all right, and it turns out she *wasn't*. She was scared to death!"

"So why come in here? Why not call the police?"

"Marissa, I don't know! She was hiding, okay? And she was real clear about not calling the police. *Real* clear. She seemed, you know, *allergic* to the idea."

"What did she do? Break out in hives?"

"Pretty much, yeah."

"Well, I'm not hanging around here until seven. . . ."

"Neither am I! Grams would kill me." I reach for the Sears bag and say, "I'll just take this home and bring it back after . . . dinner."

"What's wrong?"

"It weighs a ton...!"

"What's in it?"

I put it back down and say, "Feels like a bowling ball!" and when I look inside, what do I see?

A brand-new Barbie giving me a bubble-head smile through a bubble pack.

Obviously that didn't weigh much. And neither did the puffy yellow towel underneath it. So I pull back the towel, muttering, "There must be something else...." And that's when I see it. "Marissa," I gasp. "Look!"

It was bigger than a bomb.

Scarier than a bomb.

And it wouldn't be long before shrapnel went flying.

TWO

I grabbed the bag and charged out of the arcade. In a panic I flew around the whole central courtyard, looking up the escalator, looking down the corridors. It hadn't been *that* long. Where had she gone?

Marissa was right behind me, dragging our backpacks along. "Do you see her?"

"No!"

"What does she look like?"

"Long black hair. Curly. Pulled back in a scrunchie." I spun around and whimpered, "I can't *believe* this!"

Marissa leaned over to look in the bag. "You don't think it's . . . *dead* . . . do you?"

I peeked in, too, and there it was—the scariest thing I'd ever seen.

A baby.

I got in a little closer and said, "It doesn't *look* dead."

"I can't believe it slept through all that *noise*. Don't you think you should pick it up and find out?"

"No!"

"Why not?"

"I'm not touching it! I'm going to find that girl and give it back!"

Marissa looks around and shakes her head. "Sorry to break it to you, but she is long gone."

"But...I can't believe she'd..." I looked in the bag one more time. "Marissa, it's a *baby*."

"Exactly. Now make sure it's all right, would you?"

"Why am *I* the one who's always got to investigate? Why am *I* always the one checking pulses and—"

"Because *you're* the one who accepts unidentified packages from strangers, that's why. She could've been handing you a *bomb*, Sammy. Why didn't you look?"

"A bomb I could handle! And it happened so fast! One minute she's shaking and quaking like she's about to *die*, and the next she's shoving this thing at me and running out the door! This is not my fault!"

Marissa gives me a closed little smile, then says, "It never is."

In a flash she's squatting beside the bag, digging under the towel to check out the baby. "Look," she says to me. "He's fine! He's moving."

I looked in at the little head with the wispy black hair. It had such tiny ears. Such a tiny nose. Such a tiny mouth. And sure enough, it was moving. "Great," I whispered. "So now what?"

She didn't have time to answer. That tiny mouth let out an enormous *"Wwwwwaaaaaaaahhhhhh!"*

"Marissa! You woke it up!"

"It would've woken up anyway. Now pick it up, would you?"

"Wwwwwaaaaaaaahhhhhh!" went the bag, and you

better believe I picked it up! I grabbed those Sears-bag handles and made a beeline for the elevator.

"Sammy! Where are you going?"

"She said something about leaving stuff in the elevator. I'm gonna go find it!"

"Sammy! Sammy, that is *not* how you carry a baby!"

I held the screaming bag out to her. "Oh, really? Well, here! You hold it!"

She just stood there, her eyes wide open.

I resumed my dash to the elevator with Marissa chasing after me. "Sammy, *I* didn't take the baby—"

"Wwwwwaaaaahhhhhhhhhhh!"

"—and *I* didn't—"

"Wwwwwaaaaahhhhhhhhhhh!"

"—promise to meet some stranger back here at seven—"

"Wwwwwaaaaahhhhhhhhhhh!"

"—and *I* didn't—"

"Wwwwwaaaaahhhhhhhhhhh!"

She blocked my path and cried, "Would you just pick up the baby!"

I dodged around her, and believe me, people were staring at us. When I reached the elevator, I punched the button about five hundred times and stood by with a screaming bag on one side and a bossy friend on the other.

Finally Marissa says through her teeth, "I just don't understand why you aren't picking it up!"

I spin around and say, "Because I don't know *how* to, all right? I've never even *touched* one before! I keep ask-

14

ing *you* to do it, but you're too focused on whose *fault* all of this is to help me out."

She pulls a little face and says, "Well, *I* don't know anything about it, either!"

"Then why are you acting like you do?"

By now the baby's kicking and punching the sides of the bag. Marissa shouts over the crying, "I *do* know you're not supposed to carry a baby around under towels and a Barbie in a Sears bag, though! And when they cry, you're supposed to pick them up and feed them or change their diaper or rock them or, you know, do *something*. You're not supposed to leave them to punch a hole in the side of a sack!"

Just then the elevator door opens and an elderly couple steps out. They frown at us and our Sears bag as we scoot past them to get on board. And from their whispers and gasps, I can tell it won't be long before they notify security about two teenagers on the loose with a wailing, flailing Sears sack.

So I smile at them as the doors close and call, "It's a Dolly Scream-A-Lot. The switch is stuck!"

Marissa rolls her eyes and says, "A Dolly Scream-A-Lot?" But then she points and cries, "Look!"

Propped in the corner is a stroller. A collapsible stroller, all folded up so it looks like a double-handled umbrella on wheels. The corners of a blue knitted blanket are peeking out the sides, and there's a rubbery-looking bag wrapped over the handles.

"This must be what she was talking about, don't you think?" Marissa asks me.

The Sears bag is still wailing, and the elevator's cruising up to the second floor. "You know how to work it?" I shouted.

She fumbles with the stroller, then screams, *"Would you take the baby out of the bag!"*

"Okay! Okay!"

I started to. Really, I did. But then the elevator came to a stop and the door opened up and a herd of kids shuffled in. So I grabbed the bag and bolted, leaving a screaming *"Wwwaahhhhahhhh"* in my wake.

Marissa struggled out behind me with the stroller, yelling, "Where are you *going*?"

I just marched down the corridor, around a bend, and blasted straight through an Employees Only door.

"Sammy! Sammy, stop!" She knew where I was headed. We'd been there before.

"I can't think, all right? And I don't want to figure this thing out with everyone staring at us!"

Down a maze of back corridors we went, right, left, then right again. Then up some cement steps, through the roof access door, and into the sunlight.

Marissa drags the stroller and plastic bag and our backpacks up with her, yelling, "If you don't pick that baby up *now*, I'm going to . . ."

She never did say what she would do, but I could tell she was serious. And I wanted the thing to shut up as much as she did, so the minute we were on the roof I reached in, grabbed the baby under the arms, and lifted.

So there I am, holding a baby for the first time in my entire life, and what's it do?

Screams even louder.

Marissa says, "You can't hold it *out* like that, Sammy! You've got to hold it close to you. On your shoulder!"

I put it on my shoulder and look at Marissa like, Well?

"It's not a sack of potatoes! *Hold* it."

I yank it off my shoulder and give it to Marissa. "*You* hold it!"

She did. One hand under the rump, one hand on the back, the baby's head against her shoulder. And after about a minute of bouncing up and down, the wailing quieted into gasps and hiccups.

I let out a huge breath and said, "Oh, *thank* you. How did you *do* that?"

She shrugged. "Haven't you ever seen someone hold a baby?"

I felt pretty much like an idiot. I mean, sure, I'd seen women with babies. They're everywhere. And I can't really explain why this one felt like a bomb instead of a baby, but it did. That's *exactly* what it felt like.

"I think he's hungry," Marissa was saying. "He's rooting around like crazy! Is there a bottle in that bag? He also needs a new diaper—pee-yew!"

I dug through the bag. "Bottle, check!" I held it out to her. "Diaper, check!"

"Let's feed him first."

She sat down cross-legged on the graveled tar paper and held the baby in the crook of her arm. The baby grabbed the bottle with both hands and sucked like it hadn't been fed in days.

"Wow, look at that," I said.

Marissa grinned. "He was just hungry."

I sat down next to her. "Why do you think it's a him?"

"Looks like a him, don't you think?"

"It looks like an it. And there's a *Barbie* in the bag."

"Yeah, but the blanket's blue. And his outfit's mostly blue. Mothers are very blue and pink oriented at this stage."

"Is that so." I shook my head at her. "For someone who doesn't know anything about babies, you're sure sounding like a pediatric pro."

"Well, *here*. Have some experience."

Before I could stop her, she'd transferred the baby into my lap. "See?" she says. "It's just a baby."

Nuh-uh, I thought. This thing's a *bomb*. But I sat there and watched it chugalug the bottle, and when there were all of two drops left, the baby pushed the bottle aside and started fussing again. "What?" I asked it. "What do you want *now*?"

"I think you're supposed to burp him now."

"How do I do that?"

"I don't know. Hold him on your shoulder and tap his back?"

I tried, but it started fussing even more.

"Maybe bounce a little?"

So there I am, cross-legged on the roof of the mall, bouncing and patting and sort of trying to shake the bubbles out of him, when all of a sudden he goes, *"Aaaarp!"*

"Yeah! You did it!"

I was about to say, "Hey, I did!" but before I got the

chance, he *bombed* me. Half that bottle came up. And it was *hot,* too. It spread all over my shoulder and down my back, and all I could say was "Oh! Oh, *yuck*!" I held the baby away from me and cried, "Why'd you do *that*?" And you know what that little monster did? He smiled. Smiled and *cooed*.

"Oh, great. Just great!" I practically threw the Bomber to Marissa and dug through the bag. One small package of Kleenex, a can of baby formula, a tube of baby wipes, a plastic mat, five diapers, and a thin flannel towel.

I sacrificed the towel, but it was hopeless. I had baby barf all over my shirt and it wasn't coming off. And I'm barely coming to grips with the barf when Marissa says, "We'd better change him and go, Sammy. What if they lock that door or something?"

I was more worried about Grams worrying about why I was so late than I was about the door getting locked. So I decided, All right. Let's change this puppy and get a move on. Pit stop at home for dinner and then back out to the mall at seven. It'd be over before my shirt was done tumbling dry.

I opened up the plastic mat and said, "Let's do it."

She laid him down and said, "Smell that? This boy's pretty poopy."

"Oh, great." I unsnapped the jumper, ripped the side tabs of the diaper open, and it turns out Marissa was right. It was stinky. It was poopy.

And it was, indeed, a boy.

"I told you so," Marissa said with a grin.

He starts kicking and cooing, and the more I tried to

clean him up, the more he giggled and pumped those legs. Finally I grabbed both his feet with one hand and cleaned him up with the other. And as I'm shoving a new diaper under his bouncing bottom, he suddenly stops struggling, looks right at me, and opens his eyes real big.

"What?" I ask him. "Why are you looking at me like that?"

He holds my gaze, then lets loose.

Not with a wail.

Not with a burp or barf.

No, this time he shoots a fountain of *pee,* straight up in the air.

And since what goes up must come down—down it came. All over him, all over the new diaper, all over the changing mat, and all over me.

So I'm kneeling there with pee on my hands, pee in my hair, pee *every*where, when he starts kicking again. And cooing. Like, Whipee! Wasn't that fun!

Marissa's trying hard not to, but she can't help it. She just cracks up.

I grab the flannel towel and clean everything the best I can; then I wrap him in his diaper, snap up his jumper, flip open the stroller, and strap him in. I stuff everything else into the Sears bag, whip on my backpack, and say, "Let's go."

Marissa holds open the door and helps me carry him in the stroller down to the back-corridor maze. Then we jet out of the mall and over to where Marissa's parked her bike. She looks at all the stuff I've got and asks, "How are you going to get into the apartment?"

Now, this is a very good question, seeing how I'm living in a seniors-only apartment complex where kids are not allowed to live. But for once, I don't have to give her a plan that involves the fire escape and bubble gum in the doorjamb. For once I get to say, "I'm going to walk right in."

"Oh, of course," she says. "That way you can walk right back out."

"Exactly. And after I give this baby back, *then* I'll sneak in for the night."

I should have known it wouldn't be that easy.